THE CONJURER

THE CONJURER

LUANNE
G. SMITH

Published by 47North, Seattle

www.apub.com

Amazon, the Amazon logo, and 47North are trademarks of Amazon.com, Inc., or its affiliates.

ISBN-13: 9781542019606
ISBN-10: 1542019605

Cover design by Micaela Alcaino

Printed in the United States of America

THE CONJURER

CHAPTER ONE

The perfume was long gone, the last drop dabbed against her skin years ago, yet the sweet scent from the jasmine lingered inside the bottle. The essence of a broken promise. All the tomorrows that would never be made to swirl in the mind by a single inhale. Close the eyes, breathe deep the sorrow of loss, and remember the dream of what might have been.

Sidra shifted inside the bottle, swirling languidly as she curled up at the bottom like a snake made of smoke and mournful regret. She could recline there for a thousand years, lost in memories of things past without a soul to disturb her. Safely shut up, she was free of her pursuers, free of the troubles of the world, free of obligation and pain.

A fingernail tapped against the glass. The noise disturbed the quiet like a clanging bell of a clock tower. She swore she would turn the girl to ash for breaking her hard-found peace.

Yvette wiggled the stopper loose. "Out," she said.

The girl stepped away so that Sidra could no longer see her pale eye peering down at her through the neck of the bottle. The scent of Yvette's cigarette smoke, however, wafted over the opening, stale and pungent. Sidra shrank away, refusing to acknowledge the interruption.

Another tap, only this time Yvette gave the bottle a shake too. Sidra's anger flared. Her melancholia dissolved as her ire churned, her heart and mind spinning, ready to spring forward. She shot out of the bottle, a creature born of fire and air, a funnel of roiling energy, soaring on unseen currents that yielded to her command. Willing herself visible, her spirit, mind, flesh, and bone coalesced in the open air until the weight of gravity anchored her animated body to the earth. Or wherever this light-filled realm was that she'd smuggled herself into.

"I thought you jinn had to obey whoever opened your bottle."

"And I thought you were forbidden to smoke in the home of your ancestors." Sidra advanced on Yvette to puncture her self-assuredness, but the girl no longer retreated. Not now that she'd stepped into the river of her free-flowing *Fée* powers.

"Guess we're breaking all the rules today." Yvette glowed softly as she stubbed her cigarette out in a golden chalice. "Grand-Père found out you're here. He's requested a 'chat' by the stream."

Curse that Oberon. She'd conjured a way to escape the stinking city of infidels despite the magic bond imprisoning her there, and now this fairy king could ruin everything with his meddling. But this, too, was partially foretold by the fire.

Sidra waited for Yvette to gather her cigarettes and lighter from her vanity and stuff them deep in her pockets, then followed the spritely girl outside her grotto and through the forest. The path stretched out beneath a canopy of trees festooned with moss and lichen that smelled of fresh green growth. Bulbous red-and-white mushrooms sprouted in the soil at their feet while tiny frogs croaked in the undergrowth. Bluebells tinkled a subtle tune in the wake of their passing.

Sidra despised every step through the damp air. She craved the searing heat and brittle-bone dryness of the desert sirocco. She yearned for the company of lizards with their beaded skin as they skimmed over grains of sand to find shelter from the midday sun. A ransom she would pay to sit cross-legged once more beneath the palm trees with their sparse leaves worn as a crown. Now those were trees that made you appreciate life, not these water-fat monstrosities that dropped their shiny green leaves in one's path like cheap souvenirs for the taking.

"They said to look for him by the standing stones." Yvette levitated off the ground a mere foot to see over the top of a flowering bush, her shining and glittering nothing but an added boast. The girl had recently learned how to use her powers to rise in the air and showed off her skill at every opportunity. As if traveling on air currents were anything but child's play. Jinn were born on the air. Unseen. Free to fly wherever the wind took them in whatever shape they wished.

The chattering of tiny winged creatures hiding behind tufts of moss and lumps of stone prompted Sidra to lift the hem of her caftan in disgust so that the beastly things wouldn't hitch on. If she'd known the insufferable beings inhabited the forest like lice, she might have thought twice about her plan to escape to the *Fée* lands. But no, she'd not been ready to confront her enemy. The one who'd entrapped her in the city. Not yet. And so she had to suffer in this hideous realm for as long as it took.

A leathery-faced imp flew in her face and squirted nectar at her from a plump flower head he'd plucked from the path. She swatted the thing away. The touch of her skin sizzled its wings off in a puff of smoke. She took a small pleasure from the act, knowing she had such an effect on the nuisance beings.

Yvette pointed to the circle of standing stones. Her gauzy new clothes, much too elegant for a *sharmoota*, shifted in the breeze, clinging to her body like second skin. Another one of their fairy tricks because she knew the girl had slipped several bulky items in her pockets, yet there was no proof of them in her lithe silhouette. Enviable magic. A pocket like that could come in handy for one with her sticky-fingered talents, but the girl no longer carried the air of a street thief. Cleared of a murder she hadn't committed, Yvette had taken on the role of a daughter of the court with more dignity than Sidra might have expected. Grudgingly, she admired the girl's audacity. She was foul-mouthed and inappropriate at every turn, but the jinni supposed she was merely true to the ways of her kind.

"Greetings."

The tall woman, the queen of this place, hailed them with a wave and a dagger smile from a throne made of interlaced willow branches. At her feet sat two of the tiny winged fiends, shelling hazelnuts and piling up the nutmeat in a woven basket. They hissed at Sidra as if they'd seen what she'd done to the third creature that ought to be there with them.

"Titania," Yvette said and lowered her head.

"Nonsense. Call me Grand-Mère, child."

The girl turned to face the man with the antlers sprouting out of his temple and bowed. "Oberon . . . er, Grand-Père."

"Your luminescence is improving," he said. "May you continue to shine."

"Thank you." Yvette still carried praise uneasily in her grubby hands, but she was getting better at accepting kind words without swatting them away like flies. The girl nudged her head toward Sidra. "I brought her like you asked."

The jinni had stood tall and impassive during their formal exchanges. These trifling *Fée* with their featherlight bodies and narcissistic posturing were of little concern to her. All she cared about was the safe haven the occlusion of their realm provided from the rest of the world. Still, when Oberon finally turned his attention on her—his golden eyes lit with the hues of the forest, unblinking in the morning light—she could not deny she felt the full heft of a king's prerogative weigh on her head. She had heard tales about the king of the *Fée*. How proud he was. How indulgent. She saw now the truth in the rumors as he twirled a wineglass in his hand before draining the contents in one gluttonous gulp.

Oberon wiped his mouth with the back of his hand. "We are open to guests in our realm," he began. "We are a social people by nature.

Proud of our ways and gifts, which we freely share." He set the glass down and leaned forward, brows like oak leaves tightening. "But we are not accustomed to harboring stowaways whose only wish is to hide from the troubles of the world."

Sidra tried to remain impassive, but her upper lip curled of its own volition. "Was it the girl who revealed me?"

Oberon sat back as if amused by the question. "Do you think a king relies on his granddaughter to tell him what goes on in his own kingdom? Your presence made itself known like a hot ember among the snowdrops from the moment you arrived."

She'd lost track of time. How long had he known she was there and done nothing? Weeks? Months? Had she made the mistake of underestimating this being of light and frivolity?

"My apologies, Oberon." The words tasted of ash on her tongue, but it was all she could think to say to preserve her toehold in this realm.

"Accepted. However, your false humility will do you no good here."

Anger simmered beneath Sidra's skin, flushing her with prickling heat. How would her magic work in the *Fée* lands against a king? The dampness of the woods gave her pause, surrounded as she was by so much mist. Her fire might only smolder and hiss.

"It's not her fault," Yvette said in a rare show of contrition. "It was me. I stole a wish from Sidra, so I owed her a favor. She was hiding inside a bottle I was keeping safe for her when we landed here. The secret was mine. I should have told you."

Sidra lifted her chin a proud notch. "We were following the trail of a fire omen."

Oberon seemed to consider the notion as he inhaled a scent floating on the air. "I am aware of the prognosticating powers of the jinn," he said, gazing at Sidra. "The spark from which your magic flares is perhaps older than the font from which my people sprung, but you would do well to keep in mind you are not the only one here with abilities to see the future."

The king stood and walked to a birdbath nestled between two standing stones beside his twiggy throne. A trio of sprites had been dipping their feet into the water, splashing and laughing at the faces they made in the reflective surface. He shooed them away, sending the creatures flying into hiding in the long mossy robe he wore. Oberon spread his hand over the surface to still the water. His eyes tracked something momentarily as it darted across the surface. He half smiled, then grimaced as he raised an oaky eyebrow at the girl's grandmother. She demurred and sheathed her smile as the king dipped a finger into the water and swirled it around seven times until it flowed in a tiny whirlpool. He watched the water go around, then cast his hand over the surface of the font as if to seal its magic. With a sigh he strode before Sidra and Yvette. Behind him his queen bit her lower lip.

"The long curl of fate will devour itself if allowed to spin in a circle too long," he said, eyes firmly locked on Sidra's as he towered over her. "A dog chasing its tail. A snake that eats itself. An end undone by a hungry beginning." His eyes glimmered with the sheen of prophecy, as if he were still trapped halfway inside the vision. "Though I understand your kind prefers to remain in shadow, you do not belong here. You may no longer hide within my borders," he said and returned to his seat beside Titania.

The fire that had crept into Sidra's fingertips pulsed, begging for release. Curse that fairy for looking into the beyond. Had he seen her pain and desolate future? Did he care so little about her fate that he would toss her off like a leaf falling from one of his grotesque trees? The tittering creatures took to the air as if to mock her, daring to get near enough to tug at her robes.

"But what if she has a good reason to stay?" Yvette implored as only a granddaughter could.

The king cast a doubtful look that made the limbs on the trees shudder.

Sidra flicked a fallen leaf from her shoulder. "I won't beg a host for shelter where it is not freely given."

"But you can't go back. You'll be blown to smithereens by that creep."

"I do not need you to plead my case, girl."

"Oh là là, I was only trying to help. Fine, go ahead and get yourself banished. And good riddance."

A creature no bigger than a hummingbird fluttered in front of Sidra's face. It was naked except for the chestnut twigs tied to either side of its head meant to mimic Oberon's antlers. The sprite grinned before urinating on Sidra's caftan.

"This is an example of your famous *Fée* hospitality?" she said, holding up the sleeve of her ruined silk for all to see. "Then it is better I am gone."

Yvette rolled her eyes. "It's only a trickle."

Sidra blew hot breath on the filthy creature, not quite burning him to a crisp, but what hair he had on his head was singed down to the bare scalp. His twiggy antlers disintegrated to ash before he fluttered off to pout beside his queen.

"Enough!" Oberon stood. His winged subjects froze in the air, waiting to see which way the fickle royal wind would blow. "While I harbor no ill will toward you or your kind, jinni, you do not belong in these lands. Not because you are unwelcome but because your fate awaits your return to the other world. Life's consequences will not simply go away because you found a temporary place of safety."

"I will abide the laws of fate, but know there is only death for me if I return to that city of infidels."

"Someone put a binding spell on her," Yvette added, giving Sidra a sideways glance. "She tends to bring out the hate in people like that."

Sidra showed her teeth, but her hostility did not last. The jinni backed down uncharacteristically, turning away when her emotions threatened to dampen her fire. "I cannot return there," she said resolutely once she'd regained her control. "Do not bind my fire by tossing me back into that place. I would rather sink to the bottom of the bottle for an eternity than be thrown into that whirlwind of grief again."

Oberon took his wife's hand in his and considered the jinni's plea. "And yet the laws by which we all abide do not allow you to remain in passivity and stagnation. No one's path stops midlife. It must continue toward its end."

Titania made a barely perceptible noise in the back of her throat before covering her mouth with her hand to hide her whispers. Her king leaned in to listen. After a moment he straightened, his eyes gleaming with the spark of an idea. The jinni hugged her slightly damp caftan around her arms as if to shield herself from his verdict.

The King of the Fairies was handed a wooden staff with a crystal affixed on top by one of his winged minions. "Upon consideration, I will grant you your escape from the city in which you were bound," he said to her enormous relief. And then he added a "however" that filled the jinni with the sort of dread that made her wish she'd grabbed hold of something solid first.

The word left hanging in the air was the last thing she remembered before being squeezed through a narrow seam between worlds, where glittery lights, like sunlight on water, flared in her peripheral vision.

CHAPTER TWO

A tiny green tendril unfurled in Elena's hand. So small and fragile now, but in weeks it would become a tenacious anchor strong enough to hold up the vine when the fruit grew fat and heavy. She placed her hand on the cane and closed her eyes, listening for the rush of life inside. Cells inflated and deflated as nutrients from the soil fattened out the roots, holding on to the energy needed to create new growth. Satisfied with the plant's prospects, she hooked the tendril around the vine's woody cane and hung a charm of mustard and rosemary to protect the plant row from any shadow spells creeping around the root crowns at night, hoping for a place to deposit fungus.

A bee buzzed in Elena's ear, offering his good opinion of the vineyard.

"Yes, they are spreading quickly this year," she said. The sun overhead had as much to do with the progress as the gentle morning rains they'd received over the last three days. All in all, she and the bees agreed it could be a bountiful year. And not just for the vines. The cellar was filled with fat barrels from the previous year's vintage—her first since returning after the curse that had nearly destroyed everything. Only a few more months and they would bottle the wine and offer it for sale to customers all over the continent ready to buy by the case. If luck was with them, they might eke out enough profit to fix the leaky roof on the house before the attic beams rotted.

Three rows over, Jean-Paul was busy tying down the canes, coaxing them into position to bear the heavy grape clusters needed for the wine. Though a mortal, he had a natural rapport with the vines. He didn't know it, but they leaned toward him ever so slightly whenever he bent down to dig around their feet.

Jean-Paul clipped a pair of redundant buds, then removed his flat cap. The work was physical, dirty, never ending, but there was no place either of them would rather be than standing among the vines, except perhaps lying in their wedding bed. He wiped his brow with the back of his sleeve and took a drink of water from his flask. As he drank, his eye caught sight of something on the hill.

"There it is again," he said, pointing. "That dog I was telling you about."

Elena followed his gaze but saw only the brown curl of its tail as the animal ducked behind the row of plants.

"He's been hanging around the place for three days now." Jean-Paul put his cap back on and grinned. "One of yours?"

He'd meant it as a joke, but transmogrification was always conceivable. Elena shielded her eyes and watched for movement in the vine row. A leaf shook, and she spotted the animal staring at her from the top of the hillside a hundred yards away. His movement seemed unnaturally fast, even for a dog.

"Three days you say?"

"Might be coming from the old Du Monde place. A new owner moved in."

"Possibly." Elena lowered her hand and went back to work training the vines so they'd lean against the stakes in the most comfortable position for the long growing season. Her gold wedding ring glinted in the sun as she smoothed her hand over the canes. After the events of last fall that had nearly stripped her of her livelihood as a vine witch, she took more care with each task, appreciating every new leaf and bud that opened to the world. She'd nearly succumbed to the pull of her mother's bloodline, delving deeper into the art of poison until the knowledge coalesced at her fingertips at the mere touch of the underside of a toadstool or the hard shell of the belladonna seed. In the end she'd resisted the call by renouncing her mother's influence. And now the positive flow of energy she'd fought for met no resistance as it swam through her heart and hands to encourage the vine and coax the fruit forward.

Still, something kicked inside, demanding her intuition's attention. She looked up again at the dog on the hill. The animal stared straight at her. His ears remained relaxed yet wary until the left one suddenly twitched. He'd heard something. He turned his nose in the direction of the sound to sniff the air. Elena stretched her neck to see what had aroused the dog's attention. There on the road walked two figures heading straight for the vineyard. One, at least a foot taller than the man beside him, was dressed in a black pinstripe suit and hard-topped derby. The other wore a long white tunic and straw field hat.

Ah, Brother Anselm.

"Your intuition is as good as Grand-Mère's was," she said, letting her voice ride on the back of a spell until it reached the dog's ear. The animal startled when the words landed and squared his head to watch her again.

"What's that you said?" Jean-Paul asked.

"We have company."

The couple set their *sécateurs* in a basket and walked out of the vine row to greet the visitors in the courtyard of Château Renard, the name of which implied a much grander estate than the modest six-room house that overlooked the Chanceaux Valley. Before the men were within speaking distance, the dog on the hill trotted away, his head and tail dropped low.

Jean-Paul wiped the sweat from his forehead with a handkerchief before tying it around his neck. Brother Anselm waved from the road, though the man with him made no similar attempt to be friendly. No, that one carried the whiff of bad news on him, Elena thought, seeing how stiff and uncomfortable he walked in his suit.

She returned the wave, then wiped her hands on her apron, not that it did much good for the green grime that permanently resided under her thumbnails from pinching off leaves.

"Bonjour," the monk said when he reached her. He removed his hat. A fringe of gray hair stood on end above his ears.

Elena kissed him on each cheek, welcoming him. As usual, the old man smelled of yeast and vinegar and aged cheese. She stepped back and waited while Jean-Paul embraced the monk and shook his hand. The stranger's eyes, judging by their slight squint, watched her with a hint of suspicion.

"I do apologize for showing up unannounced," Brother Anselm said, "but the gentleman says his business is of an urgent nature." The monk turned the brim of his hat around in his hands. "May I introduce Jamra—"

"You are Elena Boureanu?" The man didn't extend a hand in introduction or even a friendly gaze.

"It's Elena Martel now," she said, looking up at his unusual height.

"Ah, congratulations, madame." He cleared his throat and quickly moved on. "Pardon the intrusion, but I am hoping to find someone you're familiar with."

"Certainly," she said, though already her instinct was telling her lips to say as little as possible. She did not read omens like Grand-Mère had, but she could imagine the old woman clutching her chest at this man's arrival. What was it about him that sent her intuition into alarm? On closer inspection the man's complexion had the sheen of spoiled meat—greasy, sallow, poorly nourished. Or perhaps he suffered from an ulcer, and the pain of all that sour bile had risen to the surface, where the effect showed in his skin. If he'd come for healing advice, there were witches better attuned to that particular craft than she with her herbs.

"It is you I've come to speak with," he said, almost as if he'd trailed her thoughts.

Brother Anselm attempted to explain. "Jamra is a businessman. From the city. I believe he—"

"Sidra," the man said, cutting the monk off in his impatience again. "It was you who helped her get out of the city, was it not? You must tell me now where I can find her. It is most urgent."

The scent of charred earth rose from the place where the man stood. She'd thought at first the smell had come from the ashes of a *brouette* they'd dumped at the foot of the old vines in the winter. But no. The smell came from the man. She took a sharper look at his frame. No aural spectrum but supernatural all the same. He must be a jinni, though not one like Sidra. Where her fire gave off genuine warmth, his was reminiscent of a blazing roof caving in.

Jean-Paul stiffened. "What kind of business did you say you were in again?"

"I was not speaking to you." Jamra stared at Jean-Paul with a look that warned against further interruption before returning his attention to Elena. "Where is she?"

So, he'd come with bad tidings and a worse temperament. "I'm not sure that's any of your concern," Elena said, cooling quickly to this stranger.

Jean-Paul's jaw clenched as he took a step to position himself beside Elena to confront the man if need be. Sweet, really, the way he always felt he could protect her better than she could protect herself, but then mortal men always did have high opinions of their rather ordinary abilities.

"You will tell me what you know," the man said. Elena felt a pinch against her instinct, as if the stranger were trying to tap into her memories. Well, that was downright rude.

Brother Anselm cleared his throat in what Elena had come to appreciate as assertiveness from the monk. "It appears I've made an error in judgment," he said, braving a stern look at the stranger before speaking again to Elena and Jean-Paul. "I apologize if I've caused any trouble by coming out here today."

Before the men could do more than posture at each other, Elena asked, "How do you know Sidra?"

Jamra's coal-black eyes turned to Elena's. "She is my sister through marriage. I fear she is in trouble she cannot handle."

Hmm, possibly. Yet she didn't get the feeling he was telling the entire truth. "I'm afraid you've come all this way for nothing," Elena said. "Sidra doesn't keep me informed of her comings and goings. If she left the city, it was of her own accord."

"No, witch, I assure you she could not have done that." The man glared as if he believed her to be a liar.

Jean-Paul had had enough. Hospitality did not include putting up with rudeness from strangers standing on the paving stones of one's own courtyard. "She told you what she knows," he said. "Now, I think it's time for you to leave."

The acrid scent of sooty charcoal permeated the air. Jamra smiled, a snake about to spring on its prey.

And then his mood turned vengeful.

Jamra pushed past Jean-Paul, bumping him hard in the chest. Jean-Paul followed, his anger and bruised ego showing with each hard step against the stones, but he couldn't keep up with the fast-moving man in the black suit. The jinni stopped in front of the nearest vine row, the old canes Grand-Père had planted in his youth. "You will not tell me what you know? Very well." The jinni waved his hand, fingers spread, palm outward.

"No! Please," Anselm called out.

The row of vines withered, shriveling brown and black like a shed beetle carapace, until they crumbled to the ground in a heap of brittle leaves that disintegrated into a million pieces.

The space under Elena's ribs clenched sharp, as if she'd had the wind knocked out of her. The sheer maliciousness of destroying something so grand and revered caught her off guard. She had to stand for a moment in her shock, blinking at the vision. Once the tally of loss became clear, she gathered her anger into a funnel of energy. It churned inside her, forcing itself higher and higher until the kinesis electrified her skin. Jean-Paul, as if tingling from the energy radiating off her, stepped aside, his arm raised over his eyes. Anselm, too, backed away in awe.

"Wind and fire, twist and spin, release this power held within."

Elena's hands shook as fire materialized in one palm and the power of the wind in the other. She rotated her hands, mixing the two until they spun in the air, then cast the tornado of fire at the man with all the force her magic could sustain. When the thrust of her energy had been expelled, she swept the hair out of her eyes, ready to strike again before the jinni had recovered. Instead she found him standing ten feet to the right with his hand stretched out, deflecting the force of her spell onto a second row of vines, smiling as half an acre of mature canes caught on fire.

Jean-Paul, his hands clutched to the top of his head, made a noise like a wounded animal at the sight of the damage.

"You cannot use witch fire against me and hope to win," Jamra said, slowly rubbing his palms together. "I will ask one last time. Tell me where to find Sidra." He narrowed his eyes, as if studying Elena's openmouthed horror at the destruction her fire had done. "Tell me, and I will spare you further infliction of the pain the destruction of these living things seems to cause you."

What magic was he conjuring in the heat and static between his hands? What thoughts was he reading that she hadn't been able to keep veiled from him? They could still recover from the damage if he left now. She and Grand-Mère had suffered worse from hailstorms, replanting after the vines had been smashed to a pulp. She and Jean-Paul could do so too.

Brother Anselm placed his hand at her elbow, as if encouraging her forward. "If you know where this Sidra woman is, might it be best to tell him?" he asked. "At least spare yourselves any more harm."

"I can't tell what I don't know." And even if she did know, she wouldn't tell, she thought as she glared at the madman in the black derby, willing him to leave.

"Then you have made your choice," said the jinni. With the speed of a falcon diving for prey, he swooped over Jean-Paul, clapping his hands on either side of his head. Jean-Paul struggled to free himself of the jinni's grip, but before Elena could utter a second feckless spell, her husband crumpled to the ground.

CHAPTER THREE

The pungent fragrance of mimosa in bloom floated on the air. Acrid, stinging, prodding memories. Sidra shook free of the shimmer of sliding from one world to the next. She blinked and was overtaken by dread. Water doused the fire in her veins as her surroundings came into focus. Red roof tiles, palm trees stretching up to kiss a generous sun, and the vast stretch of a coastal horizon, one that touched sea to shore with her homeland. If her heart wished it, she could make her eyes see that long-abandoned continent in the distance. Instead, she wrapped her robe around her and turned away.

"I can't believe he threw us both out!" Yvette shook off her gown where dirt from the dusty earth had collected on her hem. "My own grandfather."

He'd seen something in the water. Sidra had taken the old king for a fool, but Oberon's eyes saw more than he let on. What image swam in the font that made him send her *here*? And with the yellow-haired girl? Would she never be free of this chained fate with fools?

"Wow, would you look at that." Yvette shaded her eyes and gazed out at the distant sea sparkling under the midday sun. "Where do you reckon we landed?"

Sidra didn't need to guess. They'd been deposited on a hill twenty miles inland, one where the glimpse of the calm blue sea could break your heart if you lingered too long on the view. "We are in the south of your country."

"Do you smell that? Roses and oranges, and—"

"Jasmine." Sidra had almost forgotten the strange mix of the crosswind when it gathered up the scents of the fields at bud break and carried them to the hilltop. The scent had embedded itself in her memory like no other substance. The tether between the fragrance and grief inseverable no matter the years.

"Right, the flower fields. And the cathedral bell tower. The mountains. I know where we are now. We used to swing through here when I worked the carnival." Yvette scrunched up her nose. "So, why did he send us to a village where they make perfume? What's he expect us to do here?"

"We?" Damn that meddling Oberon. "There is no 'we.' Go back to your misty, damp home. You're not needed here."

"I haven't learned how to slide between realms yet." The girl crossed her arms and glared. Her skin glowed with temper. "So, you poof off. I don't need your complaining, either." Yvette gave her the once-over with her eyes. "Well, can you?"

Could she?

The bonds of the spell that had kept her confined inside the city couldn't still have their hold on her, could they? She'd escaped. Slipped through the crevice of time and space. Clever that, smuggling herself into the *Fée* lands. Fate and fortune had seen her through to a safe place where she could curl up and forget. And, she'd hoped, be forgotten. But Oberon's interference had brought her back to this place with its scented memories. Already they twined around her heart, making her suspect she'd been bound all over again.

"Well?" The girl rolled her eyes and began walking down the hill. "Thought so."

"I can leave whenever I wish it." But even Sidra knew her words were as hollow as winter gourds that rattled in the wind. She was caught at the ankle by the past and future. Returned to a place that had proved the birthplace of her downfall.

Yvette spun around. "You know, I was happy where we were. Best I've ever had it. I was just learning how to master my glamour. Until *you* ruined everything by getting us tossed out." She pointed a finger. "You owe *me* now."

Curse that girl and her family to Jahannam and back. She was right. Always the wheel of fate kept turning, tipping the balance from pauper to prince back to indebted fool.

The scrub bush poked between the straps of Sidra's sandals, irritating her even more. "We don't need to walk like mules through the brush," she said. If it were mere sand, she would cherish the feel of the grains of warm quartz against her skin, but she didn't like the scrape of sticks and prickly thorns.

Yvette yelled over her shoulder. "What are you going to do, fly us down to the village on a magic carpet?"

The thought of taking to the air was tempting, though she didn't trust herself not to drop the girl headfirst on the steepest rooftop. And for good or ill she must have needed the blonde-haired one to see this unfortunate foretelling to its end. Otherwise, fate would have left her behind.

"No, girl," she called. "Come take hold of my sleeve. There's another way."

Yvette hesitated before climbing back up the hill and grabbing a handful of silk. "You better not turn me into a bird again or I swear I'll—"

Silencing the pest, if only for a brief shift in time and space, was a pleasure all its own. The transformation was nothing. Fire and smoke. Mist and air. It was what jinn were made of. The source of their being. The girl would feel nothing but light-headedness when she reanimated. But where to land? Was the apartment still safe? Was the old one still nearby?

Sidra and Yvette glided over the rooftops of the southern village, appearing as nothing but a wisp of cloud. In this state it was difficult to know the risk they'd meet on the ground. If not for the girl, Sidra would stay hidden, watching, waiting from the shadowy corners, as all jinn prefer, but she couldn't carry the *Fée* one in their present state for too long. If Yvette were still the filthy street witch Sidra once believed her to be, it would be nothing to leave her body to wither in the ether like a dried fish, but that wouldn't do for one who belonged to Oberon. And one's balance in this life and the next was something to consider always.

Curling like a trickle of smoke from a doused candle, Sidra guided them through a narrow street lined with two-story buildings, their plaster walls painted the soft ocher color of sand and shells. She slipped under an arch that connected the buildings, emerging on the other side where the corner apartment loomed above. The shutters were closed against the bright light. No scent of bread and oranges escaped beneath the door from the kitchen. No residual whiff of oud lifted from the caftan still hung on the peg. Still, she had to enter, if only to keep them safe for the night.

Spilling through the keyhole in the heavy oak door, she entered the stale space and circled the room, feeling out the darkness. The energy was cool to the touch—in the corners, under the eaves, above the bed. The apartment was as it should be, but she was saddened to know the room had been empty long enough for the heat to have dissipated. She sighed and reanimated, bringing the girl into the room with her.

"—peck your eyes out." Yvette finished her sentence, wobbling on her feet momentarily until she realized she'd already been transported. "Oh, we're there." She steadied herself against the semicircle *majlis* sofa, blinking as she took in the new surroundings. "Where are we exactly?"

Sidra wiped a finger through the dust on the mosaic tray where the brass *dallah* and glass *finjan* were displayed. "It is my home," she said. "Or at least it was for a time."

Yvette let out a breath of surprise. "You live here? In an apartment?" She gestured broadly at the lush silk and wool fabrics lining the walls, the sofa set low on the floor, and the round hassocks trimmed in leather. "But this is fabulous."

A bowl of figs and oranges appeared on the small octagon table beside the sofa. She offered them to the girl as a matter of hospitality, though it was only a shadow gesture done out of obligation to the custom. *Was* the apartment still her home? Could it be such a place with only one occupant? She stepped deeper into the room until the spicy scent embedded in the textiles reached her nose.

"We can stay here for the night. Perhaps longer, should the need arise." She produced a steaming *dallah* full of aromatic coffee. "Help yourself to the food. It won't poison you. I promise."

Yvette picked up an orange and peeled back the skin. She didn't sit as she ate, which made the jinni nervous. Instead the girl wandered around the room, taking in the personal details of the apartment—the hanging brass lamps with colored glass panels, the woven tapestries on the walls in hues of red and blue and gold, the incense burner carved out of a stone still filled with *bakhoor*, and the man's robes hanging on a peg on the wall above a pair of worn black leather *balgha*.

The girl spun around, the thrill of discovery bright on her pale pixie face. "And who do these belong to?" she asked, eyeing the slippers.

Sidra looked up, heavy with grief. "The man I killed," she said and sank onto the sofa with the weight of a log collapsing in a fire.

CHAPTER FOUR

Elena knelt in the courtyard beside Jean-Paul's limp body, adrenaline looping through her circulatory system. "He's burning up." She glared at the jinni, hoping to sear him with her anger. "What did you do to him?"

"His mind is wandering in the desert of my people." Jamra gave a flick of his hand, as if it were of little difference. "It is up to you if he finds his way out or not."

With her heart galloping, Elena reached in her pocket for a sprig of rosemary and chamomile. She ground them between her shaking fingers and sprinkled the crushed leaves on Jean-Paul's forehead.

When he didn't rouse from her magic, she dabbed at the beads of sweat rising on his skin with the corner of her apron as Brother Anselm felt for a pulse, his fingers pressed against Jean-Paul's neck.

"Your witch's words will do no good against my magic."

Brother Anselm stood and crossed himself. "I'll fetch a pail of cool water and a cloth."

"Neither will your mortal gestures of faith," Jamra said over his shoulder as the monk ran to the pump beside the cellar.

Elena rose to her feet. She had renounced her mother's magic, but she wasn't immune to temptation, not when anger flared and the desire for revenge raged. She called a thread of dark energy into her palms, harnessing the sting of the nettle, the scratch of the bramble, the prick of the rose. "Bite and scratch, strike the match. Stab the skin of this wicked jinn." The magic tore her fingers as she hurled her rage at Jamra's face. But the jinni merely opened his mouth and sucked the energy inside him. He chewed and swallowed, then grinned at her, greedy and vindictive, revealing a row of teeth engraved with copper scrollwork gone verdigris. The green tinge only enhanced the foulness of his smile against his sallow skin.

"I can't help you," she yelled. "I know nothing of Sidra's whereabouts. Release this man from your spell. He's a mortal. He has nothing to do with you or your grievance against her."

"Grievance?" The jinni pressed his palms together and touched his fingers to his forehead, as if fighting for blessed calm. "Do you have any idea what that *jinniyah* is capable of? What she has done to my family?"

"Whatever she did, it happened before I was acquainted with her." Elena returned to Jean-Paul's side, lifting his head to let him rest in her lap.

"But you knew her soon after. In prison. You befriended her, even knowing she was a murderer."

The man Sidra had killed. The reason she was to be executed before she escaped through fire. Was that what this was about? "The man she killed. Who was he to you?"

The jinni picked a thorn out of his teeth. "My brother."

Ah. The crux of the matter.

"It was she who led Hariq astray and then abandoned him to the ever after, cursing my family by weakening our clan and our fight against the infidels. And for that you will lead me to her so I can strike her from this earth forever."

"How can I? Sidra is gone. If she's no longer in the city, then she's in the ether. *You'd* have a better chance finding her than I would."

"Except she could not have left the city without the help of sorcery. If *you* released her from the bonds I placed there, then she owes you a debt. This she must answer. You must call her."

"What bonds?"

The jinni's lip curled slightly under his thin mustache. "Are you toying with me, witch?" He stared at her with glittering eyes that telegraphed the pain he was willing to inflict.

"On my husband's life, I don't know what you're on about. She confessed she was confined to the city, but I have no idea how she freed herself."

He inhaled, calculating the truth or lie as Brother Anselm returned with the water. The jinni withdrew three paces, his hand tugging at the thin trail of beard on his chin. The monk knelt beside Jean-Paul, who appeared to be breathing normally despite the slight shiver he'd developed. The jinni watched the monk administer a cool cloth, though he didn't smirk at the effort as she expected.

"I knew Sidra would return to the city," he said as he circled behind the trio hunkered on the flagstones, "like a cat slinking into an alley at dark looking for scraps. I still bear the mark of her fire on my skin from our previous encounter, crossing my back as if I'd been whipped. A fire like that does not simply fade and go away." He revealed a nasty burn on his neck. Elena felt no pang of sympathy at the sight.

"She did this after murdering my brother. Do not doubt she is a danger that must be stopped." He wandered toward the cellar entrance and spread his hand against the oak door as if feeling for hidden energy. "I, too, know sorcerers. It is how I bound Sidra to the city. A spell cast over the fire using her true jinn name." He took his hand away and smiled, seemingly at his own shrewdness. "The spell was designed to let her slip into the city, but once she crossed the boundary, the trap was set. The snare triggered. I was this close to flushing her out when she disappeared."

For all his arrogance, he must have missed something in his planning. "A flaw in your spell?" she suggested.

He nearly lashed out. "No! I do not miss. The only flaw in the magic was being too broad. It is very difficult to catch smoke in one's fingers." He brushed his hands free of whatever he'd detected at the door.

"Yet you believe I could have somehow freed her?"

"She could not have escaped the spell around the city, either by magic or force, without outside help." He nudged his chin at her, offering the mildest hint of deference. "I saw a vision of you and she together in the flames of a prophecy. Sidra could not have freed herself on her own power. She is too green, too impulsive. But perhaps someone experienced with witchcraft found a way to disrupt the spell long enough for her to escape." He turned his eyes on Elena. "There is a rumor you broke a curse you had been afflicted with. That you worked this magic while transformed. One who can break their own curse might be cunning enough to slip an alley cat like her through a trap."

And yet she hadn't. She knew Sidra had been bound to the city when they'd shared a coffee inside the illusion of a tent atop the butte in the city. Elena hadn't even offered to help. Hadn't been asked to. She regretted that now, knowing this vile man was the one who'd entrapped her friend. Elena thought back to the last time she'd seen Sidra. The night at the museum when Yvette had been reunited with her family in the *Fée* lands. Yes, curious circumstances there. She hadn't seen or heard from Sidra since. Her brow twitched in thought.

He'd noticed.

"What is it? What have you seen?" The tenor of his voice dropped to a threatening whisper.

Elena considered her choices and relented. "I didn't assist her, but it's possible I may know where to find Sidra after all."

"Tell me at once!"

Brother Anselm removed the cloth from Jean-Paul's forehead and dipped it back in the water. As he wrung it damp, Elena slid out from beneath her unconscious husband, resting his head gently on the hard stones. She kissed Jean-Paul's forehead and cheek, feeling the heat of his skin against her lips, then sent a silent plea with her eyes to her old friend to watch over him. He returned a nod, understanding her meaning.

"You will free my husband from this illness you inflicted upon him first," she said, standing to face the jinni.

Jamra grinned as if amused. "No." He shrugged and shook his head, enjoying his power over her. "But I will agree not to kill him outright if you can prove you are not lying to me."

"Agree to return him to his proper health"—she held up a hand to silence the jinni's objection—"or, if Sidra is in the place I believe her to be, you will never find her again. She's out of your reach."

It was a gamble, but she could see no other way to save her husband's life other than to bargain with the one thing she had that Jamra wanted: information. She folded her arms and waited for his answer.

"Cooperate and your man will get no worse. Find the *jinniyah* for me and I will take away the fever." Jamra waved his hand as if to seal their agreement, then pointed his finger in Elena's face, his breath hot like the steam from a winter cauldron. "But I will burn his brains from the inside out with the flame of a thousand fires if I discover you are lying to me."

Elena nodded, relieved to have learned that it was possible for the fever to be reversed. She made the deal with the jinni while Brother Anselm crossed himself.

CHAPTER FIVE

Sidra never fidgeted, never bit her nails, never fretted over the things she couldn't control. She believed one's destiny marched forward on the single road it was meant to follow. Yet being back among her possessions, among *his* possessions, made the fire in her blood recede until she actually felt a chill on the back of her neck. Exposed. Vulnerable. As if still waiting for the sharpened edge of *la demi-lune* to fall.

Curse that Oberon! She didn't wish to feel anything ever again, and yet here she was in a pit of emotions slithering over her skin like cool-bellied snakes.

"Are you going to tell me why Grand-Père sent us here of all places?" Yvette dropped on the sofa beside Sidra. "Bit of a coincidence, don't you think? I mean, how did he even know?"

Sidra rubbed the back of her neck. The girl wasn't as stupid as she usually took her to be. She'd known that before, seeing the way Yvette had survived the city streets in the throes of her wish without resorting to her thieving ways, but for once life would be easier if her assumptions were true. She wished, too, that the girl had a destiny disconnected from her own instead of being here tangled in the web of life at her side.

Sidra stared at the abandoned shoes by the door. "Your grandfather was right to return us here. This is where the path we must walk lies, no matter how painful the next steps we take."

"Right. The two of you love your prophecies." Yvette chewed her last orange slice. "So, who was he, the man you . . . you know?" She nudged her chin toward the shoes as she drew her finger across her neck.

Sidra turned away to stare at a cobweb dangling in the window, then closed her eyes. "My husband."

There, she said it. And it didn't kill her.

"You're married? Or, well, *were* married, I suppose." Yvette sat back, flabbergasted, as her eyes scanned the room a second time with the new information. *"Merde."*

Sidra sprang up from the sofa. She wanted to dissipate. Disappear. Burn the apartment to the ground. Instead she gathered her scarf over her head and wrapped the ends tight around her arms.

"How long were you married?"

The faintest of smiles still found its way to her lips at the thought. "Three hundred years."

"Oh là là. How's that even possible?" Yvette poured herself a cup of coffee, admiring the gold inlay on the cup as she brought it to her lips.

"Three centuries is not long for my kind. We were still newlyweds."

The scent of orange blossoms infiltrated the cracks in the window frame and under the door, filling the room with shadow memories. Sidra did not know before that a heart could shrivel to the size of a raisin and die and yet leave the rest of the body and spirit to live for centuries.

Yvette whistled low. "What happened?"

"We weren't meant to fall in love, but we did. We tried to outrun the All Seeing's plan for us, and we got snapped up in its teeth in the end."

Yvette prodded her for more, but there was no reason to tell the details of her story. Spilling her heart like a common mortal who couldn't control her emotions or mouth. And to a girl who knew nothing about love. Only the coarse, hard transaction of physical pleasure for money.

"I have to go out," she said, suddenly unable to bear the antsy jitters in her blood. "Stay. Drink your coffee. Do not leave. You'll be safe within these walls until I return. They're safeguarded. But venture out and I cannot protect you."

Yvette set her cup down. "Protect me against what?"

Sidra curled her lip and drew her finger across her neck. "Certain, torturous death."

⬥

The breeze rustled the highest treetops, signifying an omen of change. Sidra sailed on the currents, a wisp of invisible smoke in a cloudless sky. The concealment spell she'd placed around the apartment was still as strong as the day she'd cast it, made of good, solid magic. The girl would be fine as long as she did as she was told and stayed inside. But with that one you never knew which impulse she would follow next. Was that why they'd been chained at the wrist on this journey? There was always a place for the unpredictable in life, but she didn't like it. Not one bit.

She passed over a crop of budding roses, inhaling the fragrance of the flowers as she flew. Her mood improved from the floral perfume until she was more resolute than desperate. Had this been her life before, she would have stayed among those heavenly scents as long as her heart desired, but today she must relent and fly. She turned to the west and headed for the hills.

The opening to the cave, once so perfectly hidden in the rocky ground, was now marked by an atrocity of a stone monument and a wooden gate. Mortals disturbed everything they came across. Tours, they called it. And yet the old one refused to leave the place. He merely burrowed in deeper beyond the reach of idle curiosity.

The gate had been secured for the day. Such locks were made for clay-footed mortals, but if the light could get through, so could she. Sidra drifted through the cracks at the entrance where the wooden gate and stone wall didn't quite meet. Inside, the cavern yawned before her. The great room echoed with cool, expansive emptiness. She reanimated on a stone ledge on the lip of darkness. Removing an oil lamp from the wall, she lit the wick and blew her fire magic inside the glass so it shone with the light of ten lanterns. In the illuminated space at her feet, a row of stalagmites with a pinkish hue stood waist-high like teeth inside a mythical beast that had swallowed the world. A great tongue of solid ground, newly carved with steps for goggle-eyed tourists, descended deeper into the cavern. To find her answers, she would need to go very deep into the abyss to find the old one, beyond the reach of mortals and their rudimentary tools.

Sidra crossed her legs and sat on a cushion of air. Steadily, she floated through the dark with her lantern held out before her, winding her way down through openings in the rock, large and small, brushing against the limestone walls with their mud-slick slime and coiled fossils embedded in time. She didn't care for the damp. And though the lure of hiding in dark places was fitting for her kind, she had never personally been drawn to them. Not until she'd felt the tugging loss of her husband's death pull her down. "Live long enough," she'd been told by those older than she, "and one day you, too, will seek out a hollow place at the bottom of the world to bury your sorrows in."

She was getting closer. The spicy scents of turmeric and cumin began to overtake the wet beach smell of the limestone. She sank deeper, past the garbage left behind by the tourists, past the dripping water from the aquifer, until she came to a cave within the cave, a sideways tunnel gleaming with the reddish color of iron oxide, the color a talisman for luck and courage.

The air stirred. A noise like small stones tumbling over a ledge reached her ears from deeper inside. *Ah, good. He is already awake.* Touching her feet down again to walk, she dimmed her lantern to a tolerable level. Even jinn needed time to adjust their eyes after so much time in shadow. Especially one as old as Rajul Hakim.

Sidra approached the door, a curtain of darkness sewn from threads of cosmic magic. *"As-salaam-alaykum,"* she said and passed through the veil.

Inside, the air grew dry and comfortably warm. A small whirlwind of sediment and tiny pebbles kicked up from the stony ground. She could remember the first time she'd come to the cave and the fierce storm he'd produced in her presence. But time robbed even seasoned warriors of their hot breath eventually.

Rajul Hakim, called the wise one for his many centuries of gathering knowledge in the folds of his caftan, reanimated in front of her. He'd shrunk again. Though he once had been a giant among his kind, age had knocked a few more inches off his spine so that he stood not much taller than she. His golden-yellow robe puddled on the ground, and his graying hair needed trimming, particularly his brows, which had grown into splayed pigeon wings above his eyes. Despite his disheveled physical appearance, she knew his mental power had merely concentrated after being forced to live in a smaller body. He was still a formidable jinni to be cautious of.

"As-salaam-alaykum," he said, though he had yet to open his eyes. Perhaps he needed more time than first thought to accept the light. She dimmed the lantern again.

The old man blinked and scratched his scraggly beard. "Ah, Sidra." He seemed pleased to see her, but then his forehead wrinkled in confusion. He glanced at the wall of his cave where several spiral markings had been scratched into the limestone. A sort of cosmic calendar he conferred with to keep track of the outside world. "Your tribute is not due for another sixty years," he said. "Where is Hariq? Did he not come with you?"

"No."

Rajul Hakim seemed then to remember what happened to her husband. His face showed the proper remorse before checking his calendar again. After a quick calculation, he nodded to himself and gestured for her to sit with much more solemnity than normal. When she smiled weakly back at him, finding nowhere to sit, he mumbled an excuse about his aging mind before presenting an illusion of comfort by introducing two plush hassocks beneath a silken canopy. A brass *dallah* full of coffee appeared on a table beside a bowl of shriveled dates. Sidra sat and inhaled the scent of cardamom wafting from the cup, pleased to let the aroma filter through her lungs. She passed on the dates, believing them to be from an ancient and outdated spell.

The old jinni crossed his legs atop the hassock. "So, you do not bring tribute. Why then have you come?" He waved a finger, and a trio of hanging lamps came to life over their heads. In the brighter light his skin appeared ashen and sun deprived. Lizard-like.

"You should get out of this cave for a change," she chided gently. "Go to a bazaar. Indulge in some sun and soft desert wind at a streetside café."

"I do go out. Whenever I hear the little mortal children shouting in the cave on one of their tours, I send a whoosh of air that hits them on the back of their heads and makes the sound of *ooooohhhh* in their ears." The old man laughed until he coughed. "They turn heel and run every time."

"That's not what I meant."

"Bah." He waved a hand. "I have seen enough of the earth above and its inhabitants. The world is darker up there than it is here in my corner of the underground. Here I see what I need to see and nothing more, nothing less."

"Do the people not call for you? Ask you for favor using their talismans?"

"A few, but the calling is not as it once was. Too many of our people have let the old ways fall on the side of the road." He made a gesture with his fingers as if they were two legs walking. "Now they are gone."

Not all, she thought, but let it rest. He was older and wiser than most she'd known. Old enough that he'd escorted the people when they traveled north to this foreign land centuries ago, carrying their beliefs and their customs with them on their backs and in their hearts. He'd answered the call to join them, saying he'd seen it foretold in the fire that he must go. The travelers asked for protection, guidance, and blessings from the jinn in the earthly realm as they built their new lives on unfamiliar soil. Now it was Sidra who flew to him needing guidance and assurance.

A glass-and-metal pipe appeared at the old jinni's side. He slipped the mouthpiece of the *shisha* between his lips and inhaled. His eyes shut for one pleasurable moment. "So," he said, as if reading printed words on the insides of his eyelids, "you sail freely to my door, yet you are still held in bondage."

The truth spoken out loud sent a hot flame dancing along her spine. "I am."

He opened his eyes, leaning into the lamplight to reveal clouded cataracts that had thickened. Though he had become nearly cave-blind, the depth of his *sight* had been retained, regardless. "The feud continues, then."

"Jamra put a spell around his northern citadel. For a time, I could not leave the stinking place." She fidgeted helplessly with the seam on her headscarf, nearly pulling it loose from atop her head. "He might have found me had I not discovered a third way out in time."

"You've always been resourceful. And the authorities?"

"They are little more than clay figures grasping after smoke."

"Yet they caught you once before."

Shrewd old one.

"I was too deep in my grief and didn't see the snare until it was too late."

"Hmm, and now?"

"They still search, but with no heart for the chase." She thought of that pale, yellow-haired Inspector Nettles and the look of failure on his face as she disappeared before his eyes. His expression was a memory she would tuck away for nights when she needed amusement to distract her.

Rajul Hakim seemed pleased to hear her report, nodding. He took another hit off his pipe, inhaling the tobacco smoke with the relish of a man satisfying a hunger. He nodded again, though this time in contemplation. "Jamra will not be so easily eluded a second time. His hatred is an oil fire that only grows the more you try to put out the flames."

The feud between Jamra's clan and hers had been more than a millennium in the making. Wounds of pride torn open over and over again and left to fester between those of the sunrise lands and those of the sunset in the west. Two jinn houses divided by a broken ideology, skirmishing under the All-Seeing Eye. But she, born of the east, and Hariq, born of the west, had looked past the worn-out grievances between their families and found love in each other's arms. And were punished for it. Relentlessly. Ostracized by members of both clans for not defending their family's side in the feud. And yet they endured, creating their own oasis in the middle of the storm.

Until the unspeakable happened.

Hariq wasn't supposed to die. He was wise and bright and beautiful. Charming and playful, he made her laugh like no other, with his harmless tricks on humans done to entertain her while they swam in the ether together. Tapping men on the shoulder at the train station to make them turn around. Sliding a diner's coffee cup out of reach while they read the newspaper at a street-side café. Reversing a laundress's shirts so they hung upside down on the line. They should have had a thousand carefree years together, but one cannot always predict the rock in the road that will next make them stumble.

"Jamra will come," she said. "He always does. But the All-Seeing Eye has set my feet down here again. With you. With the memory of Hariq." She stared at the spirals on the wall with vague curiosity. "I had once known great peace here, but this village is now the source of my greatest sorrow. I'm pleased to meet my enemy in such a wasteland."

The old jinni puffed out a circle of smoke, his eyes fluttering at a vision. He cocked his head to the left. "And the other binding?"

Other?

"There's a frilly yellow creature shadowing you, is there not?"

Sidra nodded. "Fate has tied us together by our wrists in a knot I cannot seem to undo. There's another as well, though her magic at times is worthy of the bind."

He considered this, seeing beyond into the cosmos. "It is good," he said and set down the pipe's mouthpiece. "Jamra will come, but you will not be alone."

She hadn't thought of it like that before. The girl's presence had always felt like a burden to her. A hindrance to clear thought and inner peace. But on reflection she saw how Yvette's presence with her in the apartment had kept her from sinking into a despair so deep she would have shut the blinds and stared at the blank wall for an eternity.

"It is good," she agreed.

Beside her the brass *dallah* full of coffee disappeared. The canopy and lamps disintegrated. The hassock beneath her collapsed so that she had to float to her feet. The old one's pipe turned to smoke, followed by the jinni himself. Sidra stood for a moment in the dark with only the faint lamplight from her borrowed lantern to illuminate her thoughts. It *was* good, she convinced herself. It would have to be. For she knew what Jamra was coming for in addition to her life.

CHAPTER SIX

They laid Jean-Paul on a sofa in the salon with a pillow for his fevered head, a blanket for his body, and a sprig of rosemary tied to an amethyst crystal tucked inside his jacket pocket. Though she didn't know what good it would do, Elena spoke a protection spell to keep Jean-Paul from further harm, then squeezed Brother Anselm's hand in thanks for agreeing to stay and watch over him. Without time to consult *The Book of the Seven Stars*, she could do little to reverse the jinni's magic. Fortunately, she believed she knew where to find Sidra. That fragment of information was the only leverage she had.

"Thank you for letting my husband stay in the care of my friend," she said to Jamra as he escorted her into the courtyard.

"How do you keep a man like that as a friend?"

Yes, to an outsider it would look strange for a witch and monk to have developed a friendship, but Brother Anselm was much like Jean-Paul—he didn't shut his mind to the existence of the supernatural outside his own faith. Well, not anymore. Both men had needed convincing at first. But she supposed their curious minds, convinced by the weight of undeniable empirical evidence, were predisposed to accept the truth in whatever form it took.

"He's a good man. Unlike some," she said pointedly and marched toward the wine cellar. Elena had agreed to find Sidra and lead the jinni to her in exchange for Jean-Paul's life, but she didn't have to be cordial. She opened the door to the cellar and lit a lamp with a snap of her fingers.

The jinni peered into the dark beyond her flame. "What is this place?"

"It's where we keep the wine. My workroom is also down there. I'll require my spell book and a few supplies if you want me to find her," she said without looking back. If he struck her down, so be it. But she wouldn't suffer this jinni bullying her another moment.

After he sniffed and gave his approval, Elena pressed her palm to the lock on the workshop door at the bottom of the stairs and whispered, "Vinaria." The door swung open with a creak. Inside, she ran her finger quickly over her jars of herbs, bits of dragonfly wing that had nearly crumbled with age, and a pouch of salt. Yes, she might want to keep some of that with her. But what else?

"Why do you need a book of spells? Isn't your being your source of magic?"

Is that how jinn magic worked?

"No, I . . . witches are merely a conduit for the energy they express, though I can call up the magic I need as readily as if it were a part of me. It's just that some spells are more complicated than others. They require the right combinations of words and offerings to conjure the desired outcome. To pinpoint Sidra's location, I may need an additional spell to bolster my ability to track her." A lie.

Jamra picked up the grimoire on her worktable to inspect the contents. Elena made a silent plea for the book to behave while in his hands. She also hoped the jinni's touch wouldn't singe the poor thing's edges. She'd accidentally dropped it once near the kitchen stove, and the book didn't let her open its pages for a week.

He turned the grimoire over, unimpressed, and handed it back to her. "Collect what you need to find Sidra. Quickly. We are already losing time."

"Of course," she said and slid the spell book inside her leather satchel, which she slung over her shoulder.

The only thing she truly required was Yvette's hairpin, which Minister Durant of the Lineages and Licenses office had returned to her when he no longer held any sway over her future. Elena removed it from the drawer, along with a handful of items she thought might come in handy, including her athame, and slipped them inside her bag.

The jinni rested his hand on her forearm. The heat of his touch penetrated to the bone. "I say again, cooperate and your man will recover. Deceive me or defy me and he will die. Let's go."

Jamra stole a bottle of wine from the cellar before forcing Elena back into the courtyard and ordering her to do her magic. She hesitated to enter the shadow world with him standing so near. She was exposed and vulnerable while her vision was elsewhere, but it was the only way to know for sure if Sidra and Yvette were in the *Fée* lands as she suspected. *If* her vision would even let her see that far.

If not, there was always the athame. As far as she knew, jinn bled as readily as witches.

She took a seat on the bench by the door where Jean-Paul often kicked off his muddy boots before entering the house. She ought to remove a few items from her satchel besides the hairpin, she supposed, to make it look more like a spell, so she set a calcite crystal and feather on the bench beside her. With the jinni watching her every move, she closed her eyes and concentrated on Yvette's hairpin. A buzzy sort of energy danced against her palm, encouraging her to follow its trail.

Soon her mind's eye opened in a meadow near a stream. A grove of trees with standing stones in the middle of a clearing came into view. Two chairs made out of bent branches posed beside a stone font. But no one was there. The forest was eerily quiet. No birdsong, no rustle of leaves. She felt hot breath that reeked of charcoal on her neck and for an instant thought she should reel herself back in, but then a woman approached at the edge of her vision. She wore a metallic-green gown that reminded Elena of the beetle shells she sometimes collected near a rotting log on her walking path. The woman's shimmering gown floated just above the periwinkles poking out of the earth. On her head she wore a crown made of tiny seed pearls and dragonfly wings, and around her neck hung a silver chain bearing an agate stone no bigger than a thumb. The woman's eyes glittered when she smiled.

"Welcome," she said, staring straight at Elena as if she were truly standing in front of her. "I've been waiting for your arrival."

"Titania?" Elena couldn't be certain if she said the name out loud or not.

The fairy queen nodded, then looked past her as if meeting another's gaze. The sparkle she'd carried dimmed, replaced by a hard glint full of warning. For the briefest moment her countenance changed from ineffable beauty to something wraithlike and threatening. But it was only a flash before she was herself again.

The heat on Elena's neck flared at the sight. Jamra. A nasty trick by the jinni, piggybacking on her vision. She'd have to cleanse with salt for a week to get the trace of him out of her mind. Titania had seen him and somehow made him withdraw with her brief, bizarre transformation. Was this queen's power strong enough to make the jinni take flight? The women exchanged half smiles in the shadow world as their minds met on the same ground.

"Yvette and her guest are no longer here," said the queen, anticipating the reason for Elena's intrusion.

So, she'd been right about Sidra escaping to the *Fée* lands with Yvette. That would explain how she'd slipped through Jamra's binding spell. He'd been careless after all by restricting his spell to the earthly realm. Pity for him, but good for resourceful Sidra for figuring a way out.

Elena was about to ask the fairy queen if she knew where the two had gone when Titania held a finger to her lips.

"I do not know the mortal place-name, but I can show you. She and my granddaughter are there together," she said and held out her sleeve. Elena reached out with her spirit hand, and soon her mind was flying over fields of flowers that grew in neat agricultural rows. Fields of roses, lilacs, irises, violets, and jasmine. Though her body was not truly there, the heady scent of the flowers intoxicated with their magnificent fragrance as she breathed in the southern air between mountain and sea.

As soon as the place was fixed in Elena's mind, the scene faded at the edges. Her sight was at its limit. Titania, perhaps sensing their connection was nearly undone, made a request. "My granddaughter was hastily sent abroad before I could fully inform her of the risk." The queen looked from side to side as if checking for another's presence. "Please, you must warn them."

The connection quickly failed. Elena gasped for breath as she was yanked home to her own time and place. Waking from her trance, she swayed on the bench as she acclimated to her physical surroundings again.

Jamra stood before her, his arm outstretched as if he'd summoned her back with his jinni magic. He relaxed his fingers and rested his arms behind his back. "The witch queen told you they were not there, so why did you stay with her?"

"How did you go there with me?"

He leaned forward, his gaze uncomfortably piercing the space between them. "Jinn are master travelers of the mind, able to see into the dimensions of thought when left unguarded."

His boast unnerved her. But, thank the All Knowing, he'd back-tracked out of the vision before the rest was revealed. She could tell him anything, lead him anywhere. Though she had not seen Sidra in her vision, she now knew the jinni had gone to the southern province where the perfume witches made their famous scented concoctions. Titania claimed she would also find Yvette with her. But why had they gone *there*?

Elena had to think quickly. "I know her granddaughter," she said, standing and straightening her skirt. "I helped her reunite with her family in the *Fée* lands. Titania wished to thank me for my assistance."

"But where is Sidra? The witch queen must know where they went."

"Why the city?" Elena asked abruptly.

"What?" He looked at her as if she were a gnat that kept buzzing in his nostrils.

His annoyance was growing. She needed to be careful. "That's where you set your trap for Sidra. So why there? Why the city? Why were you so certain she would show up there, of all places?"

"Because it is where I sometimes live so that I may observe the ways of mortals. The spell was as much for my protection as it was to ensnare her."

"You thought she'd come looking for you?"

His eyes sharpened like a hawk singling out its prey. "There is a blood feud between our clans. Neither can abide the other drawing breath in this world. But she, as green as she is, has hurt me like no other."

"Because you believe she took your brother's life?"

"No, witch, because he fell in love with one who is our enemy. And then she robbed his dead body of an object of indescribable worth. One that she continues to taunt me with. And I will have it returned."

Jamra hit the end of his patience. Before Elena understood what was happening, her feet violently lifted off the ground. Her body sailed backward onto something soft yet sturdy that seemed to be moving. Her legs dangled over the edge of—she looked down—the Aubusson tapestry from her salon wall?

Horrified, she gripped the edge of the tapestry as they accelerated over the top of Château Renard's chimney. The jinni sat straight-backed beside her with his legs crossed, obviously pleased at the terror he'd provoked in her by taking to the sky.

"Put us down!"

He tugged his derby snug against his head. "Too late. Enough with your games, witch." The tapestry veered sharply right, and Elena screamed as her fingernails nearly gouged holes through the wool threads. "Tell me which way to the lying *jinniyah* this instant or I will only go faster."

She felt the wind speed increase. Her stomach lurched. With no time to think, she shouted, "South! I swear to the All Knowing she is in the south."

"You see, telling the truth is not such a hard thing to do."

Defeated and angry at herself for giving in to her fear, Elena curled on her side as the wind whipped her hair and her knuckles grew white from the effort of holding on. She cursed the hour that announced this madman into her life. Queasy and afraid, she found what solace she could in knowing Jean-Paul at least was in no further danger. So long as she cooperated. Little comfort, but it was all she could find on that tiny patch of wool, aloft on unseen currents of air.

The jinni removed the cork from the stolen bottle of wine with his teeth, then laughed as he pointed the tapestry toward the southland. "Now we will see whose magic is superior."

CHAPTER SEVEN

The market hummed from the fusion of so much color and scent mingling in the dry air. The heat from the paving stones penetrated through the soles of Sidra's sandals as palm trees swayed overhead. If not for the local women in their white linen dresses and broad straw hats, she could almost imagine she was in her homeland again.

Yvette poked her nose in the bouquet rising off a dish of red saffron. "I thought you said it wasn't safe to go out."

The jinni produced three coins and dropped them in the shopkeeper's hand in exchange for a packet of the threaded spice. The smell alone, like the tall grass by the river after the sickle has swept through it, worked its magic on her foul mood. She brightened a fraction, remembering how much she adored wandering the winding walkways of the village on a sunny morning. She was too much like the saffron flower, she mused, thriving in the light instead of the shadow like so many of her kind. Hariq had been the same, so eager to walk among the people, enjoying earthly delights as if there were no greater pleasures to be had. Sidra knew of jinn who spent their entire existence hidden in dim corners, never becoming more than a fingerling of touch on the back of the neck of a passerby. For some it was enough to live in shadow. But not her.

"I said it was unsafe for *you* to walk out," she said. "At least by yourself." Sidra tucked her purchase in the folds of her caftan. "With me, you can be assured that yellow head of yours will stay atop your skinny neck. For now."

The girl skipped beside her to catch up. "How did you end up living here? I thought all you jinn lived in the desert."

"My heart remains in the oasis of my homeland, but I cannot live there anymore."

Sidra turned down a side alley. Her gold bracelets rattled on her wrists as she adjusted her headscarf. The girl went silent as she traipsed behind, but her thoughts stirred like a hive of bees. The buzzy energy that radiated off the girl was not unpleasant, but it never ceased. And the mortals—men *and* women—turned their heads, gawking in wonder every time she strode past, as if she were some delicate, beautiful goddess from another time. Fairies were nothing but narcissists glowing for all the world to see, Sidra thought with an eye roll. Yet the mantle fit the girl, cloaking her in new skin that seemed to shine brighter the longer she wore it. Burnished. Polished. Shed of the scar and grimy patina she'd once brandished with pride. And her newfound perception—it, too, sparkled with the sheen of the freshly formed.

"But why *here?*" Yvette asked.

They passed a palm tree whose bushy top swayed above the terra-cotta roofs. Beside them, a clay urn held an olive tree, the branches already laden with hints of the fruit to come. Ahead, two- and three-story apartments rose up on either side of the lane they walked, ancient and sagging on their beams, their plaster walls the color of sandstone and ocher. Every third door they passed was painted blue as an omen against bad luck. In the narrowest sections of the village, walking between the buildings was like traveling through a desert canyon shaped by rare torrents of wind and water, and yet the fair one had to ask such a question.

"Look around, girl. My people have left their mark on every street in this village." Sidra stopped before an arched wooden door with black iron hinges. "I blend in. It's a place where I can remain hidden in plain sight."

The fairy looked at Sidra with her usual quizzical expression. "So Grand-Père did you a favor by returning you here?"

"He did me no such thing. He's only rushed me toward the problem I was trying to avoid."

"So that's why you don't want me out alone, because you're still wanted by *les flics*?" The girl twisted around to look behind her as if checking for a tail. If she only knew what could actually be out there waiting in the shadows between buildings, she would run back to the apartment and hide her head under a pillow. "But then why am *I* here?"

A fair question. Sidra assumed Yvette had been sent along to aid in her fated journey, but given the high probability of death, it was possible Oberon had a separate purpose for the girl. "Perhaps your grandfather merely wanted to air the place out from your smoking," she said and knocked on the arched door before them.

After a pause, the door creaked open. An older woman wearing a simple cotton abaya and hijab answered. She held a goat in the crook of her arm that bleated in protest at being restrained.

"I wondered when I'd see you again." The woman's kohl-rimmed eyes scanned both guests.

She didn't invite the two in, as was generally customary, instead blocking the door against entry. Left standing on the threshold, Sidra slipped a bangle off her wrist and held it out in offering. The woman met her gaze, accepted the gold, and shut the door. A moment later she returned, gazed briefly at Yvette in curiosity, and handed Sidra a small bottle of civet oil in an amber-colored glass vial.

"Three drops should do, but there's a little extra. The stars say you'll need it."

The women nodded at each other and the door closed. A second later the door opened again, and the woman beckoned Yvette closer.

She slipped a small leather pouch in the girl's hand. "For later," she said and shut the door. The lock slid into place.

"Is she one of yours too?" Yvette sniffed at the contents of the pouch—which resembled two dried-up figs—and made a face. She quickly closed it up again. "Smells off."

"She's closer to Elena's kind. Though perhaps a bit like you too," she said. "She, too, steals from her employer a little at a time to work her magic." Sidra held the bottle up to the light before adding it to the fold in her robe where she'd stashed the saffron. "I'd protect that if I were you. She's rarely wrong."

Yvette tucked the oddly scented pouch in her bottomless pocket. "Oh là là, I don't steal anymore."

"But you're good at it, yes?"

"I suppose I always was. So, what's the oil for? What did she mean you were going to need extra?" Yvette's skin began to glow from the heat of her rising emotions.

"In time, girl, in time. Right now, we need to find a dishonest man with one leg."

"Of course. You can find one of those in every marketplace, if you know where to look."

"Calm yourself and follow me. We need to put your skill to work. There is something I require." Sidra led them up a stone staircase that looked as if it had been carved out of the hillside with the buildings added as an afterthought. They climbed single file until they emerged into another square sequestered from the rest of the village. There a secondary market flourished, one where the usual baskets of flowers and spices were offered for sale along with an array of ingredients a jinni in trouble might be on the lookout for.

Sidra walked beneath the loggia that ran alongside the market, observing the crowd. Women in pale blue-and-white dresses and broad-brimmed straw hats sniffed at jars filled with aromatic potions. On the sidewalk, woven baskets the size of fish traps displayed mounds of pink magnolia petals that had begun to wilt from the afternoon heat. Their fragrance stirred the air with the promise of perfumed love spells. A boy scooped his hand in a bowl of cowrie shells, then held each one up to his ear to find the one that would tell him his future. And there, in the corner, sat the man with one leg. A worn *taqiyah* covered his wretched head.

"Is that him?" Yvette asked with a nudge of her chin. "The one scratching himself."

"Like a camel with fleas. That's the one. Yanis the Dishonest."

The man's stall displayed half a dozen small brass incense burners, innocuous tourist talismans, and mesh bags full of herbs and shaved tree bark for sale. There were also fuzzy yellow flower sprigs that floated in jars of marula oil. The blooms were of the mimosa flower. The mime flower. Some called it the mocker of death. But Sidra knew that to be a lie when left to his care.

"Do not let him see us approach," she said. "The coward will scream for his life, and I don't wish to be chased through a busy market." If not for the crowd and the need to keep an eye on the girl, she would dissipate and seep into the man's stall to whisper in his ear about an insect small enough to enter through the nose during sleep and chew a path through the soft tissue of the brain. A most maddening death. One she would wish upon him a thousandfold.

The man with one leg kept busy braiding sweetgrass into bundles for smudging. He didn't look up until they were standing right in front of his table. Sidra took pleasure in the way his face sank when he saw her, as if he'd been forced to abandon every ounce of comfort he'd ever known. His hands flew up, fingers spread wide, to defend himself.

"It had to be an accident," Yanis said, his voice rising in pitch. "The potency was the same in both bottles. You have to believe me."

"And yet I do not." She wanted to strike him with fire. Burn his scalp down to the white-bone skull. Melt his eyes as if they were candle wax for his part in everything that went wrong. But, curse the fates, she needed this twisted scrap of a sorcerer. Without taking her eyes off the man, she told Yvette to go behind the table and look for a jar of frankincense.

"What's it look like?" The man risked wiggling a finger as he pointed to a canister on his right beside his wooden leg. "Much obliged," Yvette said and gave a little smile. She hadn't even shown her teeth, yet Yanis smiled back at her like a lovesick puppy despite his predicament.

"Pour a scoop into this cloth and tie it up." Sidra made sure the man looked away from Yvette long enough to notice the insignia on the slip of silk she'd laid out on the table with a thud. The cloth had belonged to Hariq.

"There was nothing I could have done different," Yanis pleaded. "One potion, two bottles. Everything went according to plan."

Feeble excuse for a witch. She would sew his lips together with stingweed if he didn't stop talking about that day. "Except it didn't. Now do your spell," she said through her gilded teeth. "The one for the scent."

"Anything, anything," he begged, then jumped from his seat onto his leg while the wooden one kept him balanced like an awkward shorebird. "Give me one minute."

While the sorcerer went about his work, crushing small brown seeds with his pestle and adding drops of various oils into the mix, all the time muttering incomprehensible words about magic and jinn, Yvette tied up the cloth full of frankincense resin.

"I'm sure you'll tell me what *this* is for, too, just like you explained about the last two items." Yvette secured the knot with an extra tug for emphasis.

Sidra adjusted her headscarf, her bracelets chiming with the effort. "It's for an incantation. As soon as this goat's ass is done with his spell mixture, we can begin."

"Sidra, you have to believe me," Yanis said, looking up from his work. "It was something other than the potion. Let me explain."

"Enough!"

With a sigh, he handed her the mixture folded up in brown paper. A card was tied on top with instructions for how to use it. She sneered at him, and the hair on his arm singed until it smoked. He patted the arm and rubbed his skin against the sting.

Back in the apartment, Sidra placed the items collected from the market in a polished clamshell along with three drops of the reeking civet oil. She opened the envelope of fragrant seeds the witch had crushed under his pestle, passing it under the girl's nose with a smile. They both sighed at the strong aroma of vanilla and cardamom.

"You asked me earlier why I live in a village not in my own country." As the jinni spoke, she lit the wick of a fat candle with a finger's touch. The firelight gleamed in her eyes as they traced the dancing flame. "There's a unique magic in this place. Protective magic. *Scent* magic."

Yvette leaned in, her gauzy gown sparkling against her luminescent skin. "You mean the witches who make perfume? I met one in the city before I found my parents."

"The magic of the perfume witches is all about pleasure. Their spells are designed to entice. They focus on allure and attraction. All good and well in the right moment." Sidra poured the contents of the sorcerer's spell packet into the shell with the other ingredients, then held the bowl over the candle flame. "But what we're after is something stronger. Something to confuse the dog chasing after the fox. A repellent. A cloak in the darkness."

"You mean from *les flics?*"

"Bah. I could strike them down with one puff of breath."

The jinni shook her head as she swirled the contents of the clamshell over the fire to let the civet oil heat up.

"That smells as bad as that stuff the witch gave me." Yvette waved her hand in front of her nose. "Then who?"

Sidra added another pinch of crushed cardamom as she spoke. "Jamra, that's who." The spice flared in a puff of golden scent. She added another drop of civet oil to be sure and a chunk of frankincense resin. The scent of pine and lemon spiked in the air.

"Who's he?"

"The one who bound me to the city," the jinni said, swirling the clamshell slowly over the flame. "Our families have been at each other's throats for as long as there have been throats." Sidra sniffed the mixture. "He is my husband's brother."

The fair one started catching on as she sat back and stared at the man's clothes by the door. "Your husband was once your enemy."

"Until we fell in love."

"Well, well, well," Yvette said and whistled. "Tell me more."

Sidra paused her stirring. How to explain to this girl of twenty years the novelty of one ethereal entity discovering another in the midst of an ongoing imperial conquest that took place over three centuries earlier—Hariq drawn by the skirmish of mortal men leading the fight for territory from their horses, and she attracted by the toll of war on the women once the horses trampled past. Each had hovered above to observe the ever-creeping expansion of the mortal empire, each resisting the urge to interfere and nudge the course of events to their liking.

In the cool of the evening after a fiercely won battle, when the mood among mortals swayed between relief and misery, she spotted him. They'd each masqueraded as tiny songbirds so they might sail over the skirmish and spy on the progress of the war. In the aftermath, the pair had perched in separate trees to sing—she to lull the wounded to sleep, he to offer promise of another life for those who would not wake again. Disguised as they were, they didn't know each other as enemies, and so a game ensued where she flitted from one tree to another, only to be followed by Hariq, who landed closer each time until their wings touched as they alighted side by side. At last he revealed himself in his human form, entreating her to do the same so they might press more than shoulders together.

When she saw his robes, his hair, the curved blade on his belt, she knew him for who he was: clan of the sunset tribes. Her enemy, sworn by blood and fire! Instinct urged her to smite him and leave the cursed jinni for dead on the pile of soldiers where the hungry vultures already filled their bellies. But then he smiled full of kindness, encouraging her to appear. A man brimming with curiosity and compassion, not hate and belligerence. Some fluttering counterinstinct told her he could be trusted, overriding her impulse to do him injury. And so she animated as a woman beside him.

Instead of lashing out in recognition of a foe, he offered her a solution to their dilemma. He held his hand up and asked for her to do the same. Then he vowed that she of the sunrise and he of the sunset would be destined to know only harmony because no day under the heavens could be complete without having the sun rise and fall in tandem. "*Tawazun*," he said and pressed his palm to hers.

She never hid from him again. He made her feel seen in a way she didn't know was possible. Such a desire was foreign to most jinn, yet she discovered that the pleasure of his gaze was what she'd craved all her life. Before the mortals could wage their next battle, she knew she couldn't live without his face being the first thing she saw at dawn.

"He had a beautiful smile," Sidra said to the girl and left it at that.

"And now this Jamra fellow is after you? Because of . . ." She nudged her head again toward the clothes.

"It's more complicated than simple revenge, but yes."

Yvette picked up the card with the instructions that came with the packet of herbs. "And this spell can hide you from him?"

Sidra grinned. "It's natural for my kind to disappear in smoke and scent. But if you add a layer over that with a spell, the fragrance-infused magic will cloak my scent-trail with its perfume," she said. "*Per fumum*. Through the smoke. It is how I am hidden." She stirred the ingredients in the clamshell with the tip of her finger, unaffected by the heat of the flame. "I make Yanis perform a portion of the spell to confuse the source of the magic. It is not foolproof, but it has protected me well enough for hundreds of years."

The jinni stirred the scents together, letting the civet oil warm long enough to transform from a stench that offended the nose to an aromatic enticement. Occasionally she looked at the card, following the witch's instructions for how much and when to add another pinch or sprinkle, until the room filled with a cloud of fragrance—zesty, earthy, but with the sweetness of vanilla. Like the market at noon when the cook fires are going and the spice-goods travel from seller to buyer to saucepot to be poured over fish or lamb in a creamy sauce.

"It is done. The cloud of scent will infiltrate the village. Between that and the surrounding flower fields, there ought to be enough confusion to mask my presence, making it much more difficult for Jamra to sniff me out. Which means you should be safe here as well." Sidra inhaled and closed her eyes. Still she could see Yvette glowing through her eyelids. "Did you get the other thing I asked for?" She peeked one eye open as she waited for the answer.

Yvette tossed the bronze talisman onto the table. The medallion clattered against the wood, as if announcing how much the thievery had cost her reformed conscience.

"It, too, is for our protection," Sidra assured her.

The girl seemed to calculate the deed against the gain and agree it was worth the effort. As she drummed her fingers against the table, her eyes scanned the rest of the items they'd used. "What about the saffron?" she asked at last. "Why didn't you add that to the spell like the rest?"

Sidra retrieved the packet of spice from her caftan and tossed it at the girl with a grin. "That," she said, "is for our rice. Light the stove. I'm famished."

"You can't just poof some up for us?"

"And deny ourselves the delicious aroma while it cooks? Grab a pot."

CHAPTER EIGHT

Somewhere over the southernmost vineyards of the Chanceaux Valley, Elena grew confident enough to let go of the tapestry's thin edge with one hand. Jamra had slowed the pace through the air, though he made sure to let her know how much it annoyed him to travel so slowly with her in tow. He chewed on olives he'd produced for himself in a brass dish, spitting the pits at her feet. She kicked them off the tapestry with the heel of her clunky sabot. Honestly, she adored that wall hanging with its scene of a fox running in a field surrounded by a floral border, but she supposed it would never see the inside of her salon again. Nor did she know if she would ever see Jean-Paul again.

What if he worsened while she was away from him? What if . . .

She looked down at her wedding ring, so new the gold still glinted with a flawless shine, and was reminded not to let herself think too far ahead or fall into despair over shadow thoughts that hadn't come to pass. Not yet. Still, she allowed herself to glare at the jinni before turning her back to let him know how much it annoyed *her* to be abducted by such a boorish swine. She kept up the brave show until she got a view of a ravine below and inched back toward the center of the woven textile to keep from falling off.

"It is amusing how mortals always give witches credit for flying in their stories," he said and spit out a pit. "But you are as scared as a cat stuck in a tree. Where is your broom? Your magic ointment?" He made the tapestry swerve left, then right as an added taunt.

She imagined Jamra being the sort of child who deliberately stuck animals up in trees just to see them squirm when they couldn't figure out how to get down. If jinn ever were children. But he wasn't wrong. Though he'd assured her the makeshift magic carpet wouldn't let her fall, the unnatural sensation of moving above the earth in the open air without even a handrail to provide a sense of security was most distressing. Escalating her fear was the very real notion that the sun would be setting soon, leaving them in the dark above the clouds. Not a place she wished to be. What if they hit a tree or hillside or one of those mortal airplanes with a propeller and were cut into pieces?

"I'd like to get down now. It will be dark soon, and I cannot navigate any longer without the light to see by." It was a lie, but Elena was willing to bet Jamra didn't know truth from fiction for witches. Besides, she was cold and hungry and in need of some grounding.

He spit another pit at her. "We are not there yet."

"We won't get there tonight, regardless. I'm not like you. I need rest and warmth at night. And food," she said, glancing at the olives he'd refused to share.

Jamra exhaled in frustration. "Very well. But only because we are approaching the city at the fork of two rivers. There is a small restaurant there that serves grilled lamb the way I like it, with all the right spices. You may eat as well," he said as he lowered them toward a grassy slope.

"You're too kind."

He answered her sarcastic response by bumping the tapestry against the ground, creating a hard landing. Elena rolled off and was sent sprawling onto the grass. Jamra had the nerve to laugh as her skirt flew up over her knees. She swore then, as she straightened her hem and gathered her belongings back in her satchel, that she would die finding a spell that would stuff the insufferable jinni into the smallest container she could think of and secure him inside for a thousand years.

Jamra rolled up the tapestry by making a winding gesture with his finger, stashing the rug high in the branches of an alder. He waved his hand at the tree, as if closing a curtain, and motioned for Elena to take the path to the center of town. "After you," he said.

Instead of heading down the main road that ran beside the river, Jamra forced them to walk several blocks inland before coming around to the side street where the café sat wedged between a tobacco store and silk goods shop. No, a creature made of fire wouldn't be very fond of the water, she imagined. The sun had gone down, and the streetlamps were just coming on in the town. The lamplight gave the walls a golden old-world glow as they entered the quaint *bouchon*.

Remarkably, somewhere between crash-landing the magic carpet and sitting down at their table by the fire inside the cozy café, Jamra had changed her appearance. She no longer wore her work clothes and muddy sabots. He'd opted instead to present her in a tasteful blue dress with a lace neckline. Simple yet appropriate for dinner out in a casual café. He, in his suit and derby hat, looked like any other man of business out for a bite of local cuisine.

"Nice trick," Elena said and shook out her napkin upon being seated.

He ordered them a bottle of red wine. A good one full of strong notes of plum, smoke, cherry, and a hint of oak-barrel spice. The grapes had been grown in the south where the sun baked the hard earth, forcing the vines to dig deep for survival. As she watched him sip, she wondered how someone capable of tormenting others with the destruction of property, brain fevers, and kidnapping could so casually sit at a table like a normal being, ordering exquisite wine and grilled meat as if he were on holiday.

The drippings still sizzled on the plates as the waiter brought out their lamb, carrots, and potatoes. "There are few things mortals do well, but their talent for braising meat with just the right spice is to be admired," Jamra said.

Elena spread a pat of butter on a hunk of crusty bread. "You don't have a very high opinion of mortals, do you?" she said and took a bite.

"Every now and then you find one worthy of the air they breathe." He skewered a chunk of meat on the end of his knife with a slice of potato and stuffed the whole thing in his mouth. He smiled as he chewed. "I vow the chef in this quaint café shall never come to harm," he said after he swallowed.

Elena put her knife down. Here she was sitting in a café eating a delicious meal in a new dress while Jean-Paul lay sick in bed with a fever. And sitting across from the very jinni who'd broken into their lives and stolen the happiness they'd worked so hard to build as if it meant nothing more to him than wiping a few breadcrumbs from the tablecloth. She might be hungry, but she couldn't share another bite with her abductor. She wished there were a way for her to be alone with her thoughts, if only for a few minutes, so she could slip into the shadow world and check on Jean-Paul. But how to do it without Jamra noticing? He would undoubtedly try to invade her vision if he caught her, and she had no wish to experience that breath on her neck again. Could she make an excuse to be alone? And just how much of a prisoner was she? Jamra certainly hadn't tried to restrain her or keep her from walking away when they landed in the village, though she hadn't really made a serious attempt. No, the knowledge that he could kill Jean-Paul on a whim was manacle enough, and he knew it.

Jamra lifted his glass to drink. "You are not eating."

"It's very spicy," she said as the seed of an idea sprouted. "Makes me thirsty."

The jinni swallowed the last of his wine, then poured himself a second glass. Elena held hers out as well. Yes, the idea might work, she thought as she swirled the wine. Let him drink and eat his food. Take it in. But not too fast. Not yet.

She'd never had much practice with silent incantations, but there were ways to conjure spells without speaking a word. Intent was always the main ingredient, of course. Speaking or writing the words out loud put them into the world in the precise form. But as long as the mind stayed true to her intentions and didn't wander, she should be able to channel the magic toward her goal without him noticing.

Elena swirled her glass so the wine rotated inside like a small tempest. The aroma of the fermented fruit funneled out, wafting in the air between them. Yes, with help from the wine she could do it.

A single sip to wet the tongue. A second one, the spell's still young. Take one more the blood will thin, drain the glass let sleep begin.

She let the words of the spell run through her thoughts three times to reinforce her intention, all the while concentrating on the potency of the wine and the jinni drinking it. Candlelight reflected in the drink's ruby tones, hypnotizing with its beauty as it spun around. She sent that dizzying sensation floating to Jamra. But slowly. Something to dissolve in his blood as the alcohol worked its way through his veins, heart, and brain.

The jinni snapped his fingers at the waiter. "Don't you adore the quaint mortal gesture of paying for nourishment," he said to her. As the waiter approached with the check, Jamra waved his fingers over his palm like a common magician doing prestidigitation. A stack of coins appeared in his hand, which he tossed on the table for the waiter to sort through.

"I'm not sure that's how it's done," Elena said, then mouthed an apology to the waiter as they walked outside.

As yet, the jinni had given no indication he'd caught her at her spellcasting. Of course, there was always the off chance the silent incantation hadn't worked. Or, worse yet, had missed Jamra and hit someone else in the café. She startled at that briefly before coming back to her senses. But as they walked along the sidewalk, Jamra's feet became unsteady, and the magic that had transformed her attire began to fade so that she wore her blue wool skirt and dirty sabots again. He, too, transformed. His jacket, shirt, and tie smoldered with orange fire that nibbled at the threads until they turned to ash. He brushed them away with a giggle as he staggered in a free-flowing robe. Only his tailored trousers, black derby, and oxford shoes remained.

They'd come to a point in the neighborhood where three streets converged at an odd pointed angle, almost as if the city's original planners had meant to create a letter Y in the center of town. To their left was a short side street, which they gravitated toward. More of an alley, to be honest, except for the odd business entrance tucked at one end. The other doors all appeared to be rear entrances to cafés and small shops—rarely used, judging by the cobwebs that had collected in the frames of a few of them. At the far end a stray dog trotted by, but otherwise the alley appeared abandoned.

"Voilà!" Jamra announced for all the street to hear, then laughed at his overt attempt at a proper accent. "I love that word."

He stumbled into the alley and pointed with a flourish. "Your quarters, madame."

A majestic tent appeared before her eyes that stretched from wall to wall in the alley. Unable to resist her curiosity, Elena pushed back the cloth of the tent's opening and entered, where she was met with soft lamplight that glowed from multicolored lights suspended from the ceiling of fabric. Below she found a plush rug and narrow platform bed buried in pillows that was certainly large enough for her to curl up and sleep on. A brass washbasin, a hairbrush, and a mirror sat on a small octagonal table. It couldn't be real. Not in the center of town. And yet she could feel the silk and cotton of the tent, the wool and leather of the rugs and pillows, the cool metal of the mirror's handle.

"I'm to sleep here? In the middle of town? Won't someone discover the illusion?"

Jamra had followed her inside and sunk into the pillows on the bed, his eyes half-closed from the mixture of wine and her spell. "I create illusions within illusions within"—he burped—"illusions. Do not doubt my magic, woman."

"Nor mine," she said under her breath.

She'd assumed they'd return to the landing site where her tapestry was stashed in the tree so they might remain out of sight of mortals. Yet the tent was warm and inviting and so much better than sleeping on the cold ground. But then, he was still right there in the same tent! If he'd meant to conjure his own quarters, as any respectable man would, it was too late. His lids fluttered shut and his head tilted back against the pillows. Her spell had hit full potency.

Elena took a pillow from the bed and used it to sit on the floor. She waited a minute to see if Jamra would rouse from his sleep, but once his mouth fell open and the snoring began, she closed her eyes. She no longer needed an item belonging to Jean-Paul to find him. The bond between them had created a silver thread that coiled through the liminal space. The connection was still there for her to pick up as soon as she entered the shadow world—an encouraging sign.

At the end of the thread she saw him. Jean-Paul's head was propped on a white pillow. His glasses were on the side table beside a glass of water. His fever seemed to have lessened. She tried to press closer, but another energy held her back. Brother Anselm. He sat in a chair in the corner reading an illustrated book of Scheherazade's tales. He'd no doubt grown curious about the jinni and his powers and hoped to find answers in the pages. She looked back at Jean-Paul. Although unconscious from the jinni's curse, he looked little different from when he was in a pleasant sleep after a long day's work. His body shivered, and Brother Anselm sat forward to adjust his blanket and reapply the cool cloth to his forehead. She didn't know how the jinni's magic had sent his mind to the desert, but she asked the All Knowing to let him find some small oasis where he could find comfort until she returned.

Elena sent her love to Jean-Paul, then reeled herself back in. She opened her eyes and immediately checked to see if Jamra had awoken. But, no, he'd rolled onto his side with his face squashed against the bed so that his derby sat askew on his head like a dandy gangster, albeit a drunken one with the giggles.

She tapped her fingers against her knees, thinking over her situation. She could leave. Run. Try to return to Jean-Paul before Jamra figured out where she'd gone. But she could never return to Château Renard more quickly than the jinni could move within the ether. And then what would he do in retaliation? She was no better prepared to defend herself and her home from the jinni than she'd been that morning.

Besides, she'd begun to wonder if the farther they got from Jean-Paul, the weaker Jamra's hold over him might become. It was a possibility. Some spells worked by proximity. Then again, it was also possible Jamra might prove a man of his word, despite his despicable nature, and release his hold on Jean-Paul if she continued to put up a front of cooperation. Not likely, but also not out of the question. From what she'd learned, jinn felt a deep sense of indebtedness to those who helped them. In either case, it meant she had little choice but to stay put.

It also meant she would have to decide if she would take him to Sidra's true location or not. At first, after he'd so rudely swept her off her feet and abducted her, she'd vowed to veer him off course, claiming she had only a vague notion of where to go. She'd meant to lead him to the coast or the southern border where the mountain peaks rose up as jagged as wolf's teeth. Let him sort out which village out of a hundred Sidra was in. Oh, but she knew exactly where to find the jinni. There was no mistaking those acres and acres of flower fields.

For now, there was little more Elena could do until her incantation ran its course and her spell-drunk abductor regained consciousness. Until then, she curled up on her pillow on the floor and hoped for once Jamra's boast about his magic was true. She would still sleep uneasily, but it was reassuring to know they were hidden from the prying eyes of any villagers prone to prowling alleys at night. Cats excepted, of course.

CHAPTER NINE

Sidra placed a chunk of *bakhoor* in the incense burner and gently blew fire on it until the resin lit. She sat back against the sofa with her stomach full but her mind aloft in the clouds. The scent spell cloaking her presence in the village wouldn't be enough, despite what she'd told the girl. Not against Jamra. He'd nearly figured out the location once before, which was why she and Hariq had gone to extremes to try to be free of him. Of course, had she known then the cost, she would have given up.

That sort of thinking didn't serve one's future. Or the present. Still, the old one could have been clearer about the danger they'd faced at the time. Even now he wasn't as helpful as he could be. He'd seen something in the cave. A vision. She'd wanted to know what it was that made him puff out the pipe smoke the way he had, one ring linked to another linked to another, as they drifted up through the illusion of comfort he'd created above their heads. But it did not do to know too much about one's unlived days. For events to unfold in the manner intended, it was usually best to face life's twists and turns bereft of the knowledge of prophecy.

But facing Jamra without at least some foreshadowing of the outcome was a fool's errand. He was sly, beastly, eager to do harm to her and many others. Was that what the old one was hiding? She suspected the vision had been about Jamra, but there was no pushing Rajul Hakim when he was being stubborn. Trust the will of the All Seeing, he would say.

Regardless, the confrontation with Jamra was imminent. She and Yvette were going to need something more powerful to protect themselves than a wisp of scent and smoke. Sidra reached in her robe for the brass talisman she'd had the girl steal for her.

"What's it for?" Yvette asked as she fluffed up her pillow. The cashmere blanket had already been laid out for the girl to sleep under. She'd complained that the night air was cold. Fairies and witches were too much like mortals with their physical needs. *Wanting* things of comfort—food, drink, a soft blanket—was fine and good when one was in the mood, but it was weakness for a body to *need* them.

"It's a talisman," she said. "For luck or prosperity." Sidra rubbed her finger over the familiar engraving—a grid with nine squares inside a circle, each with a different symbol inscribed. The star in the upper right named her as one of the jinn whom the wearer asked for help. The old one was on the left in the shape of an eye. And Hariq on the bottom right corner with the wingtip of a bird. There was a fourth symbol, a moon, but the owner, an old jinni woman from across the sea, had long ago been sent to the afterlife. Struck down by a marid she'd once been married to.

"Why do I get the feeling you're expecting more trouble than you let on?"

"We're fine."

The wind rattled a loose tile on the roof. The girl looked at the ceiling as if expecting to hear the footfall of an invasion. When it didn't happen, she snuggled deeper under her blanket. Oh, but the bees kept buzzing around in her thoughts as she tapped her fingers atop the covers.

"What happened?" Yvette had been staring at her husband's clothes. "What went wrong? Did he beat you? Steal from you? Fall in love with another woman?"

"No."

"Then what could make you crazy enough to, you know, kill him?"

Sidra had already begun to dissipate into mist, to hide away and not face the shadows in the apartment for the night, but the girl's adamant nature drew her out. So curious about emotions, the *Fée*. As if that, too, were part of the sustenance their bodies craved.

Very well.

She animated again and sat on the other end of the sofa with her legs tucked under the hem of her caftan. The light from the brass lamp glowed softly above her head. "We'd made a death pact," she said.

Yvette sat up in alarm. "You were going to kill yourselves? But why?"

Sidra dimmed the lamp's flame with a wave of her hand. "Our families didn't approve of our union. It's why we fled here. Why we used the scent magic to hide ourselves. But Jamra . . . he cannot let things go. He kept looking for us. Hariq said we would never find peace if we didn't confound that jackal brother of his. We wanted to start a family."

"Couldn't you have fought Jamra? Stood up to him? It would have been two against one."

Such naivete. Such optimism. Fool of a girl.

"Jamra has aligned himself with those who would see the world and the people in it burned to an ash pile. And he will do exactly that if he gets the opportunity. For us, it was two against a thousand."

"Jiminy. So, you thought it'd be better to be dead than be chased all over the desert by that creep?"

Sidra slipped off her headscarf and freed her hair of its braid, shaking it loose so long waves fell over her shoulders. She fanned out her tresses, letting the scent of the *bakhoor* infuse her hair. "We thought if Jamra *believed* we were dead he would give up and we could live in peace. At least that was the plan."

The girl's mouth fell open. "*Believed?* You mean you were going to fake your deaths?"

They'd wanted Jamra to believe more had been lost than just their lives, but that part of the story was not for the telling. Not yet.

"There is an elder of our kind who had come here with the people many generations ago, one whom we pay tribute to," she explained. "One who has remained neutral in the fight between our families. We confided in him what we wished to do. For the sake of peace. He said there was a way to do such a thing but that the magic must be strong to convince one as consumed with hate as Jamra and his cohorts."

Yvette's radiance dimmed so that she faded to mere shadow in the low light. "What kind of magic?"

Sidra, whether lulled by the girl's genuine curiosity or a need to confess the thing that had been eating her from the inside out, bowed her head and explained.

Since they were in the land of a thousand flowers, the old jinni had learned of a bloom with a unique property. The mimic flower they called it, because of the way the bloom could impersonate breathless, pale death in one under the spell of an infusion of its nectar. After a drop was placed in each eye, physical life was suspended for hours while the innate-self floated in the safe proximity of the liminal space. It sounded like the answer to their deepest desire.

"Did you actually go through with it? Weren't you petrified?"

"It's a state I am used to. We come and go between the ether and the physical body as we please. But to sever the connection between the two, even for a few hours while both forms exist, gave us pause. And yet we consented. To be free. For that we traveled to the stinking city of infidels where Jamra would easily hear of our fate."

Yvette sat silent with her blanket pulled up to her chin, as if it might shield her from the terrible disease of bad news. She glanced again at the forgotten robe hanging on the peg by the door. "He didn't make it back?"

Sidra shook her head. "Something went wrong. The dose. The spell. A symbol marked one way instead of another."

"And they blamed you?"

"I was the only one to awake. That fool inspector arrested me for Hariq's murder several days later, but not before I confronted Jamra." Sidra ran her thumb over the engraving on the talisman, feeling the symbols tingle under her skin. "Him I would have killed, but he has always been stronger than me." She smiled wickedly at the girl. "But I did manage to leave a scar on him he'll never forget. It's why he cast that binding spell on me last time I returned to the city."

"All that time in jail together and you never once admitted any of this."

"It's strange that our fates were joined in that place," Sidra said. "And then you and I being swept back to the city after the escape."

"And Elena, too, showing up like she did. Wish she were here to hear this."

Sidra drifted back from her curious thoughts. "Be careful with your wishes, girl." She resumed studying the talisman, wondering if her precautions would be enough.

Two of the four jinn whose names were inscribed on the talisman were dead already. Only she and the old one remained, which meant the odds of the talisman's energy being linked to her grew that much stronger should someone summon her for favor. But if she could collect all the talismans remaining in the village, the connection between her and the village would be severed. The trick was remembering who else had them.

Sidra flipped the medallion over in her hand, more determined than ever to fight back against Jamra.

"How'd you know the one-legged man would have that on him?" Yvette asked.

"The people, they ask for help. They inscribe names of the jinn into the metal in the hope we'll answer." She pointed to the mark of the star. "This is me."

"But I thought he was already a sorcerer. What kind of help would he ask from a jinni?"

"Yanis? He knows a few spells. But even sorcerers have their moments of doubt. Like anyone else they look for signs. Omens. Maybe a nudge in the right direction when they cannot make up their minds about which way in life they're meant to go."

Yvette surveyed her with a sharp look of admiration. "And do you answer them?"

"Sometimes." Sidra didn't mean to be coy, but the answer was complicated. A nudge in the wrong direction could send a life careening down a perilous path. Some jinn, like Jamra and his ilk, were all too eager to engage in the sort of harmful interference that turned a man's prospects in life to dust on the whim of a false thought or implanted self-doubt. "There's a woman in an apartment two streets over. I've not seen her often, but she is one who asks for help. She wants to know if she should stay with the husband who beats her when he's had too much to drink."

"How do you know that? Can you hear her thoughts?" Yvette blanched. "Wait, can you hear *my* thoughts?"

"Thank the All Seeing I cannot," Sidra said and let her lip curl in disgust. "But this one, it's all she can think about." She tucked the talisman away in her robe with the reminder she must find a hiding place for it in the morning. "There are thoughts and then there are desires. It is desire that coalesces in the body, causing heat and scent to rise from the skin. *This* I can detect. And this one hopes to leave one day and stay the next. But what sign do I give her? Do I place a long-forgotten photo of her and her husband in happier days where she will see it and plant the suggestion in her mind that if she waits out the storm, he will change? Or perhaps I catch her eye with a suffragette pamphlet pushing for women's emancipation that nudges her out of her indecision and onto the path of independence? These are things people sometimes ask us for. To be favored. And sometimes we answer. Sometimes we don't."

"Like my wish?"

Sidra sucked in her cheeks in quick contemplation. "Wishes are different. Once they are granted, they fly like comets on their path. They cannot be stopped. I'm still not sure how yours came to be, but I still believe your heart stole that wish while my magic was in flux."

Yvette scrunched her brows together. The light had come alive inside her again, though it glowed soft as moonbeams. "That wish saved my life."

For once the girl wasn't being overdramatic. Sidra affirmed the girl's implied gratitude with a rare display of humility as she bowed her head and nodded once in return. Hopefully the result of Yvette's wish wasn't in vain. If their efforts to protect themselves from Jamra failed, they would likely both be dead in the near future.

CHAPTER TEN

Elena had curled up on her oversize pillow for the duration of the night. The thought of escape had remained a whirring fever of temptation, but in the end she concluded her cooperation was needed to help Jean-Paul. Still, she could not, would not, lead this foul-hearted man to their intended destination—where her friends, for reasons unknown, now found themselves. She would lead him south, claim ignorance as to the exact location, and then plead for her release and Jean-Paul's recovery.

Look at him, she thought, snoring slack mouthed and still reeking of wine while sprawled on his back among the bedding, asleep in a cloud of silk. *Ah, a final snort.* So, her captor was waking at last. Jamra reached an arm toward the ceiling of the tent, stretching as he opened his eyes. He yawned, blinked, and shot up when he didn't see Elena immediately beside him. When he spotted her lying in the corner, his shoulders relaxed noticeably, though he narrowed his eyes at her. "You put something in my drink."

"I did no such thing," she said, sitting up. "You're simply not accustomed to the potency of fine wine. And you drank the entire bottle."

He grunted, then stared down at his disheveled appearance. He straightened his hat and magicked his attire so his shirt, tie, and suit jacket replaced his wrinkled caftan. "Enough of these mortal comforts. We must go."

Elena collected her satchel and rose from the cushion. The tent vanished as if the vision had been blown away on the breeze until they stood once more in a damp and moldy alley that reeked of wet dog.

"Take hold of my sleeve," he said.

Feeling she had little choice, Elena grabbed a handful of pinstripes. Immediately she felt a tug as though she'd been yanked forward through time and space at incredible speed. The alley shrank behind her in a kaleidoscope tunnel. The closest comparison she had for the motion was when she'd ridden in an automobile for the first time as Yvette raced down the Chanceaux Valley road. As the car had hit top speed, Elena's hair flew out behind her, a terrifying yet freeing sensation. Only now the feeling was ten times faster so that light and shape blurred in her vision and her lungs ached for air. Then, just as suddenly as they'd accelerated, the motion stopped. Her feet touched the ground again, and the grassy slope where they'd landed the evening before came into focus. Elena was sorely tempted to ask how he'd transported them so quickly at a mere touch of his sleeve, but the inquiry would only lead to another boast.

She opted to appear unimpressed as she caught her breath. "Not one for taking in the view as you travel, I take it."

Jamra ignored her as he stared with his arms folded at the tree where he'd stashed their prime transportation. The rolled-up tapestry was gone.

Someone or something had removed it from the branches while they slept. The treachery clearly rankled him as his jaw muscle pulsed with repetitive grinding. His bad mood could also have been the effect of the hangover from the wine and the spell, but Elena wasn't going to bring it up.

"The wind?" she said and made half an effort to scour the grassy hillside for evidence of the lost tapestry. She thought it more likely some resourceful scrounger had found her lovely wool wall hanging, a beautiful mix of olive-green and powder-blue flowers with that gorgeous red fox running through a field of gold, and taken it for themselves.

"A thief!" Jamra answered. "I would punish him with the flames of eternal torment for this action."

"Couldn't we . . . ," she began, then borrowed Yvette's phrase when she couldn't think of the right term, ". . . poof off like we just did?"

"I cannot carry you that far in the ether without killing you. Believe me, I've tried it with your kind before. You would die a choking death with your lungs withering from the inside out before we got more than a few miles away."

Elena pressed a palm against her chest. "Ah, thank you for thinking of me, in that case."

"Your directions will do me no good if you're dead too soon."

Too soon?

Calculating their location using the position of the daylight stars, she judged they weren't quite halfway to the coast. She supposed the beast could simply conjure up another ride from, oh, a bit of thatch or a wooden crate perhaps, but if so, why was he so upset about the loss of that particular textile? She was the one who had ample reason to be heartbroken over the theft, not him.

"Did you protect it with a spell to prevent discovery?" she asked on a hunch.

"It would have been invisible to any mortal," he said and walked around the tree, keeping his eyes on the branches before searching the ground. Jamra sniffed the air as if trying to follow a familiar scent, then lost it again just as quickly. "Enough. We must leave this place," he said as he cast a last glance at their surroundings. For what, she didn't know, but he hurried like a man afraid.

Curious. Something had spooked him. Or someone. Elena tried to detect anything amiss on the air, but there was only the damp from the river and the scent of fish. And maybe the moldering smell of worms turning in the moist ground beneath their feet.

Again, he held out his sleeve. Recalling what he'd said about withering lungs, she reluctantly took hold. Before Elena had time to reconsider, Jamra whisked her away in a blur. He returned them to the old part of the town, reanimating inside an arched walkway that connected one building to another. A *traboule*. He hurried her along the corridor until they arrived at a shop window displaying bolts of fine silk. The shop wasn't yet open, but that did not dissuade him from barging in through the front door with a shove from his hand to create a detonation. Honestly, he was absolutely reckless with his magic.

Inside, he unfurled a bolt of red damask silk so it rolled out on the floor. The color and texture were exquisite, too fine to touch with their unwashed hands, let alone to be spread out on the floor. Yet he yanked a good ten feet off the roll, grabbed a pair of enormous scissors, and sliced through the cloth, leaving the frayed remains of the rest of the bolt on the floor.

"Get on," he said.

"Oh, you're not serious. The cloth is much too flimsy. It will never hold us both."

Between the hangover and the theft, the jinni had been confronted with one too many difficulties that morning. His anger boiled over and his eyes simmered with something dangerous. Jamra's arm swung around to attack, either with magical intent or a physical blow with the back of his hand. Elena flinched. But just before the strike made contact, she felt a tug at her back and was swept away in another blur of intense motion.

This time bright lights flashed in her periphery until she landed in yet another covered *traboule*. She stood in a maze of red stone arches before a row of small windows that overlooked the train station. She saw no one in the covered hallway, yet she knew she wasn't alone. A ticket for the train appeared in her hand, and in her ear someone whispered, *"Get on!"*

"I can't," she said to whoever was there, thinking of Jean-Paul and the jinni's hex still controlling his mind. "What if I escape and my husband dies?" But whatever force had magicked her away from Jamra wasn't taking no for an answer. A gust of wind blew hard out of the north, concentrating like a funnel inside the corridor. Elena was nearly pushed off her feet as it forced her toward the stairs to exit the *traboule*.

She didn't want to run, not like this, but instinct told her to obey whoever or whatever was manipulating her escape, and so she did. The high-pitched whistle sounded a moment after she boarded the train. A plume of gray smoke trailed over the rooftop as the engine pulled out of the station. Steam billowed out from the pistons below to envelop the passenger cars in a cloud of white. Though partially obscured by the veil of vapor, Elena dared to peek out the window for any sign of Jamra on the platform. The steam prevented a clear view, so she lowered the window a few inches to listen for threats or angry curses as the train chugged forward. When she heard none, she closed the window uneasily, but not before spotting a large shaggy dog sitting at the edge of the platform, his eyes on the passenger car. Before she could sense for any hint of shadow in the animal, the train gained speed and she was off in a puff of smoke.

Elena looked down at her ticket and read her destination. The train was heading south to the very place Sidra and Yvette had gone. She only hoped whoever was sending her there was friend and not foe, though the lines between the two had become awfully muddled of late.

CHAPTER ELEVEN

Sidra and Yvette stood on the roof of the cathedral, their bare toes curling around the lip of the clay tiles. Spread below was the hillside village still waking with the dawn.

"Tell me again what we're doing up here?" Yvette took a step back from the edge.

"Listening."

"For?"

"Tidings."

"Of course." The girl tucked her gown behind her knees and sat with her face tilted toward the scattering of morning stars. "You're not worried someone will see us up here and wonder?"

"Nobody ever looks up in a town. Ah, here they come now."

Sidra turned east toward the dawn as a flock of starlings swooped over the rooftops. They made a wide circle over the village, dipping their wings as they chased some unseen prey that zigzagged through the air. The starlings' voices cackled full of self-importance and alarm.

Yvette looked as if she might say something, then changed her mind and rested her head on her knees. The girl didn't know the power of birds. The visions they carried on their wings. The omens sung out of their mouths.

Sidra held still. The flock had grown to a thousand birds as more gathered. They painted the sky, a black cloud against the pink dawn, tipping their wings one way and then another. And then she saw her sign form as the birds swooped as one in front of her. A crescent tail. A *dog's* tail? Unmistakable. But how to interpret such a shape?

A cry came out of the south, high and piercing. The murmur of starlings scattered in a panic. Then straight as a dagger, a merlin flew into the heart of the flock, snatching a single bird in its talons before veering toward the clock tower on the opposite side of the street. There he pecked and plucked until he swallowed globules of raw meat and bone by the gullet full.

The beating-heart panic she'd seen in the birds transferred to her breast. "We must go. We must gather the other talismans. Quickly."

"Is it Jamra?"

"I believe so." And yet she couldn't be certain that was the thing making her want to disappear. She checked the sky once more, but the birds had fled, taking their squawking with them.

On the ground the girl practiced her newly learned levitation, pretending to walk when she was actually floating. Let her feel that freedom, Sidra thought. A precious thing, when all around uncertainty is closing in.

"Here," Sidra said, pointing to a blue door.

"Why can't you take the medallions back from the people yourself?"

"I'm akin to a patron. I cannot steal from my own people. Not even a small trinket like the ones we're after. How would that look if they found out the thief was me?"

"Mon Dieu." Yvette rolled her eyes and knocked on the door as soon as Sidra dissipated. A middle-aged man with a stomach that protruded under a mustard yellow *thawb* answered. The girl smiled, glowing with the power of her glamour. The man's face brightened, as if he'd been revisited by a long-forgotten dream. He stepped aside when Yvette

asked if she could come in. Five minutes later she reemerged, flipping the talisman from one palm to the next.

"What did you do to him?" Sidra asked, animating from the mist once the girl ducked into the alcove around the corner as arranged.

"I don't know how it works exactly, but mortal men turn to absolute mush when I look at them a certain way. Titania tried to explain it once, how the glittery energy that wells up in the glamour mesmerizes a certain part of their brain. Stuns them, really, so the only thing they can focus on is making sure I'm smiling at them. I can get away with just about anything while they're in that state."

"Astonishing." Sidra had to admit it was a good trick, though somehow still tawdry.

Yvette handed her the medallion, and they traveled across town to knock on the door of the second known owner, another older man who lived alone. Five minutes later the medal was in Sidra's palm, same as the last. The third bearer of the talisman was the woman Sidra had spoken about, the one who didn't know if she should leave her husband. She worked a stand in the market selling packets of anise, cardamom, cloves, and coriander. To save time, Yvette simply nicked the thing out of her apron pocket. In recompense for stealing from a woman in such doubt, she bought five packets of cardamom at full price, claiming the smell was too divine to pass up.

In possession of the last three talismans, Sidra let herself relax. There would be no summons, no whispering of her name into the ether over the village. The augury earlier hadn't given her the information she'd hoped for, though she should have known better. One shouldn't carry expectations into any conversation with birds. She had to accept the threat was getting closer. What preparations she could make must be completed.

The jinni didn't argue when the girl asked if they could walk back to the apartment so she could see the perfume shops along the way, claiming the scents had been driving her mad with curiosity since they arrived. Sidra didn't argue because she, too, had once been a young single woman attracted to pretty things and expensive, alluring smells bottled up in crystal. And, too, it was on the way, so there was time enough to give the girl this thing of pleasure in exchange for getting her the medallions. With the *Fée*, she'd learned it was best to keep things in equilibrium. Such a volatile people.

The two emerged from a narrow lane that emptied onto a larger street. A building on the corner, with an iron railing and two Greco columns flanking the front door, presented itself as a *parfumerie*, though it was obvious enough from the overly saturated scents of bergamot, jasmine, and rose seeping through the walls and windows. The fragrance lured the girl in, so she followed.

Sidra hadn't entered the shop before. Perhaps it was newly opened since her last days in the village a year earlier. The *parfumerie* was an upscale establishment, one specializing in "modern" scents created in a laboratory, as if there was anything wrong with the pure extracts derived from the distillation of centuries of knowledge.

"Isn't it divine?" Yvette asked, accepting a dab of cologne on the back of her hand from the woman working behind the counter.

Sidra detected an underlying citric fragrance that reminded her of sitting by a fountain surrounded by an orange garden on the other side of the sea, but she was otherwise unimpressed with the more pungent scent of alcohol that evaporated off the girl's skin almost immediately.

"Buy some if you like it. We have to go."

"I spent my only coins on the spices back there," Yvette said out of the side of her mouth.

The shopkeeper put the stopper back in the bottle. Her lips puckered as if drawn taut by a string of judgment. Sidra expected the woman to make a tsking sound next. If not for the tone of disapproval, she would have told the girl to leave without the perfume. Instead she waved her fingers behind her robe and produced several fat coins in her palm. She set them on the counter, and Yvette walked out with a box of perfume wrapped in a dainty blue ribbon.

Kindness toward lesser beings didn't come naturally or often, but Sidra found it buoyed her spirits on this occasion as the girl radiated with happiness at being bought a present she couldn't otherwise afford. The jinni smiled and covered her head with her scarf as they walked back to the apartment, happy in the knowledge she had collected the last of the outstanding talismans. Jamra's job of finding her was just made that much more difficult, which meant it was a good effort. Confrontation would come, but not on this day. She tilted her face to the sun, letting its glow shine bright and hot against her skin.

Minutes later, her good mood vanished. The moment they entered the apartment she knew something was off. A scent of maleness that didn't belong. The fringe on the rug out of alignment. Grains of rice scattered on the floor. And yet it could be no ordinary intruder. The apartment was kept inside an illusion inside an illusion.

Only a jinni could have found the room on their own. Or someone led there by one.

Yvette looked over Sidra's shoulder. "What's wrong?"

"Give me light."

The girl glowed bright like a lamp, illuminating the deep shadows of the room where the jinn liked to hide. Sidra sniffed the air again. Not Jamra. Nor any jinn she knew, but there was another scent hanging in the air above the male musk. The reek of nervous sweat and common market incense.

Yanis.

"Where did you hide the sorcerer's talisman?" Sidra asked.

"In the rice jar like you said."

Sidra rushed to the jar and dug her hand through the grains of rice, finding nothing.

The fourth medallion was gone again.

CHAPTER TWELVE

The dog stood on the platform, watching the train trail off through the veil of smoke and vapor as it carried the witch to her destination. That one, he observed, was motivated by love. A shiver went through his body.

"Did she make it on?"

The dog twitched his ear. The creature standing at the edge of his ear canal tickled the fur there, making him want to scratch with his paw. He refrained and nodded.

The creature whispered, "All is well, though so much scheming to get the desired outcome is proving more challenging than first imagined. Like paddling a boat with one oar."

The dog knew nothing of the water and so he yawned. The creature jumped off, disappearing into the station's woodwork. Such a small, complicated being, that one. He scratched his ear, digging deep with the nails on his rear paw.

The alliance was an unusual pact but well worth the annoyance if the outcome was what they hoped. Events had taken longer than promised, but the original scheme churned toward its conclusion at last. The dog sniffed the air and caught a familiar scent full of char and destruction swirling in the ether one street over. So angry, that one. But he would be angrier still when he could not find the witch. The dog grinned, then sprang from the platform to lope after the train.

CHAPTER THIRTEEN

Once the locomotive had pulled sufficiently far enough away from the station for her to be certain Jamra hadn't followed, Elena let herself relax. The train had been full of passengers when she got on. Some carrying shopping bags, some reading newspapers, others already leaning their heads against the windows for a quick nap between destinations. She'd finally ensconced herself inside a compartment at the rear of the train, one occupied by an elderly woman and a businessman who merely grumbled into his newspaper when she slid into the seat across from him. Her ticket stated the train was headed all the way to the coast, so she settled in for the hours-long journey. If her benefactor had other plans, she assumed they'd make their intentions known when they were ready.

And just who had been there with her in the corridor? Who knew she'd been taken by Jamra? She glanced out the window as she thought it over, and there, along the fallow fields and stalks of emerging sunflowers, where blooming apricot trees lined the road, was a dog running to keep pace with the passenger cars. She had no doubt now it was the very same quick-moving animal Jean-Paul had seen lurking around Château Renard for three days. And the one she had moments ago observed on the platform in town. So, which side did he fall on, ally or assailant in waiting?

Her new predicament had her wishing she could quietly slip off to the shadow world to check on Jean-Paul's condition, but the elderly gentleman in front of her was making a great effort to look down his nose at her over the top of his newspaper. And the woman seated beside her hadn't even uttered a *bonjour* when she sat down, merely offering one of those small smiles meant to show an effort at congeniality when the bearer felt anything but.

Elena *was* rather shabbily dressed, even for riding in a coach-class compartment on a thinly padded bench seat. Her sabots were still caked in mud, and her apron, while well stocked with various essential herbs in the pockets, was streaked with grime from working the vine row. Her outfit, a midnight-blue wool skirt and pleated chambray blouse, was otherwise respectable enough but nothing to impress. As nonchalantly as she could, she untied the strings on the apron and stuffed the article in her satchel alongside her spell book. One more thing the lady and gentleman likely wouldn't approve of either.

Elena turned her face to the window to dodge any further side glances from her compartment mates. She thought she'd caught a glimpse of the dog again, though his movements seemed much more furtive now. Elena presumed she would find evidence of shadow in the animal's eyes if she were to come face-to-face with him. She hoped the creature hadn't been cursed. She knew too well the sensation of being trapped inside another's skin not of one's own will. She wiggled her toes—minus one—inside her sabots at the thought. But whatever condition had magicked the dog into its present form—for instinct whispered in her ear that it was undoubtedly a case of transmogrification—he was keenly invested in her whereabouts. She was likewise growing more interested in his as she watched him emerge from a field of sunflowers to leap over a rock wall.

An hour later the train pulled into the station of a sprawling rural village typical of the south, with its buff-colored buildings and red roof tiles.

It was too soon to be her destination, but the gentleman gathered his belongings and disembarked, leaving Elena and the dour woman alone. For a moment she worried the station stop might allow the dog the opportunity to board and find her. What if he turned out not to be the friendly sort? But then she shook her head at such nonsensical thinking. At the speed the animal was running, he could have leaped aboard at any time while the train was moving if he'd wanted. The entire ordeal had knocked her off course emotionally as well as physically, literally flinging her farther south than she'd ever traveled before.

"May I join you?" A petite woman dressed in a powder-blue skirt and bodice with a lace-trimmed *fichu* tucked in the front entered the compartment. She wore a narrow-brimmed straw hat with a bouquet of pink roses affixed to the band, which did a decent job of hiding the few strands of gray hair beginning to show at her temples but not quite. The scent of flowers was everywhere, as if it were infused in her skin, though not so strongly as to offend the nose. And there, peeking out from her lace shawl, a violet aura that shimmered ever so slightly above her collar. A perfume witch, by all indications.

Elena sat up a little straighter, saying, *"Bonjour."*

The dour woman on the seat beside Elena gave no objection, moving her feet so the woman could sit near the window where the older man had been. Elena smiled politely and tried not to think of her clumsy muddy clogs. The perfume witch nodded in recognition, then gazed out the window as the train churned up a cloud of steam and chugged away from the station.

Once they were on their way again, the perfume witch made eye contact with Elena.

"You make wine," she said as her nose twitched. "Beaujolais?"

"Chanceaux Valley."

"Ah, of course. I should have recognized the stronger scent of the tannins."

Their exchange drew a look of bewilderment from their fellow passenger. The perfume witch lifted her left eyebrow and reached in her purse. She removed an atomizer, gave the pump three quick squeezes, and released a lemony aroma into the car. As the droplets descended through the air, a veil of illusion dropped from the compartment ceiling. The mortal was still there, but it was as if they were hidden behind a curtain.

"It's my own creation," said the witch. She smiled at her resourcefulness. "An illusion spell in a bottle. All the mortal sees are two women staring out the window at the passing countryside. As long as she doesn't look too closely and notice the same tree going past the window every minute, we may talk at will." The perfume witch put her atomizer back in her purse and smiled. "I'm Camille, by the way. Camille Joubert."

Elena introduced herself, then glanced over to make sure the other passenger wasn't listening in on their conversation. "But how does it work without an incantation?"

Camille held up a finger. "Scents affect the mortal brain in specific ways that can be rerouted. You can send their thoughts hurling in any direction you wish with the right combination of fragrances. Lemon verbena works wonders on distraction. But, to be fair, I shouldn't single out mortals. We all respond to smells in ways that can be manipulated. There's no stronger connection between thought and memory than there is with scent. I simply bond a little spell to the mixture as I pour it into the bottle. Depending on the ingredients, I can inspire passion, anger, or"—she nudged her head toward the dour woman—"complete disinterest. Works the same as any other potion meant to be ingested, only mine are airborne."

Wine was much the same, Elena reflected. The aroma was as important as the taste, adding layers of experience to the flavor. The smells detected in the glass shaped perceptions before a single sip was taken.

"Do you run your own shop?" Elena asked, curious to know how the woman plied her craft.

"I'm the eldest daughter at Le Maison des Amoureux." The woman reached in her overnight bag and removed a brown paper package. "I'm on my way there now after briefly visiting the cousins. Here, try a bite, if you like."

Camille unwrapped the paper to reveal a white nougat treat filled with nuts. Elena paused. It was always a tricky proposition to accept food or drink from a witch you didn't know, but there was something very open about this one's intent, as if she would have shared food with anyone she met as a matter of politeness. Elena accepted the offering, passing it under her nose first. The nutty, sweet smell of almonds, honey, and pistachios made her mouth water, accentuating her hunger after she'd turned away her food with the jinni the night before.

"It's not bewitched. Merely an old recipe the locals are becoming deliciously famous for. Not bad for mortals," Camille added and popped a bite of nougat in her mouth.

Elena thanked her, then stared out the window as she ate her treat. The dog reappeared, hurdling over hedgerows and dodging around fence posts to keep up with the train.

Camille followed her gaze. "Is he with you?"

"Possibly. It's complicated."

"Always is when jinn are involved."

Jinn?

"You think he's a jinni? But how could you know that?"

"Oh, several hover hereabouts. I'd developed quite a good working relationship with a young jinni in my perfume factory a time ago. Poor man was tragically killed last year. But as I understand it, a fair number of jinn gravitated to the area after being drawn by the wishes of the people who emigrated from across the sea. Been here for centuries." She raised the nougat up as an example. "The recipe traveled with the immigrants as well. Lucky thing," she said and licked a finger after putting the last of her treat in her mouth.

Elena found the woman's remark about the jinn astonishing. Until she'd been incarcerated with Sidra and later abducted by Jamra, she'd been quite ignorant about the prevalence of jinn around her. Grand-Mère had always made them out to be more myth than truth, and Elena had accepted that without further proof to contradict the idea. But she knew now that being isolated in the Chanceaux Valley, only venturing out occasionally to the city to procure essentials for spells, had left a hole in her knowledge. A great gap of understanding that others possessed from living and traveling in far-off regions of the country. Even Yvette had known more about the jinn than most simply by traveling the country while in the carnival.

"So, I have *another* jinn after me?"

"Another? Oh dear, you are in trouble."

Camille sprayed a second layer of lemon verbena mist in the compartment to be safe, then stated what she knew from personal observation and general gossip. From what she'd gathered, dogs were a very common form of animation for the jinn. It wasn't necessarily a bad sign that one was stalking her. Not all jinn relished mischief, though she couldn't be certain about that. She'd heard most were rather aloof about mortals and witches, not interested enough in their mundane behavior to interfere on most occasions. The jinn were fiery, unpredictable, yet mostly concerned with their own affairs, to which Elena concurred.

Perhaps the dog was merely a local returning home, same as this perfume witch. But no. He had been at Château Renard. At the depot. And now running alongside the train she was *told* to get on after she'd been snatched *away* from Jamra. And just when the jinni had been about to strike her. She looked again at the animal loping with ease along the fields. An ally of Jamra's? Or something else? Her intuition prickled as if brushing up against a stinging nettle, and yet the train rolled on, taking her to her destination and Sidra and Yvette. Perhaps she wasn't the only passenger on this fated journey.

CHAPTER FOURTEEN

The sorcerer's talisman was gone. Sidra stared at the three others they'd stolen from her devotees and felt ashamed. Without the fourth, they were useless to her. She would have to return them and take the chance of being called upon for a favor. Curse that Yanis for breaking into her apartment. She would flay his brain open and sear the rotten insides with flame, though she half expected to find the space hollow.

And how had a half-rate sorcerer discovered where she lived anyway? Only one of her own could have seen through the illusions. So, who was helping that camel's ass of a sorcerer?

The girl stood outside on the steps smoking a cigarette. Sidra wondered if she should order her inside. The omen in the sky had been bad. A dog was coming, death reeking on its breath. She was convinced it marked the impending arrival of her enemy. But who was the starling and who was the hawk?

Sidra ought to call the girl in from her haze of smoke. The apartment was no longer safe, not if the likes of Yanis could be led inside to rummage through her things. The scent spell should still cloak their whereabouts, but that only worked if the person looking didn't already know where to find you under the haze. And someone had led that thief Yanis straight to her door.

"Collect your things," she called. "We have to go."

"Figured," Yvette said and crushed the cigarette under the sole of her shoe. "Where to now?"

For a moment Sidra was stumped. Indecision and fretting seemed to have seeped into her psyche like smoke through a sieve. What was happening to her? She shook her head even as a new panic began to rise. If her apartment wasn't safe, what if the dagger wasn't safe either? Everything would have been for nothing if the relic was discovered. But where to fly with so many ill omens coalescing at once?

"The old one," she said as the thought flitted through her mind like a bird dipping its wings against the wind. Yes, that would settle her. His logic always did that for her. "But first, enough of these games. We need to pay another visit to Yanis the Dishonest."

"To get your talisman back?"

"To get everything back."

Yvette brightened at the thought of another excursion to the town's center. She slipped a borrowed shawl around her shoulders, then stuffed her cigarettes and new perfume in her bottomless pockets. "Lead on," she said, and they shut the door to the apartment.

When the two arrived at the market, the sorcerer wasn't at his stall. Another witch, gray-haired and knock-kneed, stood behind the counter grinding herbs with a mortar and pestle.

"Where's the hyena who owns this stall?"

The witch sprinkled a generous portion of dried marjoram and thyme into the mortar. He looked up at Sidra and gave a shrug. "Stall was abandoned, near as I could tell. Seemed a shame to let such a good location go to waste on a busy market day."

Did he take her for a fool? Sidra set fire to the witch's herbs with a hard glint from her eye, sending them up in a cloud of smoke that singed his beard.

The man fiddled his fingers against his whiskers, snuffing out the fire before it reached his chin. "There's no cause for that." He double-checked his eyebrows for damage. "He warned someone was looking for him. Didn't say you were a jinni."

"Tell me where to find Yanis or see your day's profits go up in flame." The twigs of lavender atop the stall began to smoke.

"All right, all right," the witch said, patting down the stems. "He lives that way. A few doors from the top." He pointed toward the crooked lane that wound up the hillside. Sidra followed the trail with her eyes, remembering the times she'd seen Yanis walk that way with his wooden leg thumping the sidewalk while she lurked in the shadows of the adjacent loggia to watch the people come and go.

"Come," she said to Yvette. "And do not waste a smile on that one."

They headed in the direction the witch pointed, and at the end of the winding pathway, where the buildings closed in overhead and stubborn shrubbery grew in the loose mortar between stones, Sidra caught the whiff of fear. Trembling, sweating, hormone-rich fear. Behind a door painted blue.

"He's in there."

"What are you going to do to him?" Yvette asked.

Murder generally came to mind when dealing with Yanis, but she always grappled with the balance of deeds in this world against the consequences met in the next. "Convince him to tell me the truth," Sidra said and grinned at all the ways she knew how to get someone to talk just short of death.

She tapped lightly and pressed her ear to the door. The sound of a rat scurrying inside its cage came from the other side. She tried the doorknob. Locked, naturally. Perhaps even secured with a dead bolt. Sidra would have blown the door down with the heat of a thousand fires, but a woman and child approached from the top of the lane, eyeing her and the fair one with suspicion.

"Allow me," Yvette said and nudged the jinni aside once the woman and child passed. She uttered her burglar's charm, and the locks ticked open one at a time. "You don't always have to burn the place down, you know."

Sidra stood in rare, brief awe before pushing the door open.

Inside, Yanis didn't even have the decency to look abashed when she confronted him. Instead he hobbled to a table and turned it over as if he could hide behind the solid oak top and be safe.

"It wasn't my idea," he pleaded.

"Which part?"

The sorcerer blinked. "The talisman. I knew you took mine yesterday at the market. Figured you ought to have it again after what happened. But then the lady told me I had to get it back. Didn't give me a choice."

"What lady? Who was she?"

"I don't know. I swear it. She was wearing a hood so I couldn't see her face. But she was, I don't know, forceful."

"Jinn like me?"

The rat wrung his hands together and nodded. "Could be. She magicked us to the apartment. One minute we were talking under the loggia at the market, the next I was standing among your things. She whispered that the talisman was buried in the rice, and then as soon as I dug it out, she was gone. So I ran." He reached in his pocket. "Here, have it back. It's yours. Keep the damn thing."

Sidra took the medallion from him and held it up to the light coming through the window. But it wasn't her talisman. She threw the cheap brass counterfeit at the man. "Do you toy with me?"

"What? No." He scrambled on the floor to retrieve the medallion, seemingly confused at what he found instead. "But I had your talisman in my pocket."

Yvette stepped forward and held her palm open in front of Yanis as she smiled. He placed the thrown object in her hand without question, as if mesmerized by her wordless command.

"It's an orphan's medal," she said, rubbing her thumb over the imprint of a flower girl. "The kind mothers used to leave with their babies when they had to give them up. So, where's the talisman from the rice jar?" Yvette stared at Yanis, glowing brighter with each inhale.

"I don't know. It was here. In my pocket. But I'm a simple potions witch. I can't do magic like what's happening here."

Someone was playing a game with them. Drawing Sidra out, knowing she would go to Yanis to retrieve the talisman, only to find it gone for good. Unable to silence the pleas in her name. One less protection against Jamra.

Sidra pulled up a chair and sat in front of Yanis, who knelt on his one knee. "Yes, since your muddled brain can't seem to tell us anything about the jinni who stole the talisman, let's talk about your potions," she said.

The sorcerer shook his head helplessly. "I made them exactly the same. I swear on my mother. Both potions from one bottle." He shrugged with more helplessness. "I don't know what went wrong. You must believe me."

"And yet I don't, because I woke from the supposed same potion that killed my husband." She leaned forward and grimaced to show her teeth. "Do you know all that your mistake has cost me?"

"I still can't believe you drank something from a man who sells potions from a market stall," Yvette said with a chin nudge toward Yanis.

"Bah, it was a drop in each eye. But I was given assurance from a trusted friend he knew what he was doing," Sidra said, her voice full of regret. "That friend was obviously wrong. But now we'll learn the truth." The jinni blew hot air on her fingertips, and a flame came to life. The fire danced in her palm, winding and cooling until the smoke formed into a snake, a pit viper hungry to taste the air with its tongue. She moved the snake's curious tongue closer to the man's face. "Did someone put you up to trickery? Murder?"

"What? No! You, Hariq, and the old one. It was always just the four of us who knew," he said and leaned back as far as he dared to get away from the snake. "I never said a word to anyone. I never did anything I wasn't asked to do. Ever."

Yanis's eyes had shifted from the snake to Yvette. The fact he was wary of speaking openly in front of a stranger was a good sign. The pact had been kept secret since the plan's inception, bound by a spellword each was required to speak to seal the deal. And this weasel had, as far as she could tell, abided by the terms of their agreement—aside from the potion's failure. The three of them had never told him the full truth and the real reason for the deception. Only the same story she'd told the girl.

The half-truth.

Yanis shifted his weight to abide the odd angle of his false leg, hesitant to change position too fast. Good. She preferred him scared.

Sidra bent forward with the snake sliding over her hand as she stared at the pitiful sorcerer. "So how does a single potion from the same bottle kill one and not the other? What does your experience as a sorcerer say about that?"

The man swallowed uneasily as his eyes roamed the room in search of an answer. Beads of sweat began collecting along his brow. Soon they would trickle down his face. "I'm not sure. Unless Hariq ate something that interfered with his blood? Said the wrong words for the spell?" Yanis grew more animated, as if he'd stumbled on an answer that would save him. "Or maybe he used . . . something other than what I gave him? Maybe someone else switched the potions."

Sidra stared back at the human weasel as anger built a chimney fire inside her. "Who? Who could have done such a thing if only the four of us knew?"

The fallacy of his suggestion struck home. If what he said was true, then either someone had shared the secret—impossible because of the words binding them to the pact—or the potion had been switched or altered, which was very bad news for Yanis since he was the one who created it.

Sidra stood and kicked the chair out of the way. She cooed at the snake in her hand, kissed the top of its head, then let the serpent loose on the floor, where it coiled in front of the sorcerer. Yvette touched the jinni's sleeve and the pair dissipated from the room, leaving the man to wrestle for his life against the slithering smoke and fire.

CHAPTER FIFTEEN

The train pulled into the station in a cloud of steam. When the air cleared, Elena peered out the window to see if the dog had materialized, but all she saw was the usual bustle of people, mortals all, coming and going with luggage in tow. Though if the dog was truly one of the jinn, she imagined he could take any shape he wanted. Not a comforting thought when arriving in an unfamiliar town for the first time after having been abducted on a flying carpet by an angry jinni with a vendetta.

The passengers scattered across the platform. Elena watched for a furry face and a bearded one with a scowl, just in case Jamra had followed after all. When nothing obvious presented itself, she sat on a bench to collect her thoughts. Surely whoever put her on that train had a plan for when she arrived. She could sense expectation in the air.

"Have you no luggage?" Camille glanced from the baggage attendant and his empty trolley to Elena sitting on her bench.

"I had to leave in a hurry," she said and patted her satchel.

Camille nodded her head as if she understood. "May I at least give you a ride somewhere?" The perfume witch pointed to a goose-nosed yellow automobile with a black hardtop and two rows of seats parked in the street.

"Is that yours?"

Camille grinned. "Bought and paid for with a little patchouli oil, bergamot, and jasmine potion mixed with the right words in the right order. Our Fleur de Sable perfume sells faster than we can make it."

Elena took one last look around the platform, ready to accept a ride if nothing presented itself, when the dog's tail poked up by the railing on the other side of the track. Curious brown eyes stared back as though trying to decide whether to trust her. That put both of them in the undecided camp, she thought. His ears lifted and he pointed his nose upwind. She swore he nodded to himself after that.

"Thank you for the offer, but I see my guide has arrived," she said.

"Are you sure? It's quite a way up the hill to get to the center of town." But then Camille spotted the dog and wished Elena a friendly *"Bonne chance à toi."*

Elena walked to the end of the platform. The dog trotted out from behind the railing, remaining wary, keeping his ears on alert. She knew better than to reach a hand out for fear of being bitten, so she instead nodded and said, "Hello."

The dog sat, his head reaching as tall as her midthigh. He was a rather ordinary-looking dog with brown fur that grew darker around the face, paws, and tip of a tail that curled. There was no collar, no sign of abuse or neglect that she could see, though he did look a bit hungry after his long run to keep up with the train. She was hungry herself. Unfortunately, she had nothing for either of them.

"Was it you who put me on the train?" she asked. The dog blinked once between solemn stares. "There's something we need to talk about? Something you need to show me?" The dog wagged his tail. "Very well, but first it's imperative I send a message home. Is that all right?" The dog's nose twitched, and he pointed it in the direction of the train station. "Ah, *merci.* Good thinking," she said. "It *would* be quicker to send a telegram than a dove from this far south, not to mention the more humane choice, given the distance the poor bird would have to fly."

Sometimes mortal inventions were worth the inconvenience of all that noise and bother that came with them, but they also required payment. Elena dug around in the bottom of her satchel. She usually kept a few coins for spells requiring a little copper or silver. *Hmm, but would it be enough?* She and the dog approached the operator inside the station as she jingled the coins in her palm, uncertain. The gentleman behind the counter began to explain how the cost of a message was based on the word count, but then he glanced at the dog and seemingly lost his trail of thought. Indeed, he appeared to lose all memory of what he'd just expressed to Elena about the price and instead offered to send whatever message she liked for free. She hardly thought she needed to take advantage of such manipulation of a mortal—clearly the dog had hypnotized the poor fellow in some way—but she desperately wanted to know how Jean-Paul fared and let him and Brother Anselm know she was safe enough for the moment. With the agent's offer still humming in the air between them, she borrowed a fountain pen and piece of paper and began to write. She signed off the message with a note stating she had freed herself of the "visitor" and not to worry.

Unless, of course . . .

"You don't think Jamra returned to the vineyard to cause further harm instead, do you?" She bit her lip, but the dog shook his fur out, and she took him at his word. No, the dog was right. Jamra was likely still heading south and wouldn't stop searching until he found either her or Sidra again. Which led Elena to wonder if there was more at stake than punishing the woman he believed killed his brother and stole one of his possessions. Revenge, she knew from experience, was a fire that could burn hot for years. Perhaps doubly so, if you were made of the stuff.

"Now that that's done," she said to the dog when they stepped outside, "we can carry on with the business in town you're so desperate for me to get to." She knelt so that she was eye to eye with the creature. She checked for shadow, if by chance the animal had been cursed instead of being a jinni, but all she spied were the golden eyes of a dedicated guide. And, she began to hope, an ally. Elena thanked him for the nice trick with the telegraph officer, then followed him as he hopped on the funicular that carried the train passengers up the hill. He pulled the same mesmerizing stunt on the operator, who at first tried to shoo him off, and together they rode to the top of the hillside village with its clay tile roofs and arching palm trees. The town was like no place she'd visited before yet was pleasant enough, except for the overriding scent of flowers that obscured her sense of smell when it came to sniffing out fellow witches. Still, she could sense a familiar energy synching with her intuition as they disembarked and walked along the cobblestone streets.

For a creature so determined to see her delivered to the center of the town, however, the dog walked with an overabundance of caution. His nose twitched at every intersection. Twice he skittered sideways at the sound of an engine backfiring. As a jinni, if that's indeed what her guide was, he couldn't be more different from Jamra the Belligerent.

At last they came to a narrow road lined with palm trees, shops, and a covered loggia running along a small square. Fruits, flowers, and spices were on display inside baskets, bowls, and woven mats spread out on the sidewalk. And there were magical wares too. A man with a half-singed beard was selling crystals and amulets beside bundles of dried herbs, while a woman in a turban offered small tincture bottles full of fragrant oils meant to heal a headache. The scene was instantly reminiscent of summers in the Chanceaux Valley on market days when the palm readers lined the main street to ply their trade for money. Some you could trust to reveal innocuous fragments of your future, while others were a complete sham, claiming to know how the biggest events in one's life were going to turn out. As if impending matters weren't constantly being batted around by the whims of one outcome pitted against another. But the tourists never seemed to mind being taken advantage of, as long as they received good news.

Elena turned to the dog to ask about the types of sorcery popular in the village, but he ducked his head and darted away before she could say a word. She watched his tail disappear down the street with that quicksilver speed of his and knew she wasn't possibly meant to chase after him. So, what then was she supposed to do?

The answer came sooner than expected when she heard a pair of familiar voices. Two women bickered about a snake, of all things, as they walked along the narrow lane leading from the hillside apartments adjacent to where she stood. Sidra and Yvette, her raison d'être, at least for the moment. Or at least that's what her instinct was telling her. A tingle ran up her spinal column, dispersing like a *Fête nationale* sparkler inside her cranium to make the roots of her hair stiffen, now that she'd found them. But why had the dog run away when this was obviously why she'd been brought to the plaza?

Left on her own to work it out, she waited until the pair stepped into the market street. She wasn't sure why Yvette had come to be there, but she was glowing ever so softly. Her hair was pinned up neatly, and her face appeared bare except for a hint of blush. She walked with a sense of grace she'd not displayed before reuniting with her family. Breathtaking, the way she carried herself now.

In comparison, Sidra seemed to have lost some of her luster. Her silks were fraying and dull with dirt, and her usually proud bearing had shrunk so that she walked furtively, full of tension. Elena had never seen fear in the jinni's eyes before, not even when she faced execution, but the way they stalked the crowd, searching for some expected threat, suggested she knew already that Jamra was on his way.

Elena waited for them at the corner. They hadn't spotted her yet, though they would soon. She wondered then if a public street was the safest place for a meeting. She scanned the faces at the market wondering who might be watching. Was Jamra already near? Did he have allies in the village already? She sorted through her satchel to find something suitable. She had only a moment and very few items of practical use, thanks to being abducted by an angry jinni while in the middle of vine work. But then her hand found the two coins at the bottom of her bag as she spotted a vacant storefront across the plaza. Perhaps she could minimize attention.

Holding the coins in her palm, she whispered, "Moon of silver, moon of gold, create a shop where charms are sold. Make a sign, make it shine, let them see the magic is mine." The copper coin wasn't technically gold, but the color was close enough to mimic a golden moon. The illusion took shape in a little alcove that had become the entrance to Elena's newly created charm shop. A sign hung above the door with two back-to-back gold and silver crescents shimmering in the daylight. She crossed the street and jimmied the door open by copying Yvette's spell for picking locks, then waited for the keen eyes of the jinni to discover her sign.

CHAPTER SIXTEEN

He knew the witch was clever, but to create an illusion so quickly and with such detail was admirable. Perhaps the signs in the fire prophecy had been right about her. He hoped so. So many lives depended on it.

The dog sat on the roof of the market loggia where he could watch without being seen. No one ever looked up in a town, but rooftops were where all the best omens were discovered.

"She's arrived?" asked the creature who'd previously perched on the rim of his ear. Now human-size, the being sat cross-legged on the edge of the roof, watching the street below.

"They'll meet any moment," he answered. "And then we won't have much time."

The being squinted. "We are prepared."

The animal lifted his ears as the jinni and the fair one came down the lane. Sidra would see the illusion for what it was, of this he was certain. But would she see beyond into the ether too soon? Her growing reliance on fire prophecy had become a concern, though he understood why she kept looking. The path behind her had been sealed, so there was only the future upon which to gaze.

"It's like watching a game board and waiting to see who will move next," he said. "How do you resist the urge to intervene?"

The creature flipped Yanis's talisman in the air, then caught it in an open palm. "I don't always. Though after a while you grow detached to the sensation of so many lives interacting under your nose. But this is no time for grand apathy. The alliance was the right choice, strange as our acquaintance must seem to you."

The dog nodded, then stood and padded along the roof's edge when Sidra stopped midstride. She'd seen the sign.

"You honestly don't know where the dagger is hidden?"

He ought to know. Perhaps he could even guess correctly. But the vision wouldn't come to him. "I cannot see the damned thing."

He felt the being studying him, but his face remained placid, only because he remained in his canine state. So unnerving the way her eyes could bore into you, searching beneath the surface for ethereal truth. The creature turned away, and he released his breath slowly so as not to reveal his unease.

"There, we've managed that objective," the being said, tracking the jinni and fair one as they entered the shop. "Everyone delivered safe and reunited. We'll meet again at the crossroads, and then we'll see what progress we've made."

The dog wagged his tail. When he looked again, he was alone on the rooftop.

There were many moments he'd second-guessed his choice. And it had been a choice. His will to see the endeavor through to the end. He'd watched wish magic churn like a storm through people's lives to meet its desired end before, but never from a rooftop looking down on those unaware of the force bearing down on them. And him powerless to do anything to stop it.

CHAPTER SEVENTEEN

"You left him alone in a room with a snake." Yvette crossed her arms as she walked, as if sulking. "What if he dies?"

Sidra admitted she'd thought about such a gesture, but she was no murderer, despite her threats. "Bah. The snake looked real enough but was merely made of smoke. Yanis will figure it out soon enough. A little deadly fear is a good thing for a man to feel course through him. Especially when he lies like a snake in the grass himself."

They came to the end of the lane. Sidra stopped as soon as they turned the corner. Two moons glittered on a tin sign—one silver, one gold. Her eyes scanned the street in either direction, then squinted at the sign over the door of the abandoned shop again. She knew every stall in the market plaza, every shop that sold goods on its perimeter. This one had sold coffee and tobacco, but the owner had died and the doors had closed. How had the moon sign been magicked into being in the short time they'd visited Yanis? And by whom?

"What's wrong?" Yvette asked, sensing Sidra's wariness. The fairy glanced around as obvious as a meerkat on sentry duty, elevating a few inches off the ground to see over the heads of a couple shopping next to her.

Sidra sniffed the air. "Stop that and follow me." The jinni walked to the front door of the shuttered mercantile, where it now read ELENA'S

CHARMS AND STAR-CROSSED SUNDRIES in a metallic sheen that seemed to float above the glass. She peered through the window but could see the store was still vacant. A scale for measuring coffee was mounted on the counter, but the shelves were empty. Straw and discarded packing paper littered the floor.

"Do your trick with the lock," she said.

"Honestly, I'm good for more than just being your servant." Yvette put her palm over the mechanism, but the door proved unlocked when she tried the handle.

Sidra stepped inside. Her eyes searched the corners of the room, but it was her nose that sorted out the mystery. Ah, the scent of wine and oak wood, with a whiff of familiar smoke too.

"Hello, Sidra."

The vine witch came out of the back room. Her hair hung loose about her shoulders, and her clothes were wrinkled and smelling of earth and fire. Their eyes met, exchanging messages of unspoken worry and warning.

"Elena?" Yvette burst through the door and hugged her friend in a tasteless show of affection, as the *Fée* are prone to do. "When did you get here?"

"Look at you." Elena held Yvette's arms out. "You're absolutely glowing."

"I'm still an apprentice, but watch this." Yvette levitated six inches off the ground. "Grand-Mère says it's why people assume we have wings."

"Impressive."

Sidra locked the door behind them and pulled the shade. "She didn't travel hundreds of miles to see you float, Yvette."

The girl dropped hard on the wooden floor and made a rude gesture with her fingers under her chin toward Sidra.

"She's right," Elena said, though in a kinder tone. "I came to warn you. I was abducted by someone I think you're familiar with. He tried to force me to find you."

"Jamra is here?"

"No, not yet. At least I don't think so. I escaped before arriving."

"But you aren't burned?" Sidra looked Elena over in disbelief. "You aren't harmed?"

"Someone helped me get free of him. They put me on the train south."

"Someone? Who?"

"Another jinni, as far as I can tell. One who likes to roam the countryside as a dog."

The dog's tail?

"Wait, didn't you see a dog in the bird omen thing in the sky?" Yvette asked.

"Bird omen?" Elena's brow tightened.

Yvette nudged her chin toward the jinni. "Obsessed with signs, this one."

Sidra shivered, too perplexed to scold the girl for her ignorance. A dog could be anyone. Then again, it couldn't. The animal must be jinn. "I have no allies left except the old one, and he doesn't leave the cave."

"Sounds about right," Yvette said and added a mocking laugh.

Elena intervened with hands held in a truce motion before Sidra could push up her sleeve to draw fire. "The dog led me here to the plaza. Made sure we found each other. If he'd meant to do harm, he could have ambushed you at any time. So, it might be fair to say at least four people are on your side."

"Four?" Yvette scrunched up her nose, then realized what the witch was saying. "Oh, right. Lucky you, you've got us too," she said and lit a cigarette.

Sidra nodded, thinking about what the old one had said about their reunion being good magic. The trio had been brought together for a reason, their fates linked one to the other. Almost as if foretold. But he'd never said anything about another jinni. And she wasn't convinced the dog was an ally. Not after her home had been burgled by one of her own kind.

"What is it?" Elena asked.

"I need to look into the fire."

Yvette blew smoke up to the ceiling. "Again, with the omens? Titania says magic has to be respected. Some of *les anciennes* in the *Fée* lands even worry it could run out someday."

For once the girl had a point. "One shouldn't look too often at the shadows lining the future, true, but this moment needs clarifying." Sidra gathered the scraps of straw and crumpled paper from the floor and tossed them onto the plates of the scale mounted on the counter. The setup was crude but would suffice.

"Come, girl, and see how superior magic is done."

"Last time I saw you read a fire you abandoned me on top of a tower to fend for myself against your wish magic." Yvette smirked and floated five feet over to the scales.

Sidra gently blew fire onto the paper and straw until they caught. The paper curled and turned black as the fire feasted. The straw crackled, glowing like orange filaments before turning black and drooping. The three huddled around the scales. In the distance, a whistle announced the train's departure.

"You see how the paper curls and holds its shape even when it turns to ash? It means plans cannot be altered. The path is set. That's not always so with the future."

"Which path?" Elena asked, unable to hide the genuine worry in her eyes.

Sidra pointed to how the filaments of straw crossed each other before collapsing. "The conflict I've been expecting. But there's something else here," she said and watched how the fire died out and trailed into smoke.

"What? That we're all going to die?" Yvette had meant it half in jest, but no one laughed.

"Perhaps only some of us." Sidra smiled inwardly at making the girl uncomfortable, then turned back to her pyromancy. "The smoke twists uniformly instead of wafting naturally. It spirals in a controlled manner. Almost as if by design. As if the future were . . ."

"Compelled by wish magic?"

Sidra met Elena's gaze with a nod. "You have sensed this too?"

Yvette visibly shivered. "*Merde*, you think someone wished for us to be killed by Jamra?"

Elena peered closer at the smoke. "My intuition isn't compelled to act the same way it was in the city with your wish, but there is a feeling of some grander scheme at work, drawing us all together."

The smoke dissipated, carrying with it any further insight. Sidra shook her head, still not convinced anything like wish magic was at work. And yet she, too, had the sense that events were being manipulated. The way her medallion was stolen. The coincidence of Elena being abducted by Jamra and then freed so she could be led to the village. Even the annoying girl being sent to this place at her side had the whiff of coordination. As if someone kept correcting a master plan.

Elena sorted through the ashes left in the tray.

"What else do you seek?" Sidra asked.

"I thought maybe . . . I'm not as good at reading ashes as you, but I hoped I might see a sign."

"You have to first ask the fire a question before it burns through to find an answer in the ashes."

Elena straightened. "In that case, I have to go. Whatever's going on here, I've done my part. I warned you about Jamra and what he intends to do, but now I must return home as quickly as possible. Jean-Paul was hexed before I was taken."

"What did that jackal do?"

The vine witch rarely showed fear, but her eyes brimmed with concern. "He did something to Jean-Paul's mind. Gave him a fever as if his brain was on fire. Jamra said he sent his mind to wander the desert. It was the only way he could compel me to find you."

Sidra understood his treachery. She had used such spells on her enemies in the past too. Mortals were particularly vulnerable to magic that affected their soft-tissue brains.

"What kind of magic can send a man's mind to swelter in a desert?" Elena asked. "Can he recover? Please, is there a spell to cure him? He seemed to improve the farther away Jamra and I flew."

"You know this for sure?"

"Last night I was able to make Jamra pass out long enough for me to use my shadow vision." She paused as Sidra's brows raised at such a feat. "I used a wine spell that doubled the alcohol's potency with a little sleep spell mixed in for good measure. In my vision Jean-Paul's fever seemed to have lessened, even though he remained unconscious. I haven't been able to check since."

Sidra confirmed her speculation with a nod. "If Jamra has come south, the tether of magic may have weakened. The hold over your man could have lessened, but distance alone won't be enough to help him recover."

"What can I do? My healing charms had no effect on him."

Predictably, there was little a witch could do for one whose mind had been sentenced to wander in the sand under an unrelenting sun. Most victims ended up in asylums, unable to care for themselves any longer. "No, in this case your herbs will not work."

"There must be something you can do. Jinni magic against jinni magic. Can't I make a wish? Let the magic find him in the desert and bring him back?"

"Yes, grant her a wish," Yvette said. "Those things are powerful stuff."

"It doesn't work that way." Sidra reached in the fold of her caftan. "However . . ."

The witch's cat eyes flared with hope. "Yes?"

Sidra fished out the three medallions. Without the fourth, they were useless for the purpose she'd had in mind. All had to be in her possession to ensure they were not used to entreat her help and reveal her location to Jamra. The instinct to be hidden was strong, but there was a force working against her. Perhaps not a true enemy, or they would have already informed Jamra of her whereabouts. As the fire revealed, some other plan had been set on its own trajectory and couldn't be altered. One that determined she should not hide. The confrontation had to take place. Sidra exhaled, knowing the truth she'd seen in the fire.

"There is a way," she said. "Both of you take a medallion. You must grip it in your hand and ask me for help. Invoke my name. Only then can I try to help him."

"Wait," Yvette said, accepting one of the charms. "Won't that alert Jamra to where you are?"

Elena looked up from the bronze talisman in her hand. "Is that true?"

The elements of Elena's shop illusion disintegrated as the spell ran its course. The letters on the glass scattered with the breeze, and the sign of the two moons above the door faded into shadow. Change was coming for them all.

"It is true." Sidra gathered her silk around her. "But it's what the fire has shown us. Events cannot be altered. They must proceed. This is the fate we've been shown."

"But can you fight him by yourself?"

"I don't think I'm meant to," Sidra said, daring to meet each woman's eye.

"Right. We're in this together," Yvette affirmed. "Always have been, it seems."

"But I can't. You have to understand. I must return home to tend to Jean-Paul."

"And how will you get there?"

"The train . . ." Elena searched her satchel. "Though I may have to borrow the fare."

"This is not the city. The train has already left. The next one won't depart until tomorrow."

The jinni had briefly wondered what her odds of defeating Jamra would be without the vine witch to complete the bond between the three of them. But again, the fire didn't lie. The witch wouldn't be going anywhere despite her proclamations. They were meant to stand as one. Though nothing was without cost.

"Give me a chance to free your man's mind of Jamra's influence. We'll use your shadow vision. It is the only way. Afterward you'll see if he is restored. Ease your mind of this worry."

"But the talisman. You'll draw Jamra here like a beacon. He and his followers will find you."

"It's as it should be."

Someone jiggled the door handle. All three startled and backed away, but it was only a curious tourist thinking the store might be open. Sidra waved her hand to obscure them from view behind a veil of darkness.

"Jamra will find me. The fire has spoken. But my life is not what he's truly coming for, though he'll try to claim it all the same." Sidra lowered her voice as she approached the cusp of telling the entire truth for the first time since Hariq had died. "No, what that blackhearted one is after is the dagger of Zimbarra and the powerful sigil embedded in its handle."

Yvette stubbed out her cigarette in the ash left in the scales. "Jiminy, that doesn't sound good."

"Zimbarra? But . . . but that isn't real," Elena said.

"I believe you once said the same about my kind." Sidra attempted a smile, despite her cursed nerves.

"What's Zimbarra?" Yvette glowed eerily, as if sensing something supernatural in the wake of speaking the word out loud.

"Not what—where." Elena opened her satchel and removed her spell book to show the girl. She laid it on the counter and thumbed through the pages until she hit on an old love spell she claimed her grandmother had passed on to her when she was a teen. "Zimbarra," she said to Yvette, "is a mythical floating island."

"Not mythical," Sidra corrected.

Yvette eagerly leaned over Elena's shoulder to get a better look at the page for herself. "Here," Elena said, her finger trailing under the words as she read. "A spell for conjuring commitment from a boy who ignores you one day and can't stop staring at you the next. The directions for the incantation say to work the word 'Zimbarra' into the spell because it refers to the dynamic nature of the mythical island, said to float from one location to another, the way a young man's attentions may at times fluctuate."

"This is what they teach you?" Sidra's bracelets rattled as she turned the book around to see for herself. She read half a page, which proved more than enough. "Just because someone wrote something down in a book doesn't make a lie a truth, though it may reveal the depth of the author's ignorance."

The book snapped itself shut and turned its spine on the jinni. Elena opened her mouth to argue, then admitted her mentor *had* been wrong about a few things in the past.

The book shuddered and locked itself.

"What makes you so certain this Zimbarra place is real?" Yvette asked.

"Because I've seen it," the jinni said. She conjured a sitting area in the back of the shop for the women to be comfortable. She provided coffee, dates, and flatbread. A small oasis created in the midst of looming danger.

"Your book was not wrong about the nature of the island," she said as she sank onto a pouf. "It *is* a fickle place, moving from one coordinate to the next. Many a pilot in their dhow has sailed to his death looking for its shores over the centuries. The silhouette of the island rises, barely visible on the sea's horizon, and then disappears the nearer one gets. Nothing more than a mirage for most."

"But not you?"

Sidra shook her head.

"How'd you find the place if it's always moving around like that?" Yvette asked.

"The birds," she said, her eyes glancing up to the sky where the creatures reigned. "Their vision is better than any human's. They keep track of the island so they have a place to land when migrating. The terns revealed its beaches to Hariq and me as a belated wedding present. A place where we could be alone and hide from our feuding families undisturbed, if only for a little while. Hariq was the one who discovered the dagger."

"Where'd it come from?" Yvette asked.

"There were no other people on the island, but there were bones," Sidra said. "We found a skeleton above the beach. Sun-bleached and scattered by scavengers."

The girl gawked. "You found a body?"

"The bones of a magus. A priest. At least that's what Hariq believed. There were rings and amulets among the skeleton as well as the dagger. Either he had been shipwrecked by chance or magicked there and never returned."

"Or banished," Elena added in a warning tone. The witch's mind was clearly evaluating what she'd heard against what she'd been taught. At last she shook her head. "I can recall a few childhood stories about magical knives and swords, but I'm not familiar with one about a knife empowered by a sigil. What does it do?"

"Tell your grimoire to open again and I'll try to explain."

The vine witch looked doubtful. She stood and approached the book on the counter, speaking to it as if it were a stubborn child refusing to eat. Rebuffed, she carried it back to the soft pillows and poufs and set it on the ottoman in the center. At last she coaxed the spell book to open again by promising it could sleep with its pages spread out and free to flutter for the night under the draping silk ceiling. Sidra resisted the urge to roll her eyes to the heavens. Finally, the book cooperated.

"You will allow?" Sidra asked. After Elena gave a stern warning to the book, the jinni turned it toward her and thumbed through the pages until she came to the inevitable section on sigils. Some were familiar to her, others complete nonsense. She scanned her finger over the various symbols until she landed on a shape that looked similar to the one on the dagger Hariq had found, though the design in the book was not nearly as elaborate. "Sigils like these can be used to harness great power," she explained. "Though often the power imbued in the symbol is incumbent on the skill of the sorcerer who created it. Or who controls it."

"What kind of power?" Yvette asked softly.

"This one can control weather in the hands of a master sorcerer." Sidra pointed to another. "This one, if only slightly altered with a line or two and paired with one's malicious intent, can bring on famine and pestilence."

"I'm guessing the dagger's sigil aligns more with the destructive side of things," Elena said.

"It's a mark that carries a terrible curse."

"What kind of curse?" Yvette asked. The girl glanced at Elena before popping a date in her mouth.

"Chaos," Sidra said. "The kind that could set the world spinning into despair if the dagger were to fall into the wrong hands."

"Jamra," Elena whispered. "But what could he do with it?"

Sidra balled up her fist as if gripping the handle of the dagger. "The balance between order and chaos is held together by the tension between opposing forces. They serve as counterweights to each other, creating stability. But it's a delicate line, as if always resting on a knife's edge. This is why the sigil was embedded in the handle of a dagger.

Whispered tradition says the one who wields the dagger, applying his will to tilting it just a little toward chaos, will gain dominion over an army of demons whose only mission is to create havoc and pain."

Yvette stopped chewing and swallowed the date in one hard gulp. Her glow dwindled. "But don't *you* have the dagger now? Doesn't that make *you* the, you know, wielder of . . . demons? *Merde*, do you have it on you?"

The girl's ignorance was at times astounding.

"Do you look in my eyes and see reckless stupidity?" Sidra showed her teeth and still the fairy didn't balk. *Good, she would need her nerve.* "I have no ambition to bring humanity to heel. The world is a wild thing that doesn't deserve to suffer more than it has already. But there are those like Jamra who would see the human race shackled and forced to do their bidding in return for past insults and degradations done against our kind. The dagger, in his hands, could do this. Intention, always, is the force behind any magic."

"But where is it?" The vine witch set her grimoire aside, leaving the pages open as promised. "How does Jamra know you have the knife?"

Sidra explained how she and Hariq had brought the dagger back from the island, before they knew exactly what they'd found. The couple knew only that it was a powerful magical relic. They left the bones behind but collected the rings and amulets in the hope they might help identify the magus who'd died on the island.

"We asked at the markets if anyone recognized the jewelry so we might know who the priest was and what he carried. Many offered to buy the trinkets, but an old sorcerer in a village shop across the sea got a strange look on his face when we brought out the dagger to ask about the owner. The scent of char rose around him, the kind that hungers for destruction."

"He knew what you'd found," Elena said.

She nodded. "He was no market sorcerer. Behind his eyes he was jinn. But not of any clan. One of the dispossessed."

"Dispossessed?"

"Outcasts. Unwanteds. The marauders who ride before the storm, their horses' hooves kicking up the dust to create the great haboob. We fled to the ether as soon as we recognized him for what he was, but not before he'd seen the mark on the dagger. Afterward we took the sigil straight to the jinn leader we pay tribute to. He is a wise one with a great gift for envisioning the future." Sidra recalled the look on Rajul Hakim's face when they unveiled the dagger, full of astonishment, as if they'd found one of the lost treasures of the world. "When he told us of its power, we understood the mistake we'd made in returning it to the mainland."

Sidra raised her palms to ask forgiveness from the All Seeing. "It was the dispossessed one who told Jamra about the dagger, I'm certain. It is they who he's aligned with."

"Where's the dagger now?" Elena asked. "Somewhere safe? Shouldn't it be in the hands of an official custodian or protector?"

"The dagger is safe for now. But anything can be thought safe until it's found."

The fairy and witch grew silent. Such beings of air and light, earth and herb. The thought of fire and death made their skin glow with the sheen of nervous perspiration. Their mood was as it should be. For it was their hands now, together with hers, that held the balance propped in place. One slip in the wrong direction and they might all be flung into chaos.

The balance between them must be held. Debt and indebtedness. One gesture in exchange for another. It, too, was as it should be. She would do this thing for the witch's husband, and then Elena would stay until the other was done. *Tawazun.*

CHAPTER EIGHTEEN

The anonymity of the abandoned shop proved the wisest place to hunker down for the remainder of the day, especially after learning that there was more at stake with Jamra's impending arrival than mere murder. Elena held the talisman in her hand. Invoking Sidra's name for help could draw attention to the jinni's whereabouts, but without her help Jean-Paul might be lost forever. She felt the jinni's glittering eyes on her as she wrestled with what to do.

"We cannot stop Jamra," Sidra said. "The fire isn't wrong. The confrontation has already been willed. But we can still try to help your man."

"Go on," Yvette said, turning her medallion over in her hand. "You have to try. I'll say it too."

The bronze felt warm in her palm, as if urging her to use the magic. Elena ran her finger over the symbols engraved on its surface. Small glyphs in the shape of an eye, a moon, a star, and a bird's wing. Such different magic, yet similar too, the way it used symbols instead of words to connect with the source. Elena met Sidra's eye one last time. She had no choice. If the jinni had already accepted her fate should the talisman's energy reveal her location, then she must trust in the generosity of the offer. She closed her fingers over the metal and spoke Sidra's name while envisioning the help she desired.

"It shall be done." Sidra scooted closer on the sofa. "We're lucky. You have the gift of second sight. Without it, he would be doomed. But we have a chance. First you must look into your world of shadows. Find your husband. I will follow you there. Now, for we must act quickly."

So, she meant to heal him by piggybacking on her vision the same way Jamra had. The notion made her uneasy. They would both be vulnerable while in this state, with only Yvette to keep vigil in their absence. And yet the young woman had never failed her. With that in mind, Elena settled into the soft pillow and closed her eyes. A moment later her vision, only slightly slowed by the acknowledged presence of the jinni in the liminal space, followed the silver thread to Jean-Paul. He was still unconscious, though he'd been moved and was now in their bed. Stubble shadowed his jaw and his eyes darted beneath their closed lids, but otherwise he appeared as he had before. Brother Anselm wasn't in the bedside chair. Turning her vision east, she sensed the monk moving in the kitchen below. The scent of sautéed chicken wafted up from the stove. She took it as a positive sign before feeling a psychic nudge to get out of the way.

An odd sensation filtered in behind Elena's eyes. Warmth, as if she'd been staring into the fireplace, filled her vision. Her sight dimmed until she no longer sensed the light around her. Panic crept in at the edge of her thoughts until the calming scent of ripening grapes, just as the sugar rises before peak harvest, infiltrated her olfactory senses, soothing her while Sidra overtook her shadow vision. A good trick, that. And though she couldn't see her, she sensed the jinni smile at her thought. Once Elena relaxed, the light seeped back in and her sight returned, though she no longer controlled where her line of vision was cast.

Sidra concentrated on Jean-Paul's eye movement, the way it flitted rapidly under the lids. Frantic. Frenetic. Elena saw her hand reach out and presumed she no longer controlled her own limbs in the shadow world either. It was as if she and the jinni occupied the same space in her body yet remained side by side in her brain. She thought about

Jamra nearly invading her this way and her body shivered, knowing he wouldn't have preserved her mind.

Keep control of your reactions, an unspoken voice communicated inside her head. *Concentrate on the scent of the vineyard while I jump.* Elena let go of her image of Jamra so Sidra could do her work. The jinni then slipped free of Elena's mind, stepping inside the room as if she had physically transported herself. She laid her hands over Jean-Paul's brow. His head tossed from one side to the other, resisting. Beads of sweat gathered on his skin, slick and shiny. Sidra rubbed her fingers over her thumbs as if she didn't wish to touch his moist skin. Instead she cupped her hands over his ear and whispered some message or incantation incoherent to Elena. Jean-Paul convulsed on the bed. His body writhed as if he fought against a pain that clawed at him from the inside out. He twisted and screamed, throwing off his blankets. Just when Elena didn't think she could watch another moment of his torture, knowing she'd brought this pain on him, his eyes opened and he rolled to his side, where he coughed up a handful of cinders still steaming with smoke.

The sound of the monk running up the stairs caught Sidra's attention.

It is done. She shimmered softly, then dissipated, as the warmth rose again behind Elena's eyes before receding.

Elena waited to see Jean-Paul sit up and recover from coughing before telling Brother Anselm he'd had the strangest dream. When he was assured it wasn't a dream, he nodded as if he understood how that might be so. Though his voice was choked, he appeared restored as he asked about Elena. Brother Anselm handed him her telegram from the nightstand. While he read, she reeled herself back in, opening her eyes with a start as she regained consciousness.

"*Merde,* I didn't think you would ever get back." Yvette rubbed the gooseflesh on her arms. "Jiminy, it's creepy sitting here alone while you're passed out in zombie land."

"It's all right now."

Sidra materialized at Elena's side. Her thumbnail was jammed firmly between her teeth as she seemed to fret in a very un-jinni-like way.

"What was it that Jean-Paul coughed up?" Elena asked when the jinni was fully back in her body. "Is he going to be all right?"

Sidra jumped up and checked the street, the rooftops, and the clouds through the veiled front window of the shop. "It was merely the remnants of Jamra's foul magic. He'd sent your man's mind into the desert, as he said. I found him following a dog deeper and deeper into the land of endless sands. If a storm had come to erase his tracks, he would have been lost for good."

Elena absorbed the news of how dangerous the curse had been and how close she'd come to losing Jean-Paul. A lump of pity for Sidra formed in her throat. And yet her mind was curious about the peculiar magic. "A dog? You mean like the one that brought me here?"

"It's a common-enough form among my kind, but this one was ifrit." Sidra's brow tensed, as if she didn't believe the words she'd spoken. Her eyes searched the sky once again.

"Ifrit? What's that?"

"Jinn but not jinn. The dispossessed ones I spoke of. Made of fire and smoke. Jamra has made a pact with the ifrit. It is they who will come with him."

Elena and Yvette exchanged a worried glance.

Sidra stopped to listen when the walls of the shop creaked, as if speaking the very word had summoned the fire demons. She sniffed the air, then continued. "We should prepare for the inevitable."

Elena agreed. Now that Sidra had successfully freed Jean-Paul's mind from the desert, she owed the jinni her help. It was impossible to return home, at least not yet, so she needed to stay and do what she could to aid her friend. But until she could summon a more effectual magic to wield against Jamra, she was as useless as a mortal.

"And how, exactly, does one defend themselves against these ifrit?" Yvette asked.

"Or Jamra, for that matter," Elena added. "My fiercest defensive spells had no effect against him when he attacked the vineyard. He merely absorbed the magic as if it fed his power. Swallowing it whole. He was barely scathed."

Sidra got that look on her face that said it was to be expected going against a superior being. "Ah, but that was because you were trapped in the moment. But given time for your mind and your book to work together, I'm sure you can form a spell to meet the need. Sorcerers are known for devising all sorts of tricks."

"But how much time?"

Sidra tilted her head as if listening for something. The wind? The cosmos? The sound of ifrit gathering in the ether? A straight answer was all Elena needed.

"There's a spell over the village already," Sidra said. "It will hold him off for a short while. A day perhaps, if luck is with us."

"What kind of spell?" Elena stuck her hand out to try and sense the magic, but there were no filaments of a spell she could detect. Leastwise not within the walls of the abandoned shop.

"We did a scent spell together." Yvette beamed at having been a part of creating an incantation. "We gathered ingredients from the market and then read the words the one-legged sorcerer wrote down."

Now it was Elena's turn to tilt her head. "One-legged—"

"He's not a jinni, but he makes talismans and amulets to help people summon them."

"He's a thief and a liar, but his sorcery masks my presence," Sidra said. "Still, the spell isn't foolproof. A determined enemy could see through the veil easy enough, once he knows where to look."

The town was already full of perfume. The scent wafted everywhere, from the distilleries to the flower fields to the women who bathed in the stuff. But wasn't that what Camille Joubert, the perfume witch on the train, had been talking about? The witch was quite proud of how scent could manipulate matters of the mind.

"That's it," Elena said, struck with an idea. "We're in the midst of the fragrance capital of the world. Run, at least in part, by witches. There has to be a way we can use that against him."

"Their spells are all trifling sweet notions meant to attract a lover," Sidra said, tossing her hand in dismissal. "The art of allure is their only magic. And I do *not* wish to attract Jamra any sooner than I must."

Elena shook her head. "Oh, I think there's more they can do than attract a paramour. In the right combination, scent can be as powerful a concoction as anything a potions witch could come up with." Already her mind was racing with possibility. "I think we need to pay a visit to the *parfumerie* at Le Maison des Amoureux."

"I'm going with you," Yvette said. "I think I'd like to be surrounded by some trifling sweet notions for a change."

She and Elena left the shop through the back alley, while Sidra chose to retreat to the rooftop, where she could watch for the impending signs of her enemy. Following the directions given to them by an elderly woman pruning dead flower heads off a potted geranium, Elena and Yvette climbed the narrow steps leading to the next hilltop terrace. There on the left, in a distinctly villa-esque two-story building overlooking the seaside valley, sat the *parfumerie* at Le Maison des Amoureux. The factory was a distinct terra-cotta color with blue shutters flanking each of the six windows. There were two doors: one for the factory and one for the shop where the perfume was sold. Bottles of Fleur de Sable, with their distinguishing crystal bird stoppers, lined the front window.

Elena approached the main entrance to the factory before a flutter of curiosity brushed up against her intuition, making her pause.

"What's the matter?" Yvette asked.

"Do you smell that?"

The young woman inhaled and smiled. "Smells like lemon and thyme. Like the tonic Tante Isadora used to soothe my sore throat when I was little. Always made me feel better."

"Really?" Elena had caught the scent of woodsmoke and grapevine, reviving happy recollections of summer picnics on green fields with Grand-Mère and Grand-Père when she was a girl. She was going to comment on the discrepancy but then stopped, recognizing the potency of the magic. "It's a spell. To manipulate memories. I'll bet each person experiences a different scent when they enter to put them in a pleasant mood." She smiled at the cleverness and entered the factory with even more determination.

A receptionist behind a huge mahogany desk greeted them with the obligatory "*Bonjour*." Elena stated her business; then she and Yvette waited in the lobby while the woman relayed their message. To bide their time, they perused the museum-like displays arranged around the lobby. Housed under glass domes were delicate crystal bottles with bejeweled finials, an opaline perfume locket on a chain decorated with gold filigree, and four antique bottles filled with botanical oils. The prism-like bottles stood nearly a foot tall and were perched on glass stems with pedestals that had the imperfect patina of handblown glass. They'd been carefully crafted to showcase the essential oils contained within—patchouli, jasmine, rose, and davana. The heart of the fragrance industry for Le Maison des Amoureux, according to the placard propped at their feet.

"Don't you want to jump in and douse yourself in the divine stuff?" Yvette asked, coveting the contents of the bottles with the same rapture as one might express for a diamond necklace.

The receptionist returned and cleared her throat just as Yvette got a little too close to the glass displays. "This way," she said and led them to an upstairs office where Camille Joubert donned a white lab coat over the pale-blue skirt she'd been wearing on the morning train. Behind her were backlit glass shelves filled not only with dazzlingly beautiful perfume bottles but also several stoppered brown jugs with plain white labels, beakers in three sizes, and a line of tiny test tubes held in a wooden rack. On her desk sat a pestle and mortar stuffed with dried seedpods waiting to be ground. Beside the mortar rested a well-worn grimoire open to a page showing a drawing of a five-petaled flower. The witch gave a test tube filled with purple liquid a shake as they entered, looking every inch a scientist about to embark on a magical chemical experiment. And perhaps she was.

"Ah, we meet again." Camille set the test tube in the rack and extended her hand in greeting. "Elena, was it?"

The women shook hands. Elena then introduced Yvette, who glowed ever so slightly from the excitement of the place. The young woman had improved her control so much while in the *Fée* lands that it was difficult to read exactly what her aura was doing, even for a fellow witch. Camille paused, obviously trying not to be rude yet completely aware that there was something different about Yvette's shimmer.

"So, what can I do for you?" Camille asked, letting her eyes rest a second longer on Yvette.

Elena shut the door to the office and explained the situation, though out of an abundance of caution, she omitted the part concerning a powerful ancient relic capable of wreaking havoc on the world and its mortal inhabitants. After all, she'd only met the perfume witch on the train that morning. Best not to overplay her trust in the woman, despite the need for her unique help. A pointed glance at Yvette when Elena had finished her explanation seemed to convey the need to keep that portion of the story quiet for now.

"Ah, I did wonder what had persuaded that jinni to follow you so closely. Apparently he can smell trouble like a bloodhound." Camille reached for a bottle on the top shelf. "Now, if I understand you correctly, you wish to deploy a defense against this Jamra fellow using fragrance?"

Elena had to admit the plan sounded absurd once said out loud. "Am I being ridiculous?"

Camille practically winked at them. "Not ridiculous in the least. As I mentioned on the train earlier, scent often proves the most potent element of all. And, as luck would have it, that is especially true when it comes to its effect on jinn."

"How's that?" Yvette asked.

The perfume witch sat behind her desk and gestured for Elena and Yvette to take a seat in the chairs opposite. She slipped on a pair of round wire-rimmed glasses before digging through the contents of a bottom desk drawer, out of which she pulled a small vial with a dropper for a lid. "Brace yourselves," she warned. She opened the bottle, used the dropper to dab a single tear of clear liquid onto a strip of paper, then wafted it in the air so that the fragrance drifted toward them.

Yvette fell back in her chair. "*Mon Dieu*, what's in that stuff? Smells like heaven."

Elena, too, was overtaken by the allure of the scent, though she couldn't quite place the source of such heady magic.

"This," Camille said, "is the pure concentrated form." She put the lid back on and smiled. "As it happens, I've had the pleasure of working closely with one of the jinn before. My bestselling Fleur de Sable perfume was actually a collaboration with the rarest of jinn gentleman. An absolute charmer." She spun around to show them a crystal bottle with a pair of doves for the stopper.

Yvette nudged Elena. "But that's Sidra's bottle."

"Yes, that's right," Camille said, her voice infused with surprise and curiosity. "She was his wife, his inspiration. How did you know?"

Elena's neck tingled from the featherlight touch of her intuition paying attention. "She's the jinni in the midst of this mess we're in."

"But she was arrested for Hariq's murder. I assumed she'd been executed already. Such a tragedy. They seemed to truly be in love."

Elena looked to Yvette, who nodded. "We escaped prison before that could take place."

"*We?*"

It took a little convincing, but Elena managed to explain their history with Sidra so that Camille was satisfied the two of them posed no threat. Still, while Elena and Yvette had both been exonerated for the crimes they were accused of, there was no such condition for Sidra. She was still wanted for the murder of her husband.

While Camille pondered this new information, Elena sat forward to peek at the grimoire lying open on the desk. "What was it you were going to say about the jinn and the power of fragrance?"

The perfume witch waved the scented paper once under her nose and closed her eyes as if in a fragrant dream. When she opened them again, she relented. "It was his idea. Hariq's. He wanted a scent that encapsulated the beauty of his homeland and the woman he loved. Fleur de Sable. He called her his sand flower." She took down the crystal bottle from the shelf behind her and removed the stopper. She motioned for Yvette to hold out her wrist, then dabbed a drop on her skin. A milder version of the concentrate permeated the air, floating in a cloud of smoky, citrusy musk.

"The top note is a hint of bergamot," she explained. "Then there's a line of jasmine holding the middle in pure ecstasy. The heart of the scent. And at the end is the bass note, a delicate incense-like musk that lingers on the skin, reminiscent of a mystical night spent in the desert under a silken canopy as the scent of trade spices and exotic flowers sails on the summer air."

Elena recognized a kindred spirit in the perfume witch and the way she blended scents to get the perfect flavor she was after. But how could they use this magic to help them with the jinn? As if anticipating the question, Camille put the stopper back in the bottle. She turned to her grimoire, flipping through the pages until she came to her handwritten notes at the back.

"I wrote this note down at the time, which was, goodness, twenty years ago," she said, checking the date beside the entry. "Hariq said he and Sidra wished to stay here in the village, but there was some trouble with their families, as I recall. They wanted a way to ensure they wouldn't be found easily. They were looking for a spell to cover their tracks." She ran her finger under her words as she read. "The jinn are attracted to smoke, botanic fragrances, and incense. All of them natural substances. But each jinni is different. What attracts one jinni might repel another. The allure is dependent on their nature. If one's intentions are harmless, they will often be drawn to scents infused with qualities that enhance beauty, happiness, and satisfaction. But if one's will is set on creating mischief or destruction, it's likely they will be attracted to aromas that heighten or reinforce those intentions—scents of char, decay, bitter reed grass. Even the modern odors of locomotive smoke, car petrol, and exhaust fumes can attract and enliven a wicked jinn."

"How can we use that against Jamra?" Elena asked.

Camille looked over the top of her glasses and grinned. "Well, from what I've gathered, he and his colleagues are not prone to being the helpful sort of jinn. Which means they wouldn't be overly fond of my concoctions."

"So, we blast him with this heavenly scent," Yvette said, sniffing her wrist again.

"Perhaps we won't deploy my bestselling perfume. However, there are certainly other aromas we can combine to achieve the same effect."

"Jinni repellent," Yvette said and smiled.

Elena leaned in to her intuition. "It could work. It's why Sidra and Hariq chose to settle here. The flowers, the perfume. The fragrances protected them." At least until Hariq's untimely death. "We're in a dreadful hurry," Elena said. "Jamra may arrive at any moment. He destroyed a good portion of my vineyard already. I don't think the village will fare much better against his wrath if he senses he's close to finding what he's after."

"Perhaps your jinni friend should consider leaving to spare the village."

A fair assessment. Elena had wondered the same thing, but there was a final destiny in Sidra's demeanor. As much as she feared Jamra, she also seemed determined to face him. And this town was where she meant to do it. "There's an element of fate involved. She believes this is where she must face Jamra, according to the omens she's seen."

"I'm well aware of the jinn and their faith in prophecies. Hariq was much the same. But I can't do the spellwork alone, not on the scale required to protect an entire town. You'd better leave this one here with me," Camille said, pointing to Yvette.

"Me? But what can I do?"

"Oh, with that glamour of yours I think there's plenty you can add to help create what we're after. I'm quite curious to see the results. Yes, most curious."

With Yvette already giddy at the prospect of working with the perfume witch, Elena left the young woman and headed downstairs. Before exiting the factory, she ducked into the store adjacent to the lobby, where the fragrances were sold. Dozens of bottles of perfume with crystal birds for stoppers were on sale. A bestselling scent, indeed. A dozen other bottles and fragrances were available too. So many there must be one for every woman. Standing in the middle of so many scents and thinking of the unique spellwork Yvette and Camille were embarking upon gave her an idea, one that had her exit the perfume shop and head for the marketplace of magical goods.

CHAPTER NINETEEN

There in the open air, riding on the heat and gray smoke that wafted out from the top of a chimney, Sidra recognized herself again. Her fire smoldered within her once more so that she felt it in the tips of her fingers and soles of her feet. Still, she would never again experience the exquisite heat she'd once known from a single touch. A glance. A shared bed.

At first she'd cursed the fairy king for returning her to this place of cold remorse, but his instinct proved correct. She was even glad the girl had been sent with her. Sitting above the rooftops, gazing over the village where she'd once been consumed with the happiness of a thousand dancing flames after marrying Hariq, she knew she'd been set on the good path again. Her only regret was not understanding earlier the fragility of love. How a heart was housed in brittle glass. So easily shattered.

But now the fire inside her had returned. The old one had been right. There were circles within circles in the continuity between past and future. Let Jamra come, she thought. Enough of this jittery, nervous energy. Enough fretting over what might be. Hariq was gone to the next world. Soon she would join him, so might it be, and may it fill her with the scorching blaze of vengeance.

She settled within the heat wave rising from the chimney, hiding amid its smoke as she kept her eye on the sky, the street, and the ether around her. It was then, while tracing the movement of a tiny dust devil that swept along the cobblestones below, that she caught sight of a dog's tail slipping around a corner. A tail in the same crescent shape found in the omen the birds had gifted her. But whose tail?

There'd always been jinn who came and went through the village. Others had taken up residence in similar older villages in the hillsides to the east. Or there'd been nomads, clanless jinn who roamed over invisible mortal borders, curious to see the whole of the world.

If this was the same dog who'd led Elena to her, he was familiar. Knew her. Knew the village. Instinct suggested Rajul Hakim had sent him. A guard dog to lead the witch to Sidra's side and watch over the last events of her life. Perhaps the dog was one who paid tribute to the old one from a village closer to his cave. The tail disappeared up a narrow lane. She contemplated the risk. One was smart to keep watch for those about to charge the tent, but one was wisest not to neglect those already inside.

Sidra filtered through the air unseen from rooftop to street level. She followed the animal around the corner, hoping to catch a glimpse of the tail again, but the lane held only mortals. The jinni animated behind a palm tree and sniffed the air. Spice, salt, sand. Someone roasting a chicken in wine. Always in wine. But there was nothing amiss—merely the usual odors of a town steeped in the botanic oils of a thriving industry.

Except . . . yes, there. Her nose caught a whiff of something enticing in the wind, something intoxicating, yet paired with the musty odor of dog fur. She followed it down a narrow lane where small recesses had been built into the walls of the ocher-colored buildings. Residents had placed small statues and an offering of a bouquet of flowers inside one of the alcoves, adding to the layers of fragrance mingling above the pavement. Even she couldn't be sure she'd be able to detect the smoke of another jinni in the mazelike quarters. Sidra's body wavered like a candle flame in a draft, realizing the same spell she'd invoked to protect herself might also prove a vulnerability in such a tight space.

The lane ahead veered to the left as it passed under an archway bridging two apartment buildings. She couldn't see beyond the arch as the lane twisted, though she thought she heard the padding of a dog's feet against the cobblestones, the pant of breath. She ventured ahead another ten feet, following each new scent that captivated her nose, anxious to uncover the dog's motive.

But then the floral scents converged, churning in the air with the bitter odor of char and acidic ash. A smokeless flame shot up in the lane before her. A shadow of a man in a derby hat.

Jamra stood three feet before her, eyes blazing with the hunger of revenge denied too many times before.

"Jinniyah."

Sidra bared her gold-and-ivory teeth even as the torch inside her wavered at the sight of her enemy. Had he been the one she'd followed? Impossible. He wasn't worthy enough to take the form of a dog.

She grinned, seeing the whiptail end of a scar peeking out above his collar. "How fares your back?" she asked.

Jamra didn't lash out as expected, but his temper clearly simmered beneath his skin. "Give me the dagger and I promise you will feel only minimum anguish when I kill you and avenge my brother's death. Deny me, and the morning will bring nothing but destruction for you and the people of this village."

Sidra glanced quickly at the rooftops for signs of ifrit hovering about, but the sightline was clear. Had he really come alone?

"You never spared any love for your brother," she said, lowering her eyes to meet his. "You would have eagerly taken his life if his death would have delivered you what you seek."

"Now I have the pleasure of demanding that same condition from you."

Sidra grew bolder. "The dagger was not made to fit the hand of the defiled."

The jinni's eyes flashed with hatred. The insult had found its sticking place. Let the wrath of her fire do the same. Sidra conjured a wave of grease-fire and hurled the blaze at Jamra. The same spell she'd used to sear his skin the first time she'd faced him one-on-one. Only this time the fire missed. Went right through him. The flame hit the wall, licking the stone with scorching heat and black smoke.

Jamra hadn't even made a move to defend himself. Instead he grinned as a choking column of smoke billowed upward. And then he faded from view. A mirage. A trick. He'd never been there at all. He'd manipulated her mind. Her vision. Provoked her from afar until she reacted. She looked up again. The smoke climbed above the rooftops to fill the sky.

A signal. A beacon to mark her spot.

At the end of the lane the dog lowered his head after watching the trail of smoke rise higher. Even he seemed to understand that, somewhere, a pair of plotting eyes scanned the horizon.

CHAPTER TWENTY

He'd had to slink behind a mother and child while they admired the stalactites, the rows of teeth-like formations growing in the stomach of the cave. Their tour guide had been so preoccupied with assigning lanterns and pointing out the guide ropes that he hadn't noticed a dog slipping inside the gate behind the group. Not that it would have mattered. He could have easily moved through the ether, though the damp in the cave wasn't to his liking in his spirit form. Better to trod on four paws than endure the unnatural merging of moisture with his essence.

The old one slept. To mortal ears his snores were likely nothing more than echoes inside a cave. The sounds of wind and dripping water. But to the dog they were the forewarning of an ancient one's days winding down. He stared into the abyss where he knew Rajul Hakim was tucked away.

As-salaam-alaykum, Rajul Hakim. The dog sent the greeting into the old one's mind, yet the jinni didn't stir. He sighed, not wishing to do the thing he must. He waited through another chorus of snores, then reluctantly trotted inside the darkness, letting his wet nose nudge up against the coil of energy there. At last the old one grumbled awake.

"Who is there?" he asked, reanimating so that his hand reached out to touch the dog's head. "Ah, it is you. I've been expecting your arrival."

"The time is upon us," he said and transformed into the form of a man.

"Yes, so the great unwinding has begun." The jinni gathered up the front of his too-long caftan and walked the few steps to the wall where the spirals had been scratched into the limestone. He traced a finger over each one, as if sensing the churning energy—wish energy—still swirling in the cosmos. "The confrontation is imminent," he said and tapped his finger on the final spiral.

"She has already been found."

The old one studied the coiled etchings. Each like a spring releasing its kinetic energy into the world, creating ripples of outcomes that might never have been otherwise. At least that was how the energy of wishes had been explained to the young man from his earliest education in the designs of magic. But the way the elements of the wish all interacted was a thing to behold. He bowed to the old one's ingenuity and wisdom.

"It was not all my doing," Rajul Hakim said, as if reading his mind. "She had a hand in things too." He tapped his finger on the big spiral enveloping the smaller ones.

The man recalled the creature who'd sat on his shoulder to whisper in his ear and shivered. "She makes gooseflesh of my skin."

"Then you have good instincts." Rajul Hakim laughed, but it soon turned into a cough. In the outer cave a child cried out for his mother. "She is not one to trifle with. Especially if met in one's dreams."

The jinni nodded before lowering his head in thought. There was more he wished to say. Uncertainties he wanted made certain. Guarantees written in the language of the ancients. The old one's blood oath that everything would work out the way it was meant to, but he was no fool. Events would go forward as planned, with the consequences spilling out when the thing was done.

"And you still do not know where she has hidden the dagger?" the young man asked, although his instinct knew the answer even before it was confirmed with a shake of the head. The old one seemed to realize then he had not extended his hospitality to his guest by offering coffee or a pipe, but the jinni waved him off. "I must return and find my place. May the All Seeing allow us to meet again on the other side."

Aching to stretch his back, the jinni said a final farewell, then walked out of the cave on four feet. Soon, the All Seeing willing, he would live in the world as a man once again.

CHAPTER
TWENTY-ONE

Elena walked among the market's generous baskets of spices and plucked flowers. There were also shells, jewelry, boxes of fresh fruit, clay pots with olives, shawls of wool and silk and lace, and even a few bottles of red wine for sale beside salty fish wrapped in paper. She'd need to consult her grimoire with Sidra, as delicately as possible, to learn which ingredients would be the most potent against the jinn, but as she only had the few coins in her satchel, the options were limited at best.

Ingredients for potions weren't the only thing Elena browsed for. She also kept her eye on the people. She walked past each market stand until she came across a fellow in a dirty white shirt with sooty marks around the neck where a deep purple aura peeked out. He was busy tying sweetgrass into bundles for smudging—always a helpful cleanse for a spiritually sullied space. On his counter sat half a dozen brass incense burners, a bowl filled with chunks of resin she assumed was frankincense, and several bronze amulets small enough to be carried in a pocket for luck. The merchant himself appeared rather shopworn, though she supposed he had a genial-enough face and disposition. Besides, her instinct told her he and his goods might be of help.

Elena circled his shop at arm's length as she continued to browse. The man stood to help another customer, alternating his weight between his good leg and a false one. *Ah, so this was the one-legged sorcerer.* And a thief as well, according to Sidra. Elena waited for him to sell a man a scoop of dried seedpods, then approached.

"May I help you choose an incense, madame?"

"I'm more interested in your talismans and sorcery skills, actually." Sometimes it's best to get right to the point. "You are Yanis, correct?" He shifted uncomfortably on his wooden leg. "I'm a friend of Sidra's, and I'm afraid I have some bad news for you."

"Worse news than being a friend of Sidra's?"

She ignored his remark. "I'm a witch in need of assistance protecting the village from a jinni, and I have it on good authority that's something you can help me with."

He backed away and leaned on his stool. "You have the wrong man." He held his calloused hands out as if to prove they'd been depleted of anything she could want. "I'm a simple sorcerer who sells a few charms and ingredients for spells." To make clear his position, he swept two magically incriminating medallions off his counter and stowed them away.

"I understand your hesitation when it comes to dealing with the jinn. I'd rather not be here myself. I have a husband at home who requires my attention, a vineyard that desperately needs nurturing, and a monk who ought to hear a few words of forgiveness before he returns to his abbey. But unless there's another sorcerer with your particular experience in the village, I'm afraid you're it."

"Madame, you should return home to your husband. Tend to your vineyard. You will find only disappointment if you try to interfere with the jinn in this village."

Elena peered at him until he nearly shriveled from the scrutiny. Had she heard wrong? Was he a mere charlatan selling charms to tourists?

No, he was the one. The shiver running up and down her neck was rarely wrong.

"But it is possible? There are amulets or spells that can help? Potions perhaps?"

The man shook his head. "If you try to interfere in magic you know nothing about, you will find yourself at the mercy of the jinn. There are symbols. Rituals. But one false move and the jinn can easily overtake you." He pointed a finger to his temple to insinuate they could get inside her head.

"Sounds like you know more than you let on."

He grumbled something about another lifetime before accepting a coin from a woman for a packet of incense. He wished the woman well, smiling at her as she walked away, then let his annoyance show when he saw Elena still standing at his counter.

"I could compel you to help," she said. "The matter is that urgent."

"It's against your laws."

"Only when used against mortals." That got his attention. To convince him she was serious, she took a pinch of herbs from a bowl on his counter and ground them up with her fingers, letting the crushed bits of leaf fall in her palm. "Wind that blows, leaf that stirs, ruffle the hats of mesdames and messieurs."

She blew a puff of breath over the herbs, and the wind picked up. A whirlwind—she kept it small enough to hit only one market stand at a time—stirred up leaves and debris from the ground and kicked them into the air. Men and women turned their backs and clamped their hands over their hats to keep them from blowing off their heads. Yanis, too, had to spread his arms over his merchandise to keep the items from blowing away. Elena closed her fingers to form a fist, and the mini storm abated as the whirlwind lifted over their heads and vanished.

"All right, all right," he said. "No reason to show off."

"We haven't much time," she said. "It's probably best you close shop for the day and come with me. We have a protection spell to design, you and I. Unless you'd rather see the town burned to the ground by a horde of angry jinn. Because I assure you, monsieur, that's exactly who we need protection from."

Yanis raised his eyes to the sky. "Am I to be plagued with unruly women of magic all my life?"

"Gather any items you think you might need for a spell," she said.

He shook his head, collected his items from the counter to pack them away, and closed his market stand, securing it with a padlock.

The man grumbled all the way to the abandoned shop about lost income and the debts he had to pay. It was little use explaining that there were other obvious metaphysical rewards and debts at stake. Elena entered the alley behind the abandoned shop so they might go in through the back door unnoticed. The man stopped halfway, as if having second thoughts.

"She tried to kill me, you know."

"Sidra? Believe me, if she'd wanted you dead you wouldn't be talking to me now."

Yanis limped closer. "Yes, but she blames me," he said with a nod toward the store.

"For what?"

"Her husband's death. But it wasn't me. And I don't believe it was her, either." His eyes seemed to sink into his skull, his expression remorseful. "I was careful with the incantation, with the amounts. You understand. I can tell you've worked with potions. It was one batch for the both of them. Each the same. But something went wrong."

"Why did the inspector arrest Sidra for his murder?"

The man swallowed and shook his head. "He said it was a classic lovers' quarrel. And she still had the potion bottle when the police finally caught up to her. They claimed she poisoned him. But there was no poison."

"What was in the tincture?"

"Mimosa flower. It's a spell to mimic death, but one wakes after two or three days. Sometimes people need to start over. Leave an old life behind and start afresh." He shrugged as if to say he was merely the messenger. "But even a double dose shouldn't have killed him."

Elena's first thought was to wonder *if* a jinni could die by poison. But the authorities obviously thought so. And they'd have happily executed Sidra for the crime of murder if she hadn't escaped through fire. But poison? Yanis was right. It didn't make any sense. Then again, nothing in life had made sense since she'd broken the curse that had transformed her into a toad. Nothing except perhaps finding Jean-Paul. Love was the one curious remedy that had emerged through all the turmoil.

Right. The sooner they faced this next challenge, the sooner she could return home. She opened the door and waited for Yanis. "We have work to do," she said. Recognizing there was little choice in the matter, he limped forward like a man marching toward his own execution.

Sidra was not there when they entered, which pleased Yanis. Elena watched as his eyes traveled around the room, taking in the fine silk canopy, brass lamps, and the rest of the accoutrements she presumed were part of his native culture as well. Did she read regret on his face? Or perhaps homesickness? She knew from experience that longing for one's home was the sort of emotion to strike at the most inopportune moments, flooding the eyes with yearning.

She looked away to allow him a moment. "You may help yourself to the coffee, if you like. It's charmed to stay constantly hot."

Elena removed her apron from her satchel and tied it around her waist as Yanis ran his fingers over the seven-pointed star pattern on a pillow.

"She did all this?" he asked.

"Yes. I assume it's all an illusion, but the textures always feel very real. Better than anything I've ever feigned."

"It's no illusion. This was all manifested to be real. The work of a master conjurer."

He knelt to study the pattern on the pillow more closely. Elena felt compelled to do the same, given his interest. It was then she noticed the intricate pattern of a circle within a circle within a circle within an elaborate decorative design.

"Does it mean something?" she asked.

"Only everything," he said and managed a humble smile. "The circle in the middle represents the energy at the center of the universe. All things are drawn around it. Some near, some farther out. We are all at various distances from the center. But all strive to find the heart. The symbol is a good thing. A good reminder."

His finger maintained almost reverential contact with the circles as he stood. When he let go, he removed his frayed skullcap and nodded slowly. "I will help you," he said. "Though it will be difficult and dangerous, and there's no guarantee any of the spells will work. Not if there are jinn involved."

Elena had done difficult and dangerous before. She raised her hands in the sacred pose and welcomed his help, though she was beginning to suspect he was more learned than a mere street vendor peddling charms and trinkets to tourists. Once in agreement, they leaned over her grimoire to scan for the limited information it held on desert mysticism. There were a few drawings featuring pentagrams meant to control spirits and some spindly notes she'd scribbled from her time in school when she'd been allowed to study *The Book of the Seven Stars* but nothing of any urgent value. Yanis concurred.

"We'll simply have to start with our intuition," he said. "And what I remember from my school days as well."

Each shared their inventory of supplies, laying the items out on the counter. Yanis had brought a rope of sweetgrass, a stick of incense, an amulet bearing a quadrangle of symbols she didn't recognize, a white crystal, a candle stub, and a stick of chalk, which he explained was most important for drawing symbols on flagstones. Elena emptied her satchel next. She still carried the two coins, her athame, some bundled rosemary, a polished bloodstone, an amethyst crystal, a packet of salt, and a smudge pot full of ointment that was really only good for treating blisters. It wasn't much to work with, but Yanis disagreed, claiming intent was the most important ingredient. Elena heartily concurred, and so they set to work.

Yanis began by asking Elena to cleanse the center of the shop so they might have a sacred space in which to work. She blew on her fingers to create a small flame, which she held against the braid of sweetgrass until it smoldered. Before the flame went out, she asked if she should light the incense as well. "Wouldn't hurt," Yanis replied, so she got that to smolder too. Then with measured steps she walked around the space, letting the incense drift up into the rafters. Following the sorcerer's instructions, she let the smoke seep into the darkest crevices to assure there was no safe place for unwanted jinn to find comfort.

When she finished, Yanis lowered himself onto his knee and drew a large star within a circle on the floor with the chalk. Similar to the talismans he created to sell, he added symbols to the spaces that were created between the circle and the seven-sided star. They were unlike any marks Elena had worked with before. She asked if she could draw one to experience the energy it emitted. Yanis wasn't sure at first but then had her draw a crescent moon, Saturn, and Uranus. She was just about to ask about their meaning when Sidra reanimated inside the abandoned shop.

The jinni's energy, even before she opened her mouth, was scattered and unfocused, signaling something was wrong.

Elena stood and brushed the chalk from her fingers. "What is it? What happened?"

Sidra began to confess, but then she saw Yanis and the chalk drawing on the floor and her temper exploded. "What is he doing here?"

"We're designing a protection spell against Jamra."

"Impossible. Stay away from this man," she said to Elena. "He's nothing but a liar."

Yanis remained calm as he stood beside the symbol on the floor. "Sidra, you must believe me."

Elena knew better than to put a calming hand on Sidra once she began to boil. Instead she moved to stand in front of the sorcerer. "Yanis can help us."

"I'm warning you. He's a bringer of death."

"I didn't kill him. He did something—"

Before he finished speaking, Sidra unleashed a stream of hissing steam from her sleeve that grazed Elena's hip, making her gasp at the heat.

"No!" she screamed, turning to see if the spewed steam had hit Yanis.

But the sorcerer deflected the heat by raising his arm. Instead of burning him—or maiming the man for life—the ejection of steam halted as if hitting an invisible wall, curling and rotating into a tiny storm cloud that spun beneath Yanis's open palm. The steam never even touched him. He whispered three words, foreign to Elena's ears, and the mini storm dissipated in a final poof, leaving only a moist palm behind, which the man wiped against his soiled shirt.

Sidra stood with her hands at her sides, her fingers nervously clutching her robes as she scrutinized the man with a scathing stare. "How does a seller of charms stop my magic with the flat of his hand?"

Yanis let out a breath. His eyes seemed to judge the distance between him and the door. Sidra glared, threatening to test his resistance again if he didn't answer her. The sorcerer's demeanor changed. Some pretense fell away. His posture straightened. His jaw tightened. He was still dressed in near rags, his face was still wan and unshaven, but when he straightened his back, he somehow bore the weight of authority. Yes, there in his eyes rested complete assurance of his abilities.

"Because I am a priest of the Order of the Seven Stars," he said and replaced his skullcap.

"Liar." But even as Sidra spoke, she betrayed her own doubt by taking a step back.

"An outcast, but still ordained."

"You, a magus?" Her eyes looked him up and down, not seeing the proof of his boast in his shabby appearance.

"*Order* of the Seven Stars?" Elena asked. "As in *The Book of the Seven Stars?*"

Sidra simmered on the periphery, anxious to know more as well.

"Yes," the sorcerer said plainly but with a tone of regret. "I was training to be an acolyte."

Encouraged by Elena, Yanis explained how he'd been accepted by the Order as a teen after he'd unlocked a summoning spell that caused a roc with emerald wingtips to soar over a seaside village. The incident caught the Order's attention after the enormous bird snatched a dolphin out of the sea in front of a boatload of fishermen, who then boasted of the sighting at every café along the coast. "They trained me in sorcery until I'd mastered the skill and discipline needed to become a guardian."

"You were recruited to oversee the magic included in *The Book of the Seven Stars?*" Elena was more than impressed.

"Acolytes," he explained, "are charged with continually exploring the world of the supernatural. The mission is to push the boundaries of magical understanding and practice." He held up a finger as if making a point. "But the contents of the book aren't chiseled in stone. Guidance and advice continually evolve, manifesting new knowledge and interpretation in the pages as it's uncovered."

Sidra circled him. "And why are you not still pursuing this high calling, sorcerer?" The final word hissed out of her mouth like water on a hot skillet.

He swallowed as if he still held a sour taste on his tongue. "Much of that knowledge, as you know, comes from magical teachings first practiced in the ancient East. It's important to keep the information accurate so the contents remain relevant." Yanis wiped away the sweat on his upper lip. "The Order constantly investigates reports of unusual practices. Interactions with preternatural beings. Undocumented sightings and complaints. That sort of thing."

"What kinds of complaints?" Elena asked.

"My first mission," he said and moved to sit on the *majlis* sofa. He rubbed the knee above his wooden leg as if it pained him, along with the memory. "I was tasked with ridding a burial site of ghouls."

"Ghouls?" Elena sat beside him, and to her surprise, Sidra joined them, offering coffee and small butter biscuits filled with dates as she listened in silence. *Payment for the storyteller?* she wondered.

"I was armed with the collective knowledge of the world's greatest sorcerers, yet I was still young and green enough to think that made me invincible." He saw Sidra shake her head. "Yes, I was an arrogant fool. And it nearly got me killed." He pointed to his wooden leg. "I'd tried entering the burial site with a few protective charms, a chant, and the symbols of the seven stars painted on my body. I thought they would see I was a member of the Order and scatter." He wiped his face, reliving the horrifying moment. "The first ghoul I encountered broke through every defense I'd used as if they were made of straw. She slashed my leg clean off with one swipe."

"Mother Ghulah." Sidra's eyes lit up, impressed.

"You're saying ghouls are real?" Elena asked.

"Oh, they're real," Yanis said. "Some even suspect they're related to the jinn."

Sidra stiffened. "They are *not* jinn."

"No," Yanis said. "They are not."

That seemed to please Sidra, but still she squinted at him. "And now you sell talismans behind a wooden stall in an infidel village. Maybe your leg wasn't the only thing you lost that day."

Elena winced. "Sidra, that's hardly—"

"No, she's right. I lost my nerve after that. I left the Order. Or as much as one can. They never truly consider you done, once you've received the training."

Sidra watched him, tapping a finger against her coffee cup. "And now you think you can protect the people in this village from Jamra and his ifrit with your chalk drawings, sorcerer?"

"We're going to try," Elena said.

Sidra continued to stare at Yanis but with a different glint than she had before. When he set his cup down, she covered it with a saucer, then flipped it over, letting the remaining fluid drain out onto the saucer. "Was it Hariq who sought your help?" she asked, righting the cup again and running her finger over the lip to make a circle. "Or maybe it was the old one himself who summoned you?" She pinned her gaze sharp on Yanis before peering into the depth of his cup.

Yanis swallowed as he watched her read the dregs. "Both," he said. "The old one knew about my past. It's why he trusted me with such a delicate potion, but Hariq gave me my day-to-day instructions. I swear to you I don't know what went wrong."

Sidra curled her lip as if she'd expected to discover him in a lie yet again, but as she stared into his cup her eyes tensed in confusion. She turned the cup to see it from another angle before pushing it away. Elena wasn't sure if jinn could cry, and yet there was unmistakable sadness in Sidra's eyes when she looked up again.

"You have told the truth," she said. "Which means I am a murderer."

Sidra sank back against the cushions. Elena and Yanis didn't dare make a move while the jinni seethed in the pain of learning a truth she hadn't believed. Comfort wasn't an easy thing to administer to one made of fire. And yet Elena remembered the kindness Sidra had shown her in jail when she'd offered her a blanket against the chill. Calling fire onto her fingers, Elena lit the firewood inside the brazier until a warm glow shone on all their faces. Sidra seemed to respond, turning to stare into the flames.

"Jamra has found me," she said. "I tried following that phantom dog and instead ran into a jackal. He tricked me into revealing my location. And now he's given me until morning to hand over the dagger, or else he'll kill me and attack the village."

"What? Why didn't you say so earlier?" Elena knew time wasn't something they had in abundance, but she'd thought they at least had the advantage of being hidden a little while longer.

"I have already cheated justice once. Perhaps I should let him kill me in the name of righteousness."

Yanis leaned forward. "What dagger?"

"Do you know your sigils, priest?" Sidra sat up. "Do you know the seven signs that came into the world in the beginning? One assigned to each of the seven original kingdoms?"

"Of course. They were recorded in many of the ancient scrolls recovered from the cave of shadows. Two copies survive under the care of the Order."

"You think these seals have only been around as long as your history books?" She slowly turned toward him. "The jinn were born before ancient civilizations. Before cities, before soothsayers and magi. My kind was there when the original sigils were unleashed in the world. The tension between the symbols holding the world in equilibrium, like a seven-pointed star. But the world is full of careless men. Always they seek to tip the balance with their greed and ambition. And now Jamra believes he is this close to possessing one of these sigils without the eye of your Order watching over it. One that will hurtle us all toward chaos."

The sorcerer grew pale. "This dagger bears such a mark?"

"I have seen it with my own eyes."

Yanis tilted his head as if recalling something once forgotten. "There were objects created, embedded with the sigils to better keep track of them. A cup, a mirror, a belt. I forget the rest, but this dagger should have had a guardian. They were all assigned to magi of the highest order. Their movements traced with scrying stones. What happened to him?"

"He died alone on Zimbarra. My husband and I discovered his bones on this island. The dagger was buried in the sand beside him."

"Zimbarra? No wonder his death went unnoticed. The movement of the island would have simulated the wanderings of a magus." Yanis stood and paced, dragging his wooden leg against the floor despite the pain. "So, you found the sigil and brought it here? Did you know how dangerous that was?"

"They didn't know what they'd found until an ifrit recognized it," Elena said in Sidra's defense.

"An ifrit?" Yanis tapped his closed fist against his lips. "Where is it now? Is the dagger hidden? A relic like that must be protected."

"It is in a safe place."

"But where? The Order will need to secure the weapon. Do you understand the damage something like that could do in the hands of a . . ."

He stopped himself before the word spilled out, but Sidra had already snatched the word out of the air for him.

"A jinni?" She stood and gathered her scarf over her head. "Go back to your chalk drawings, sorcerer. And may they spare your life when the sun comes up."

CHAPTER TWENTY-TWO

Sidra dissipated from the shop, shrinking into the quiet solitude of an empty cupboard in an upstairs attic. She missed the sanctuary of the bottle and the scent of jasmine and bergamot Hariq had created for her. But that was gone now, her bottle left behind in another realm. Safe. Still, she needed a quiet place to hide, if only to regain her balance again. The fire of fury and destruction and the blaze of warmth and comfort coexisted inside her, always battling one another for control. There was no such thing as an even flame. Which was why not even she, despite the restraint of a hundred patient camels waiting to drink, could be sure of resisting the lure of the dagger's power forever. No, the weapon was where it needed to be. Gone from this realm and safe in the airy humidity of another.

Centered once more, Sidra decided she ought to go check on the girl before the morning light. A storm was coming, and the chances of she, the witch, and the fairy outlasting it would be better if they were all together when the force hit. She wondered if Yvette ever suspected the power she'd once held in her hands or, at times, stashed in her gown between her breasts. Yes, she would go find the girl and bring her back. There was no truly safe place for any of them, but perhaps the sorcerer's marks on the floor would help. With the right words spoken by the witch, a small circle of safety might withstand the damage about to be unleashed.

It was well past midnight when Sidra seeped out through a crack in the cupboard to travel within the ether to the *parfumerie* on the top of the hill. She knew the place well from the times Hariq had thought he was sneaking off to pursue his pet project, a perfume designed for her. Of course she'd known what he was up to. The scent found her every time he returned home. The fragrance clung to his robes, his hair, his skin. Even in their ethereal state, the jasmine mingled with his natural oud scent, adhering to his being. But that was years ago. A blink in time, yet a lifetime gone by.

The walls of the factory were made of stone, the windows of glass, but they proved no barrier. Shards of her energy slipped through the interstices, reforming on the other side so that when she reanimated, two stories up, she stood in a depressing walled cubicle full of bottles, paper, and mortal machinery. Lifeless things endowed with a little ingenuity but otherwise useless.

The girl shrieked down the hall. That frivolous high laughter of hers that sounded like crystal bottles clinking together. Before announcing herself, Sidra crept up to the doorframe to learn what had caused the fair one's outburst. She found Yvette in a room crowded with the hot metal bellies Hariq was so drawn to—the copper boilers used to distill the fragrant oils from the tender flowers. Heaping baskets of pink and white petals awaited the fate of having their precious scents extracted through steam. She inhaled both the smell of the flowers and the heat coming off the boilers, filling her lungs with bittersweet memories. They'd been so sure this was their safe haven.

"Sidra!" Yvette spotted her lurking in the dark. Curse her fairy instincts. "We've been at it all night. And now we've just about got a plan of attack sorted out. You won't believe how we managed it."

"What is all this?" she asked, stepping into the room, her eye steady on the witch holding the glass bottle. "What have you done?"

Yvette wiped her hands on a cloth and nudged her chin toward the witch. "This is Camille Joubert. She owns the joint. She's been letting me help her with the perfume."

"*Enchantée,*" Camille said before peering closer. "You are Sidra? Then I feel like I already know you. Hariq talked about you all the time when he was here."

Sidra's lip began to curl at the idea of this woman thinking she knew her. Yvette nudged her in the arm and mouthed, "Behave."

"Actually, I'm thrilled you're here," Camille said. "We could certainly use your opinion on this concoction we've come up with." The perfume witch crossed the room to where several beakers full of liquid sat atop a wooden table. She pulled the stopper out of a large container filled with a yellowish fluid.

The aromas of vanilla, jasmine, lavender, and a hint of something animalistic and wild clung to the air. Sidra was drawn to the scent like an aroused lover. "What is in this?" she asked, leaning her nose in. Her brain knew it was merely a mix of the petals she'd already experienced in the room, but there was something else, some magnetism to the scent that made it impossible to resist.

"Three things," Camille said. She smiled coyly as Yvette nearly squealed with delight. "First, we've made a delectable mix of some of nature's finest scent offerings. Second, Yvette was in possession of a goodly amount of castoreum, procured at the market, so we tossed it in."

"Turns out what that old witch gave me was from a beaver's ass," Yvette said, scrunching up her nose.

"Highly prized for its robust aroma." Camille held up a finger as if presenting the pièce de résistance. "And finally, there's a unique tinge of magic holding it all together. A combination of my spellwork and this young woman's glamour."

"We put a few drops of my *Fée* blood in the mixture. A pinch of fat would have been better, but, oh là là, I'm not *that* dedicated to the cause."

Camille gave a *comme ci, comme ça* shrug. "I think our jinni friend here has shown it worked as well with the castoreum replacement."

Feeling an unnatural giddiness infiltrate her mood, Sidra blocked her nose and mouth with the edge of her robe so only her eyes showed and stepped back. "What has worked? What magic is this?"

"Camille has a theory, or rather she got the idea from your . . . from Hariq. Seems perfume can awaken a person's spirit. Both the good and the bad, depending on the scent."

"And depending on the person," Camille added.

"But with jinn it also matters what their intentions are," Yvette said. "At least that's what Hariq told her when they were making that perfume of yours."

The mixture of scent and talk of her husband combined to form a whirlwind of happiness, sorrow, longing, and a deep, deep desire to forgive him anything if only he would materialize once more. Sidra kept her nose covered as she slumped against the wall. Her fire, the flame that kept her mood sharp and mind fixed, flickered within her until she felt woozy with watery emotions too complicated for her to control. She didn't think she could hold up her physical embodiment another moment. And yet her mind couldn't focus long enough to dissipate. Yvette, attuned as ever to the capricious moods of others, swept in and put an arm under her before she collapsed to the floor.

"Take her to my office," Camille said and put the stopper back in the bottle.

Yvette used her power to levitate and guide Sidra to the next room. "Strong stuff, eh?" she said as she eased the jinni down into a soft chair.

With some distance between her and the fragrance, Sidra recovered enough to gain control over her body and mind. "Hariq often took an interest in the creation of such complicated scents," she said once her head cleared. "But what was the part you said about good and bad intentions?"

"That may still be a matter of guesswork," Camille said. "The idea is these pleasant smells are attractive to jinn whose intentions are well meaning. Or at least benign." The woman paused briefly, as if only just making up her mind about Sidra. "Whereas a jinni whose intentions are of a befouling sort, his essence will be repelled by the pleasantness of such airborne aromas. They'll get in his lungs, eyes, and nose, stinging the membranes with the stench of beauty."

"My husband was often right about such things."

"So, you think our jinni repellent will work?" Yvette moved to lean against a shelf. Her glow was soft but steady, enough to distract the eye and the mind from unpleasant thoughts.

Sidra opened her mouth to speak when she saw the bottles lining the shelf behind the fairy. Rows and rows of perfume bottles like the one Hariq presented as a gift years ago. The one with her fragrance in it. The one she'd left behind in the *Fée* lands.

The girl had made a joke. She was still smiling. But then she patted her hips as if feeling for something. "Oh, that reminds me. I keep forgetting to give this back to you." Yvette reached in her pocket, the one that never showed the bulk of any of the things she hoarded, and produced a bottle. It was like the others behind her, but with one very distinct and terrifying difference the girl could never have understood.

For the second time in mere days Sidra felt a chill overtake her. "What is that doing here?"

"I picked it up on our way out of the grotto. Old habit, I suppose, keeping it safe for you. Good thing, seeing how we got kicked out right after. I know how much the bottle means to you. It's like your home away from home, right?"

Sidra stared, confounded by her bottle's physical presence in this strange room. "You stupid, interfering girl! Do you know what you've done? You must send it back to your mother's realm this instant. Back through that portal your frivolous kind slips in and out of. Now!"

"Send it back? If I knew how to send the bottle back, do you think I'd still be standing here?"

The fire surged back into Sidra. "The bottle cannot be here."

Fool of a girl! Sidra swept the container up in her fist and had to restrain herself from pulverizing the crystal into dust. Not that it would have eliminated her problem.

And then Yvette understood. Her mouth formed a small O that she covered with one hand as her eyes went to the bottle. "You mean you had it with you all that time?"

"Had what?" Camille was naturally confused, but she wouldn't find enlightenment from this jinni.

Sidra tucked the bottle in the folds of her caftan, threatened Yvette with death by a thousand fiery ants gnawing at the inside of whatever brains she had left if she said another word, then shimmered into the ether. There had to be one safe place in these infidel lands that wasn't overrun by fools.

CHAPTER
TWENTY-THREE

"She's right. These markings will help a little, but they won't stop a full-force attack from a jinni as powerful as Jamra." Yanis had removed his wooden leg so that he could sit on the floor and move without the hindrance of a limb that wouldn't bend. Leaning forward, he added the symbol for Venus in the lower right corner of his seven-sided star. Elena handed him the parcel of salt she'd brought so he could sprinkle a handful around the perimeter.

"Isn't there some way *she* can stop him?"

"She's still young, in terms of the life of a jinni," he added when he saw the doubt in Elena's eye. "Sidra is centuries old, don't get me wrong, but her will hasn't been tested. Not like those who've been around for thousands of years, who've seen the world turn over again and again."

"Is that why he was able to bind her inside the city?"

"When was this?"

Elena explained the wish magic she'd been caught up in months earlier while in the city—the tugging at her instinct and the feeling that she'd been swept inside a whirlwind of energy, driving her toward a predestined outcome. "Even Sidra couldn't resist the pull of her own magic. She'd had no intention of returning to the city, but a stolen wish landed her there anyway. Jamra had set a trap for her should she ever return. Bound her so she was physically and magically unable to leave the city limits."

"How did she escape? She couldn't have broken his binding spell on her own."

"That's what Jamra said. But she didn't exactly free herself of the spell. She's clever, our Sidra. She slipped free by using the protection of Oberon to transport her to the *Fée* lands. Apparently, changing dimensions is a little stronger magic than a binding spell that confines one to the cross sections of mortal streets."

Yanis shook his head in disbelief as he shaded in another symbol. "Oberon? As a child I'd been taught the *Fée* were a myth, characters from stories leftover from antiquity."

After Elena revealed how she, too, had been raised in ignorance of the existence of jinn, she shared her thoughts on Sidra's escape. "I can imagine her fiery temper didn't go over well with the locals in the *Fée* lands, which may be why Oberon decided to redeposit her here, where she has some history." She sorted through their remaining items to see which would be of the most help in protecting them from a jinni hellbent on destroying mankind. "Do you use knots to seal a binding?" she asked and held up the blades of sweetgrass and some string.

"Yes, but also a small ritual using a talisman." Yanis rubbed his knee as if it pained him. "There is an incantation."

"Well, that's it. Why can't we use the ritual? Bind Jamra within the village or, better yet, something smaller. A vessel of some kind. Isn't that how it's done? With an oil lamp or a bottle with a tight-fitting lid?"

Yanis shook his head. "To bind a jinni, you must know their name. Their *real* name," he said, holding his finger up to clarify his point. "The name that rises from the fire when they're born into the world." He paused then, as if distracted.

"What is it?"

"It's just the jinn make every effort to protect their true name. Simply because it can be used against them in spells. Jamra would've had to have known Sidra's true name to bind her to the city."

"Hariq," she said. "She might have confided such a thing to her husband."

"Perhaps. But then somehow Jamra got it out of him. Or, if he has an accomplished sorcerer working with him, he could have figured her name out using a code that pairs letters with numbers, such as those found on certain talismans. Sometimes the name is disguised that way. For, while their true name is something they wish to keep secret, it is also a means of invoking their power. But that's the only way he could have bound her to the city limits. Or any boundary line."

"So, we can't trap Jamra without his true name."

"No. Not unless Sidra knows what it is. Which I doubt, or she would have retaliated already."

The revelation made sense, even if the news deflated Elena's brief bout of excitement. She watched as Yanis returned to his drawing. He was absolutely meticulous when it came to his markings. Though he used a humble piece of chalk to draw his symbols, there wasn't anything sloppy or ambiguous about the lines he made. Everything was deliberate. Neat. Intentional. Which didn't comport with Sidra's derisive version of the man, calling him a charlatan and jackal.

"Nothing went wrong, did it? With the potion, I mean. I know I asked earlier, but that was before I saw how dedicated you are to your craft," Elena said.

"And before you knew about my past?"

"Well, yes." She glanced over his shoulder at the nearly complete drawing on the floor. A work of art. "You've obviously had more training than the mere street vendor you tried to pass yourself off as." She knelt beside him, feeling the energy begin to coil over the symbols, coalescing in the ether, waiting for the incantation. "But there was something else at play in Hariq's death, wasn't there."

Yanis set his chalk aside and brushed his fingertips off on his trouser leg. "Please don't say anything to Sidra, but I have often wondered if Hariq did it himself. If he added something to his dose."

"You mean . . . he took his own life?"

"I have no proof, but we had a pact, the four of us. The spell wouldn't work unless we all said our part. I wrote it myself, without error. No one could have interfered."

"But why would he do that?"

"He wouldn't. That's what doesn't make any sense. They seemed happy here." He nudged his chin toward the last place Sidra shimmered into the ether. "She used to be pleasant to me. But one never truly knows the mind of another. Or the inner workings of a marriage not your own."

"I met her not too long after Hariq died," Elena said. "In jail. Just before she was to be executed."

"You helped her escape."

"Actually, she helped *me* escape. We've been helping each other ever since."

She'd often thought about how their lives had intertwined with Yvette's, the three like vine tendrils that stretch out and anchor themselves one to the other. An odd tangle, but one that had borne fruit in friendship.

"It's finished," Yanis said.

He backtracked from the drawing, said a sort of prayer or incantation in his native language, and then blew over the chalk marks, sealing them with his breath. Yanis never claimed the magic would hold off Jamra, but with luck it would be an eye in the storm.

Elena might not have believed in the power of chalk and breath and whispered foreign words when they first met, but she had every confidence their intention was well received under the gaze of the All Knowing. And the eye of the All Seeing.

CHAPTER
TWENTY-FOUR

"Are they sleeping yet?"

The dog lifted his head to see where the voice had come from. There, at the end of the roof, legs dangling over the lip of a chimney top, sat the unnerving creature. She stared with eyes that glittered like starlight.

"The witch and sorcerer are still awake. They're trying to create a protection spell that will hold off Jamra."

"Can they do it?"

"They've underestimated him. The sorcerer's chalk magic will break like the brittle bones of birds. But there's still the chance their other talents will shine."

"And Sidra?"

"Scared. Hurt. Gone for now, but she'll be back once she processes how the bend in fate will favor the best outcome."

The creature looked up at the stars as she dangled her legs. "Whatever course the magic must take, whatever pain it causes the heart, that's how these things work."

The dog knew her words were true, but the knowledge didn't make witnessing the unfolding events any less painful to watch. That would have to be dealt with later. He changed the subject to hide his despair from the creature's glittering eyes. "Yvette has done well. You were right about her instincts."

That seemed to please the creature, though he couldn't care less about her happiness. She'd made him uncomfortable for days with her unblinking gaze, as if reading his intentions, his worries. He'd hardly slept for fear of her intrusions. She turned away from him with a crooked smile, as if reading his thoughts even now, and called her diminutive minions to heel at her side. Their black beetle shells reflected the light from the stars, drawing attention to the halters on their backs. In this form she was hideous. A nightmare to scare a man from ever wanting to close his eyes. He was glad to see her fly away in her hulled-out shell of a chariot, snapping her cricket bone whip. He wouldn't have slept anyway, but knowing her devilry was alight in the night air made him shudder as he curled up atop the roof to wait for the dawn with his tail over his nose.

CHAPTER
TWENTY-FIVE

The apartment wasn't safe. Not even a random crevice in the village wall was safe. Sidra skirted the cobblestone lane, keeping to the shadows where the glint of moonlight didn't reach. She ought to get up higher onto the rooftops, where she could anticipate the threat better, but then she, too, would be visible. A lone starling under the eye of the soaring hawk.

There had to be some haven, a temporary place where she could hide the dagger and keep chaos out of the hands of those who would use it to cut the throat of the world. "Think!" she scolded herself, but the only solution that came to mind was the one she couldn't be sure of. And yet it was her only option. She must go to the old one and confide in him and his wisdom, and quickly, before the morning announced itself on the horizon.

Sidra dissipated, ready to fly as quickly as she could to the cave. Her spirit form soared over the rooftops, a mere wisp in the night air, desperate to find help. She dipped and dived between chimneys and steeples, swooped above treetops of cypress and palm, with the speed of the desert zephyr. As she approached the tumbledown buildings form-ing the outskirts, she veered west, preparing to accelerate over the open land, when she slammed into a wall of resistance at the edge of the village. The collision forced her back, her energy curling in on itself like smoke blown into a bottle. She regrouped and pushed forward again, only to be hit by a barrier that refused to let her pass. Materializing, she reached a hand out to test the invisible blockade when a shadow rose up behind her, forcing her heart into her throat.

"You have grown careless, *jinniyah*." Jamra emerged out of the shadow, his eyes shining with the ungodly lust of a grave robber. "There was a time I could not sneak up on you."

"You've bound me to the village."

"I would not want you flying off before I get what I want. Is that not what you were about to do?"

"It isn't morning yet."

Jamra let his eyes gaze up to the stars, then pointed. "And yet there is Atarsamain, rising to spy on our conversation."

Sidra didn't dare move a finger to verify the security of the bottle within her robes. If he detected even the slightest movement at her side, he would know. And she could not—would not—lower her eyes before this jackal. "The morning star is the mother of *my* tribe," she said and forced herself to grin, letting the gold scrollwork on her teeth glint in the moonlight. She hoped it unnerved him to know she might have the blessing of the morning star during their meeting. His tribe was of the land of the sunset, and this was *not* his hour to crow. "Do you wish to continue this fool's errand beneath her eye?"

Jamra paced to his left. *Good. Let him walk on uncertain ground.* She held her feet solid on her own patch of earth as he took a turn around her. "They are not worthy, the ones you wish to protect. They are weak. Powerless. Clay-footed mortals. They do not burn bright like us. They do nothing but populate the world with more dull-hearted mortal offspring. Their only grace is that their lives are short and without importance. Playthings to dangle a wisp of hope in front of, only to see how far you can lead them astray before they run themselves off a cliff."

Jamra laughed, and the hot fire of his disdain scorched the edge of the roof tiles over their heads. "The world is better cleansed of them." He stopped in front of her, his hot breath steaming in the cool morning air. "The sigil and dagger are the reason powerful families like ours were brought into the world, sister. We were created with a greater purpose in mind. Do you doubt this?"

What Sidra doubted was his sanity. She would not have said there could be too much fire in a person before meeting Jamra, but his heat was all charred earth and blackened cinders and always would be. Yet he was also simmering with fear. It flushed through his veins like gasoline that burned, foul and choking, with the reek of ruin.

"What I doubt is that I will ever see the dagger in your unfit hand."

"Imagine," he said, "the shining cities we will build for ourselves, once the mortals and all their mundane possessions are hurled into the crevice of chaos they've earned for themselves. Oh, but I forget. The stars say you will not survive to see our visionary future."

"Perhaps you read the stars backwards. It is a common ailment of those who do not have sound vision."

"You are trapped and bound. You will deliver the dagger or I swear I will burn this village until it resembles nothing but a charred scar on a southern-facing hillside."

Her lip twitched of its own volition. "Not in this lifetime."

"Then I will send you and everyone in this village into the next one by day's end." Jamra took a step nearer and exhaled his reeking breath in her face one last time. "I know the dagger is here, *jinniyah*. The vision was foretold to me in a dream. Discovering where your devious mind has hidden it is the only reason you are still alive."

Jamra knelt and scooped up a handful of grit from the gutter, sand and sediment that had run off from the roofs and walls. He stirred his finger in the grit, a slow swirling motion, as he whispered a summoning spell.

Sidra knew the magic he called and backed away. "You cannot do this. Not here." Her eyes searched the sky, and he laughed.

"They are coming," he said and blew the dirt from his palm, invoking the fury of the fiery riders who drag the great haboob over the desert on their heels.

She'd not believed it possible, not in this land, not this far from the desert, but she felt the wind shift, smelled the sea air rise before the push, and knew he'd grown even more powerful than imagined.

"I warned you not to cross me."

Jamra shimmered into morning fog and was gone, while Sidra fought the urge to run like a frightened child through the streets, warning the ignorant sleepers in their beds of their impending deaths.

CHAPTER
TWENTY-SIX

A breeze rattled the windows of the shop, causing Elena to jump. Every little noise seemed to make her flinch once the clock ticked down to the final hour before dawn. She and Yanis had stayed up all night doing the prep work for their protection spell, and now he was meditating, calling his energy to him so they might speak the incantation at the opportune moment. He was a quiet man. Dedicated to his craft. And yet fear had taken the edge off his skill. Not his knowledge or his acuity with magic, but in the stature of his confidence. She'd very nearly succumbed to the same debilitating anxiety after her confrontation with a demon the year before, and so she understood his desire to center his energy now that the moment was nearly upon them.

She supposed she was busy doing the same thing, though to anyone else it might look like nibbling on pomegranate seeds and running her fingers over the pages of her grimoire. The book had served her all her life, or at least as long as she could remember. Grand-Mère had started it for her before she could write, adding notes and instructions that she would later amend or enhance when she had experience of her own. But as she looked at the subject matter, after having spent the evening scribbling magical symbols in orders she'd never imagined, she noticed gaps where its contents were limited. A mere portion of the world's magic was represented in the book. Yes, it was the magic she understood and wielded with confidence, but those weren't the only spells worth knowing in the world.

The grimoire, perhaps detecting the shift in her mood, began to sulk by forgetting to turn the page when she was done reading, so she laid the book beside the incense burner, where chunks of the *bakhoor* still smoked. With luck, the pages would absorb and hold the smell so she could revisit the scent again when she returned home. Of course, thinking of home set off a chain reaction of guilt, longing, and despair over not being there with Jean-Paul. Nor could she be until the next train departure, which was hours away. And only *if* she were still alive in the morning.

Still, there was a way to "be" home, if only passively. Curling up in the corner of the sofa, she centered her thoughts on the angle of Jean-Paul's jaw, the heat of his skin, and the way he looked at her in the vineyard when his heart pumped full of life and love for her and all they were building together. Soon she found the silver thread leading to him in the shadow world, but instead of taking her home at his bedside as expected, she found herself inside a small compartment. The floor shook and the outside world, though eerily dark, spun by as if the room were in the center of a tornado.

There was Jean-Paul, sitting up, asleep under a blanket. Beside a window. Was he on a train? She leaned farther into the shadow world. Yes, there across from him sat an elderly gentleman muttering in his sleep. On the seat beside him, sticking out of a valise, was a train ticket.

They were on the overnight train. The very same one she was waiting to take on the return trip back home.

Jean-Paul was on his way to her.

The gentleman let out a snort and grumbled. Not wanting to impinge on his privacy, Elena's mind whirled back through the liminal space until her eyes snapped open. No, it wasn't the gentleman on the train who'd made the noise. It was Yanis. He was seated directly opposite her, uttering a distinctly audible "huh." He looked away and apologized for interrupting, though something was clearly still on his mind.

"What is it? Has something happened?"

"No, nothing yet. Only, you're able to move in the shadow world," he said, though it came out more as a question, as if making sense of what he'd observed. "In a trance?"

Elena smoothed her hair back into place, feeling disheveled after two days away from home. "Yes," she admitted, then had to cover a yawn with her hand. "I'm able to see people I have a connection with."

Yanis pressed his finger against his lips, considering, the optimism of an idea showing on his face. But before he could speak whatever point he was about to make, the walls rattled, hit with a gust of wind. Sidra swept into the shop in a flurry, pacing the floor the minute her feet materialized on the hardwood. Yanis, still forgoing his wooden leg in the name of comfort, leaned against the shop counter and hopped over to his drawing to make certain it had survived her entrance. He wiped away a few scatterings of debris until Sidra chastised him.

"This is no time for chalk drawings, you fool. He's summoned the ifrit." She stirred a finger against her palm as she spoke at Yanis.

"Haboob?" he said with his eyes on the window. His previous optimism evaporated as terror took over.

"Who is Haboob again?" Elena asked.

"Not who—what." Yanis absentmindedly massaged the knee above his missing leg. "The haboob is a storm. Made of sand."

"A storm called up by the churning feet of the ifrit as they ride over the desert," Sidra added.

A storm? She knew there were degrees of bad weather that could be summoned, but none that justified Yanis's current wide-eyed reaction.

"A haboob could swallow the entire town," he said, as if reading her doubt. "Bury it in sand and suffocate anyone caught unprepared with a choking thick grit that gets in the nose, throat, and lungs."

His terror proved contagious as Elena thought of all the mortals about to wake from their beds. "We have to alert the village," she said, though the enormity of the task was likely beyond the time they had. "There has to be a way to warn the residents of the danger."

Sidra stomped across the floor. "There's nothing worse than a panicked mortal running through the streets thinking it will save their life."

"But if this haboob is as bad as you both say, there'll be innocent people hurt if they stay." Elena shook her head when she came to the other obvious truth. "No, you have to leave," she said to Sidra. "Get out of the village. Never mind whatever future was foretold to you. You need to take that dagger with you and hope Jamra follows. It might still spare the village."

Sidra fumed, and a puff of hot air rose around her. "I cannot."

"What do you mean you can't? Do you wish to put everyone in this village in the path of that maniac?"

Sidra advanced and spit out her words. "And what do you think will happen if Jamra gets his hands on a weapon that can affect the balance of chaos and order in the world?"

Elena stood toe-to-toe with the jinni. "You have to take the dagger and leave. Run. Go to the ends of the earth to get away from him, if you must. Find another magus who can protect the power of that sigil."

"Yes, I know, I know, but I cannot." Sidra relented, hands on her hips, while she thought. Before Elena could argue a second time, she lifted her head to speak, though she kept her eyes cast down. "He has done it again," she said. "Jamra has used a sorcerer to whisper my true name over the flames, and now I am bound within the confines of this village. He means to bury me and everyone here beneath this storm. To force me to give him the dagger. But I cannot. I will not."

"This is a disaster. All those people." Elena's stomach clenched from fear and desperation coiling into a knot. "Is there any chance you know *his* real name? Couldn't we bind him the same way he did you? Perhaps even be rid of him for good?"

"Elena sees in the shadow world," Yanis offered. "I could do the spell if we knew what to call him. She could make sure he didn't escape in the ether."

"My husband was the only one who might have known Jamra's true name. Curse the heavens, he never told me what his brother's name was or I would have shrunk that jackal down to the size of his charred heart and been free of him a century ago."

Sidra removed a small perfume bottle, like the ones lining the shelves in Camille's office, from a fold in her robe. She squeezed the crystal in her hand and held it to her lips, pacing the floor again until she stopped before the incense burner on the coffee table. "What is this?" she asked, seeing Yanis's false leg propped nearby against the sofa.

"The worn-out padding was causing me pain while I worked, so I took it off. I'll move it if you wish."

Sidra glanced from his chalk drawing to the trouser leg that had been cut off to allow for the false leg, then back to the wooden shaft with the leather straps and steel peg for a foot. "No, no, it's fine. Go back to your markings."

The jinni sat, holding the perfume bottle to her forehead. Elena and Yanis let her be and double-checked that the drawing on the floor was still intact. When they looked again at Sidra, she was wafting handfuls of scented smoke up to her face. She took in several breaths, then gripped the perfume bottle with new conviction. "I will go get the girl," she said humbly. "Their experiments are a fool's endeavor, but perhaps there's something we can do to warn the town before disaster falls upon us."

Yanis pointed out the window. "I'd say it's already descending."

Sidra and Elena joined him at the front of the shop. A storm was building against the dawn. It loomed in the distance over the rooftops, an eerie cloud of pink and tan.

"Better start reciting your protection spells, sorcerer." Sidra tapped a finger against the top of the crystal bird stopper in her hand. "I'll return before the first grains pelt the town," she said and disappeared.

Elena tried to calculate the arrival of the storm against the arrival of Jean-Paul's train. She wondered briefly if there was anything she could do to stop the locomotive from pulling into the station, but there was nothing in her power, not with the measly supplies she had with her. As for the approaching storm, she could conjure a crosswind easy enough. A quick appeal to the elementals. And yet her instinct told her it would be useless against the charge of trampling hooves bearing down on them.

"Quickly," Yanis said, standing over his seven-sided star. "We must continue adding to our protection magic."

Elena joined him, isolating her doubt so the energy and intent of the spell would flow in the proper direction. There was no more time to dawdle on speculation. The time was upon them. Jean-Paul was on a collision course with the storm, as were they all. And so she raised her hands in the sacred pose and joined Yanis at his task.

Moments later the air grew still, the first rays of dawn shed their light through the window, and the sky darkened under a cloud of sand and fury.

CHAPTER
TWENTY-SEVEN

Sidra had to reserve her energy. The binding spell had not only trapped her but had also diminished her powers so that each act drained her just a little more. If she wasn't careful, she would be helpless in the teeth of the storm. But the demons, too, would be weary. The magic Jamra had called was powerful, but the ifrit had been forced to travel from the deserts of their homeland over the open water to find her. Still, the storm would come with a ferocious appetite. One that could kill everyone in the village to fill its stomach.

The jinni reanimated at the perfume factory inside the witch's office. No light burned, and no laughter or shrill cry of excitement echoed down the corridor, though the scent of lavender hung thick in the air. Down the hall, a man in a white lab coat near the brass distillery equipment sat hunched over on a stool, his head leaning against his worktable. Sidra sidled up to the mortal and reached a finger out to touch the skin on his neck. Her skin shivered at the contact, but he was still warm and breathing. He exhaled a chorus of snores, and she retracted her hand.

Curious, Sidra dropped down to the main floor and found a similar scene in the lobby. Lavender and absolute quiet, only this time it was the night janitor who'd slumped against the wall, asleep beside his mop and bucket. She stepped over his outstretched legs to peer through the glass doors where a lamplighter, too, snored with his cheek on the pavement. It was as if she'd stepped into a bewitched fairyland where all the mortals had been put under a spell. And yet where was the girl?

For a moment Sidra contemplated if this was Jamra's doing, but the enchantment didn't carry the stench of cruelty. No, this was magic done by the girl and the perfume witch. It had to be. Which meant the building was still safe. She had a moment. She wandered nearer to the gift shop, where dozens of bottles of Fleur de Sable lined the shelves like birds on a wire. Hariq's gift. His passion. She passed through the door to be nearer to the bottles. Lying at his side before they each put a drop of mocking death in their eyes was the last time *she'd* felt safe. Staring at the bottles, she knew she would never again have those first moments after the sun rose in the morning when the heat and scent of his body reminded her she was alive and happy for one more day.

That life was gone. Memories and mist. She tucked her bottle in among the others on the shelf and said goodbye.

The girl. She shook her head, remembering her aim. She flew to the rooftop to scan the village for the fair one. Dawn had broken over the horizon. The wall of storm collided with the first rays of sunlight, turning the sky shell pink. It was still too early for most villagers to be up and about, but those she spotted—the baker, the newspaper hawkers, the train station attendants—had also collapsed in place. And then, at the bottom of the hill in the passenger seat of a bright yellow automobile, she spotted the girl's eerie glow. Using another ounce of energy she couldn't spare, she made the leap into the back seat of the car.

The girl spun around. "Sidra, you found us!"

"Goodness, you gave me a start," Camille said, adjusting her rearview mirror as she pulled over to the curb.

On the back seat beside Sidra were two canisters that reeked of lavender. "Prophets protect us, what are you doing with these?"

Yvette nodded toward the witch. "It was Camille's idea. We were ready to deploy the scent we'd been working on—"

"But we hadn't considered what the overpowering scent-magic might do to the mortals in the village," Camille finished. "Some of them are dear friends, mind you."

"So we snuck a little squirt in front of Thomas."

"He's my assistant."

"And he fell straight over asleep. Camille thinks it's all the lavender we added."

"Still not certain about that. Could as easily be the glamour in your blood that's affected their brains."

"But probably a combination of the two would be the most probable explanation," Yvette said, sounding very self-assured.

Camille concurred. "That, and my intention during the spell might have been a little too focused on my own lack of sleep."

Sidra held up her hands to stop them talking, exhausted already from trying to follow their conversation. "But why are you in this monstrosity of a vehicle with two jugs of the fragrance? Do you see that storm on the horizon? Jamra and his ifrit are going to rain sand down on this village, batter us with destructive winds, and suffocate any who stand in their way."

"Well, that's just it." Yvette sprayed a whiff of the perfume into the air with an atomizer the size of a grapefruit. "We figured maybe we could knock out two birds with one stone. Use our divine creation to offend the ifrit noses and also maybe protect the mortals by dousing them with the stuff. Put them to sleep so they don't get caught in any crossfire."

"I thought your laws forbid acts like this against mortals?"

"Oh là là. It's for the greater good! You said yourself these creeps mean business. Well, so do we."

"You can affect everyone in the village with this?"

Camille dropped her smile. "I sent doves to the witches at the other *parfumeries*, and they're helping as well. I've got them covering the upper village and the train station below with canisters of their own." The witch watched the cloud of scent drift from the car to the apartment building on the right. She whispered an incantation that carried the notes of a song in the spoken words. "Sleep, mortal, do not stir, inhale our scented elixir. Breathe in heavy, breathe in deep, sweet dreams await you as you sleep." The witch swung around in her seat to see Sidra's face once the spell was sealed. "One street at a time."

Sidra believed the women were delusional in their thinking, but perhaps their plan was better than a mass exodus of mortals running out of the city in alarm to huddle in the flower fields surrounding the village. The storm may still kill many, but an unconscious death may prove a kindness. She'd never in her life envied a mortal, but the feeling flickered in her now like a candle flame, knowing the scent had no effect on her except to stir memories of flying over purple fields in a time she thought she'd always be so happy. What she would not give now to sleep and never wake again.

CHAPTER
TWENTY-EIGHT

"Did you know he would do this?"

The dog avoided looking at the creature as the haboob took shape several miles away. "There is more of his soul eaten away than I thought," he said.

Soon this would be over and he could be free of this forced alliance and the creature's hollow murmurs of concern. Yet for now, the ifrit were worth worrying about. Their horses' feet would only gain momentum as they closed the distance to the village.

"Should we do something to stop the horde?"

Was that the vibrato of fear in the creature's voice? He shook out his fur and wrapped his tail over his feet as he sat on the edge of the roof. So, even those who can control the chess pieces when it pleases them aren't sure of where they'll land on the board? How then does one respect the ultimatum fate demands? But then there were matters of blood at stake that could sway even the noblest judgment.

"It is too late," he said. "At least for the limits of my talents. Besides, this will bring us what we've been waiting for quicker than anything else."

The creature steeled herself, as if proving she, too, could ride out the worst, if that's what her nerves must do to see things through to the end. *She* might have been able to halt the approaching storm, if he had faltered and nodded his assent, but then what of the outcome they had all agreed was necessary?

"You have to be wondering if the end will be worth the cost," she said.

But she was wrong. He was long past the frivolous notion of balancing one outcome against another. All he wanted was to be finished with the charade. Then he would stand in the headwind of the consequences and hope he remained on two feet as a man again.

The creature seemed to intuit his guarded emotions, as if drawing them out into the open with her breath. "Anger is just another energy on the spectrum of emotions," she said. "Forgiveness another. You'll know soon enough which end you've been stuck on."

She laughed and cracked her whip in the air until it splintered like thunder in his ear.

"And you?" he asked. "Will you be satisfied?"

"All debts will be paid." She exhaled, and some of the tarnish around her wore off so that he could almost look her in the eye. "It is a peculiar sort of magic, though, this wishing. The way it manifests, swirling through the cosmos like the tail of a comet. Such a fierce desire to be realized. Lives colliding, separating, and reforming again as each stage progresses." She extended her bony finger, stirring the invisible air so that a trail of stardust formed a tiny whirlpool of sparkling light at her fingertip. "Pooling in odd little eddies of commonality, tugging at filaments of swirling light that are somehow interconnected." She flicked the whirlpool into dust with her finger, letting it whoosh away on the breeze. "No care for the damage left in its wake while the recipient is granted their heart's desire."

"That's how wishes work." And even as he said it, the painful truth rattled through him, knowing he, too, may end up as collateral damage scattered on the wind. "That's why they're precious and not to be wasted."

The creature seemed satisfied that she'd made him flinch, at least emotionally. "I will intervene if blood is to be spilled. I never agreed to that."

And yet death doesn't require blood. One should not be so careless with their words. "I understand," he said.

The storm drew closer, building in height and width. He was certain the cloud was big enough to swallow the whole of the little village. And still the inhabitants slept as though . . .

It was only then he realized what an odd thing it was to see no one about on the streets. No baker to open his shop, no lamplighter out snuffing the flames, no street sweeper clearing the gutters of debris. No alarm raised. Certainly, the storm occluded the low angle of the sun, but it was still light enough out to signal the dawn. He raised up on his haunches.

"What is it?"

"Do you smell that? Lavender tainted with witch's words."

The creature stood, her nose in the air. "And fairy blood."

He swung his head around to see if she was serious.

"There," she said, pointing. A yellow car rumbled into the lane below. "They're casting a sleeping spell."

The pair peered over the roof's edge and sniffed. "Yes, that's the stuff," said the creature as a string of saliva dripped from the corner of her tiny mouth. "What dreams shall be born this morn?" she wondered aloud as her eyes lit with greedy mischief.

He cringed, watching this midwife of dreams out of the side of his eye. None he knew ever spoke of her except for when the dream turned caliginous and sour, forcing one to wake in the middle of the night with the sheets twisted around their legs as they lay in a fretting, soaking sweat. The midwife of nightmares was more apt.

"I could change back, if you prefer," she said. "But we agreed it would be more effective if we each took our alternate forms. Less risk of being spotted and derailing the task at hand."

Curse this witch. The way she eased in and out of one's thoughts was unnerving. He actually felt a pang of sympathy for the mortals whose minds he'd entered for a bit of fun.

"The wish is almost completed, and then you can do as you like," he said and trotted off to the corner of the roof to watch the yellow car wind around the building. He understood what Yvette and Camille were attempting. A noble effort, at the very least. They might not save any lives, but at least the mortals wouldn't suffer. He wished he could say the same for the rest of them as the first harsh winds of the coming storm ruffled through his fur.

CHAPTER
TWENTY-NINE

A battering wind hit the building, shaking the walls and whistling under the eaves. The haboob was nearly upon them. Elena opened the shop door to gauge how much time they had before the worst of it arrived. Thirty minutes? Five? A train whistle sounded in the distance, screaming through the air like a wild animal trying to outrun a predator. Panic pumped adrenaline through her limbs, knowing Jean-Paul was aboard the train and on a collision course with the storm. What was he thinking leaving the vineyard after he'd only just woken from his fever? But she knew why he'd done it—to find her and make sure she was safe from Jamra. She would have done no less for him.

And would do so now.

Sand pelted the terra-cotta roof tiles and the windows. But the protection spell seemed to be holding. Not a single grain of sand entered the shop while she studied the sky through the open doorway. It was something, however tenuous, in the face of the stacked cloud of sand bearing down on them.

Elena shut the door and took one last look at the pages of her grimoire, hoping to find some spell strong enough to protect a moving train without injuring everyone on board. There were illusions and halting spells, but they were meant for stopping people, not twenty-five-ton locomotives barreling toward a village at forty miles per hour. So, if she couldn't stop it, her only option was to meet the train at the station and somehow get everyone back up the hill to the safety of the shop before raining sand inundated the streets. Which meant leaving the protection of Yanis's spell.

Outside, the storm sent a whirlwind of newspapers and dirt twisting toward the market square. She could no longer see the daylight stars through the window, but she knew the time was due for the train to pull into the station.

Elena twisted the wedding band on her finger, wanting more than ever to feel the warmth of Jean-Paul's body safely beside her. "I have to get to the depot," she said, unable to put it off any longer.

"You can't truly mean to go out there." Yanis watched her gather her things. "The ifrit could already be sniffing around the town."

"My husband is on the morning train. He has no idea what he's riding into. He and the other passengers are going to need help. I have to go before it's too late." Elena slung the strap of her satchel over her head and shoulder. There wasn't anything of much use remaining in the bag, but her spell book and athame were like extensions of her arms.

"What about Sidra? And the fair one? They haven't returned yet."

Sidra had popped in an hour earlier to explain how Camille and Yvette were using perfume to put the town's mortals to sleep. They could take care of themselves. "Yvette is safe enough with Sidra. But there's no one to warn those arriving on the train."

"You'd better let me come with you, then," he said, reaching for his wooden leg. "Maybe together we can stay alive long enough for us to die with your husband."

"Have you always been such an optimist?"

"Realist," he corrected and finished strapping the leg to his thigh. Yanis slung his own bag full of loose items over his shoulder and wrapped his head and mouth with the scarf around his neck. Before he would allow Elena to leave, he yanked one of the drapes Sidra had manifested down from the ceiling. He ripped the cloth in two and offered Elena a manageable length. "Wrap it around your head and mouth like a mask. It will protect you from breathing in too much grit."

Elena accepted the red silk and tied it over her head the same way he'd done, making sure to cover her face so only her eyes showed over the top. She tied it off in the back, then nodded she was ready, and together they left, taking advantage of the last moments of relative calm before the storm.

It was slow going down the hill. Elena's legs constantly tangled in her skirt as it twisted in the wind, and her clumsy sabots felt untrustworthy on the pavement. Yanis, though, seemed to have no difficulty with his balance, limping on his false leg. She wondered if he self-spelled, given the pain he said it caused him, but it was only a passing thought as her foot finally lost traction on the grit-covered cobblestone streets. With her hair blowing wildly around her face, she slid forward on the hill and nearly tumbled; then her hand fell on a broad, hairy back. The same dog who had saved her before had bounded out of nowhere and caught her, bracing himself against the stones. Elena righted herself and was about to thank him when he tugged at her skirt. Yanis moved to intervene, but the dog bared his teeth before pulling her to the side.

"What's he doing?"

Over the howling wind, Elena shouted, "I think he wants us to go there," and pointed toward a narrow stairway leading to a two-story building.

Yanis cursed and leaned into the wind, following the dog. At the bottom of the steps, they found a large man wearing a leather apron curled up asleep beside a stone wall in the yard. The dog ran to the man, tugging at his pant leg and trying desperately to haul him toward the building. He dragged the man a mere few inches before stopping to pant. He let out a yelp as the wind whipped over their heads.

"He wants us to get the man sheltered," Elena shouted. "Before the storm buries him."

Yanis did a double take at the dog; then he and Elena grabbed the man by his legs and dragged him into the apartment on the first floor, where a woman slept upright in a chair beside her breakfast table. They leaned the man against the wall, then stopped to catch their breath. Yanis stared at the canine again. "Is this the same dog that you encountered earlier?"

"Yes," she said. "He can be very helpful when he wants to be."

The dog cocked his head to the right before trotting out to the lane. Elena and Yanis followed, shutting the apartment door against the storm. Back outside, the dog stood in the wind with his ears and tail up. He barked once with a good deal of insistence, then scampered off in the direction of the funicular.

"Will it even be operating in this wind?" Yanis asked.

Elena nudged her chin, and the pair put their heads down against the brunt of the storm as they hurried behind the animal. Sand and wind assaulted them from all directions until Elena was forced to keep her hand on the makeshift scarf covering her mouth to keep it in place. There was no one to run the funicular down to the depot, but the dog jumped inside, waited for them to follow, then barked once. The cable jerked, and the car ground into motion.

As the car traveled down the track on the village hillside, passing the second railcar as the opposite cable forced it back up to the top, they got their first clear glimpse at the size and ferocity of the approaching haboob. Elena squinted to see through the flying dirt. A massive cloud wall of swirling dust towered over the village, casting a sickly brown shadow as it smudged out the sun. Sand stung their skin with growing velocity, so they turned their heads, thankful for the masks over their faces. The railcar shuddered in the heavy wind, and its wheels jerked against the track. The dog barked and wagged his tail, and the car rolled forward, though Elena couldn't be certain it was still on the track as it seemed to float over the ground.

At last the funicular reached the platform at the bottom. The dog leaped from the car and ran for the lee side of the depot building. Down the track, a whistle sounded, loud and shrieking, as the train approached the station. The locomotive emerged through the brown cloud of debris as steam billowed sideways out of its smokestack. The wheels slowed, the brakes squealed, and the chugging of the engine gasped to a stop as the passenger cars aligned with the platform. Faces pressed against the windows, staring incredulously at the building storm and the odd trio awaiting them in front of the station, their backs turned to the wind. Elena searched for Jean-Paul through the glass, but he wasn't among the gawkers. He had to be there. Her vision couldn't have been wrong.

A strong gust battered the side of the passenger cars, rocking the train on the rails. Screams of surprise from the women inside carried over the shrill wind. The conductor leaned out the door and peered at the station, but he wouldn't find anyone inside to confer with about the storm since Camille and Yvette had done a proper job of putting them to sleep as well. The conductor cupped his hands around his mouth, about to shout for the crew, when Jean-Paul pushed him aside and jumped from the train. Elena called out for him, the wind and face covering muffling her voice. She tore the wrap from her face and shouted again. He saw her then and ran, embracing her even as the strengthening storm blew sand hard enough to scrape their skin and scratch their eyes.

"My God, are you all right?" he asked once he released her.

She nodded. "I knew you were coming. I saw you'd woken from your fever."

He hugged her again. "That damned jinni. I swear I'll kill him if I see him again."

"It's him. This storm. Jamra called it up to punish Sidra," she yelled. "Yanis says it's only going to get worse." Elena quickly introduced Jean-Paul to the village sorcerer.

"We must get everyone off the train and sheltered in the station," Yanis said to Jean-Paul after a quick handshake. He turned to Elena as another gale rocked the train, nearly tipping it off its wheels. "There's no time to get anyone back to the shop. The storm is almost at full force."

And just as he said it, the windows of the passenger cars exploded, sending shards of glass flying into the side of the depot. Panicked screams followed as people aboard ran for the exits. They pushed past each other, squeezing two and three at a time out the doors and onto the platform. Men and women tripped, falling to their knees as a strong gust whipped them from behind. But it wasn't merely the wind that assaulted them.

A pair of fiery demons, shaped like men but with a corona of flames for hair and eyes that glowed orange and red, descended from a whirlwind above. They landed on the roof of the railcar with hands ablaze. The ifrit.

They wasted no time racing atop the cars, setting the roofs on fire. In the heavy winds, the flames spread in seconds, engulfing the passenger cars before everyone had escaped.

"We have to get everyone out!" Elena shouted as women in long skirts crawled through the narrow windows, tumbling onto the wooden platform.

Yanis hobbled to the end of the train. Jean-Paul, still weak from his fever, barely kept up. Together they pulled the people free of the windows and doors, then urged them to go to the depot for safety. A dozen people still struggled to escape the front end as the cars swayed violently with each new blast of wind. Elena screamed for them not to panic, to no avail.

"What are those things?" a man shouted, cupping his hands around his eyes as he squinted at the roof of the train cars. Before Elena could answer, the dog leaped from the ground like cannon fire. He snarled and snapped his teeth at the first of the ifrit as it was about to stomp its foot through the car's roof. Elena worried the demon would plunge a plume of fire on the heads of those still inside. Instead it threw the stream of fire at the dog. The animal's fur burned bright orange, but then the flame receded as if it had been absorbed into his body. He lunged, tearing at the ifrit's leg until the demon fell backward off the roof and plummeted into the crevice between the wheels of the locomotive and the platform. The dog jumped onto the coal tender and shook out his fur. As if on command, the engine spewed a column of hissing steam from its boiler, extinguishing the fire demon so that it shriveled into a pile of wet ash, leaving a sooty smudge on the side of the platform.

The second ifrit leaped over the dog, landing in the cab of the locomotive. Elena watched in horror as the creature inhaled the seething fire glowing in the coal burner. Water! She had to find water. Or as close to it as she could muster. She reached into her satchel as the wind whipped her hair around her face. There had to be *something* of use. Sand, still hot from the desert sun, grazed her cheek with its stinging bite as her hand hit the sack of salt. Salt and sand. Of course!

Elena grabbed a handful of salt with one hand, then held out the other until she felt the grit cover her palm. Turning her back to the wind, she eyed a standpipe coming out of the ground. She rubbed the sand and salt together, focusing her intent while reciting her spell, as the dog and demon lurched at each other inside the cab. "Desert sand within my hand, fill your thirst at my command. Draw forth the water 'neath the ground, until the fire is neatly drowned."

The pipe used for filling the steam engine boilers with water creaked and moaned under the pressure of the spell. Elena called the water forth as she held her hand out to direct the flow of energy, prying open the spigot and bending the nozzle toward the train. The dog's ears went up, and he bounded out of the way just as a gush of water shot from the pipe with enormous pressure to spray the burning cars. The flames on the roof sizzled and sputtered, while the ifrit emerged from the cab of the engine looking like a wet sock. The beast spread his wings and flew off until slowly disintegrating into lavalike pieces that scattered over the rocky hillside.

The people were drenched, but at least the immediate threat was over. The howling storm, however, continued to rage. Yanis and Jean-Paul helped herd the terrified passengers into the depot and out of the path of the haboob. Some did ask, hesitantly, why the entire depot crew was asleep on the floor. In their shock, none seemed to notice when they never received an explanation.

Elena found Jean-Paul in the crowd, shivering and exhausted. She lit a fire in the lobby stove and said a quick spell to warm the room. The worst of the fear was beginning to wear off the passengers as they evaluated their injuries and came to terms with what they'd witnessed. Sand and wind continued to batter the depot, but the walls held firm. Elena chanced a look out the window and couldn't even see the village through the haze. What damage was being done atop the hill? Where was Sidra? Yvette? Camille? Were they sheltered or already battling Jamra and his demons? And where was that dog? Wasn't he one of them? Couldn't he do something? But he hadn't come inside, and he was nowhere to be seen on the platform.

She would have to go out again. She must. But first she was going to have to do something about the two dozen mortals in the depot waiting room muttering to themselves about winged fire creatures. Yanis seemed to come to the same conclusion as he approached her bearing the braid of sweetgrass and incense from his bag.

"We can do it if we work quickly but quietly," he said.

"What does he mean?" Jean-Paul removed his glasses to wipe the dirt off the lenses.

"I'm sorry, my love, but we have to go help the others."

"Others?"

"Sidra and Yvette. Camille and the dog too. They could already be in danger."

"A dog? You can't be serious." He slipped his glasses back on. "It's mayhem out there."

"Which is why we have to go. They can't face this alone."

Jean-Paul pulled her aside. "Elena, we should all get on the train and head in the other direction. Go back home. Whatever those things are, they just tried to kill dozens of people. They have wings made out of fire, for God's sake."

"They want to do more than just kill a few passengers," she said. "This is Jamra's doing. He's the one who called up this storm. He's the one who summoned those demons. If he has his way, he'll unleash havoc on the world and kill every mortal he can. But, yes, let's go home to our quiet vineyard and wait it out and hope for the best, while people we know and care about are left to face him alone."

Jean-Paul's lawyerly side was ready to argue still. Elena held a finger to his lips. No magic, no spell, just waiting for him to see what must be done.

"Right," he said at last, dropping his shoulders as he looked at the beaten and shocked faces of the passengers around him. "You're right. That maniac jinni has to be stopped before he does this to anyone else." He wiped away the tiny particles of sand that clung to her cheek. "Can you do it? Can your magic stop him?"

She didn't want to lie or give him false hope, but if she didn't believe it possible, she would never be able to summon the courage to go back outside. "If we all work together, but we must hurry."

He kissed her hand, held her tight, then got out of the way.

Elena began by setting the end of the sweetgrass rope in the stove and quietly cleansing her athame with the smoke. Once satisfied it had been purified, she paced the room in a circle, which often meant waiting for a woman in a drenched hat with drooping ostrich feathers to move out of her way so she could continue the ritual unnoticed. When she'd completed the circle, Yanis lit the incense, letting the scent fill the room. As nonchalantly as possible, the two stood in the center of the circle and cast a quick calming spell. Not quite a sleeping spell, but the warmth from the stove and the scent of the smoldering sweetgrass wove together with the incantation to keep those in the room sedated.

Elena hoped Jean-Paul would forgive her, but there'd been no way to exclude him, being a mortal. She raised her hands in the sacred pose and thanked the All Knowing for hearing her intentions. Yanis finished his acknowledgment to the All Seeing, and then they pulled their scarves over their faces. She'd meant to kiss Jean-Paul once more before leaving but couldn't find him in the crowd of slumped bodies. She stepped over outstretched legs and tilted the heads of the few young men in the room, yet he was nowhere to be found. And then she knew.

Elena left the safety of the building, entering the swirling sand and wind, and there was Jean-Paul waiting on the platform, a woman's lace-trimmed *fichu* tied over his nose and mouth.

"We go together or not at all," he shouted over the din.

Yanis and Elena looked at each other, then back at Jean-Paul. Elena handed him a chunk of amethyst. Yanis offered him a bronze talisman from his pocket. And then the three of them trudged up the hill to where the storm spun in a violent vortex above the village. The dog emerged from the train and limped quietly behind, stopping every few feet to look over his shoulder.

CHAPTER THIRTY

A whirling funnel descended onto the roof of the clock tower below. From it spun Jamra, flanked by two fire demons. Sidra had been waiting, watching the storm develop from atop the cathedral's bell tower across the street. This, she knew from observing the birds, was where she would meet her nemesis.

The girl and the perfume witch, exhausted from their night's effort, were tucked away in the shop several streets over. There was little long-term protection inside those walls, but it would do for the moment. They had put the town of mortals to sleep, then hunkered down to wait for the worst of the storm to land. When the wind and sand hit full force, Sidra escaped to the rooftop to meet her enemy. And there he was, staring up at her with the searing blaze of hate smoldering in his eyes.

So be it.

Sidra held her arms out to welcome him. The sleeves of her caftan, now tattered and dirty, fluttered in the wind. Her bangles rattled as she raised her arms higher. *Come,* she thought. *Try and take what you think is yours.*

In a flash, Jamra vanished from the clock tower and reappeared at Sidra's side atop the cathedral. He'd ditched his Western suit and put on his finery: an indigo-blue caftan jacket with gold embroidery and matching leggings that ballooned slightly over the tops of soft leather boots, as if he'd arrived at an improvised coronation of his own making. The demons, meanwhile, smelling of rotten meat and foul waste from the back end of a cow, squatted on the wall behind him, one on each corner. Their tails dangled over the side of the building as their fetid breath steamed in the air. Sidra focused her eyes on Jamra. The wind swirled around them in a dizzying motion, though once he landed it did not touch them. They stood in the eye of the vortex, cut off from the rest of the devastation.

Jamra folded his arms. "In the name of sanity, I hope you have the dagger with you."

"In the name of all that's sacred, it will never belong to you."

They were mere spoken words, a puff of breath in the dirty air, but their meaning burned as they struck Jamra's ear with the heat of rebellion. His face contorted from its usual sneer into a full-frowned expression of loathing.

"Enough of this game playing." His hand lunged out lightning fast and gripped her by the throat. He lifted her off the ground. Sidra clutched at his fingers against her neck, fighting for release. "You will not dissipate. You will not change form. There is nowhere for you to go. You are bound here. There is no crevice I cannot find you in this filthy human village." He set her down again, and she gasped for air. "I am done asking, *jinniyah*. If you do not produce the dagger, now, you will watch your friends die."

Jamra snapped his fingers, and behind him both demons took a dive off the roof. Sidra felt for damage along her neck as she coughed up smoky phlegm. She'd been singed by his touch. He'd grown stronger since their last encounter. And she, her power bound within the village, had grown weaker. She straightened and sent a blow to his stomach with a jolt of energy stolen from the storm. He stumbled backward, dirtying his fancy coat as he hit the roof tiles.

Sidra braced for more violence, but instead of retaliating, Jamra stood and laughed at her pathetic effort. He brushed grit from his fine blue jacket a speck at a time as the fire demons rose up behind him. It had been no bluff. Each carried a struggling woman in their grip— Yvette, shimmering with anger, and Camille, wide-eyed and out of her depth. The ifrits' scaled hands were pressed tightly over the women's mouths, though the beasts kept their noses turned away as if trying to avoid inhaling the women's stench. Jamra was wrong if he thought she believed he'd keep his word. He'd never said he would let them go, even if she were to falter and give him the dagger and its dangerous sigil. And so she could show only indifference.

"They're nothing to me," she said and hoped the shaking of her leg didn't show under her caftan.

Jamra approached Camille. "Was this the one with you in prison?" He sniffed her hair and turned his nose away as if the scent disgusted him. "They all begin to look alike to me after a while. Though this one's reek I would remember."

Camille had been trembling uncontrollably, her eyes brimming with tears, until he said that. The woman was still scared, but something changed. She stopped clutching at the demon's arm, letting her hands slip inside her lab coat pockets instead.

"Where is it?"

Sidra drained the emotion from her eyes. He would find only hooded apathy in them. Nothing more. When she did not answer, Jamra put his hands on her, feeling under her robes, patting her sides, fumbling over her breasts. She stared at the clock tower across the lane as she suffered through the indignity of his unclean hands on her body. As if she were so stupid as to wear the thing on her person once dawn arrived.

Frustrated, Jamra pushed her away. "I warned you," he said.

He reached for Camille's hair and yanked her out of the arms of the fire demon. Behind him, Yvette struggled and let out a muffled scream. Her breath heaved under the scaly arm that covered her mouth.

Sidra twitched her nose as if she smelled something in the air, looked at Camille, then turned away. As subtly as possible, she put the thought in the witch's head that she wasn't powerless.

Held only by her hair, Camille pulled an atomizer filled with the enchanted perfume out of her lab coat. She pointed it directly in Jamra's face and sprayed. The jinni reeled, spinning away from the witch. Incandescent with rage, he coughed and spewed the sensuous, beautiful fragrance out of his lungs and mouth. Camille jerked free of his grip, but not before he flung the back of his hand out, connecting with her jaw. She fell to the ground as the cathedral bells began to chime.

The clanging noise rattled the roof, giving Sidra a moment of distraction. She took hold of Camille and jumped from the tower onto the tile roof below. Camille began to slip on the landing, but the jinni held firm and lowered the witch to the street. Before the ifrit could dive down to reclaim her, Sidra ran up the side of the tower and hurled the fiery demon into the wall of the raging vortex. His body ricocheted through the storm and was spit out on the other side of the ether. The burst of magic cost her dearly. She doubled over to catch her breath, wary for the next blow.

Jamra wiped his eyes with the sleeve of his caftan. Combustible with anger, he ordered the second ifrit to throw Yvette from the roof. The girl screamed and wriggled in the creature's grip before managing to free her mouth. "Let go of me, you *fils de pute*!" The ifrit, struggling to contain Yvette's manic energy, dangled her over the side of the roof. She grabbed the creature by the wing, the arm, and finally the leg before it successfully disentangled itself from her and kicked her body over the edge.

Sidra lunged half a step to intervene before halting herself. There was a pause while the ifrit leaned over the side to see the mess he'd made on the pavement below. But he'd obviously never dealt with a fairy before. As soon as the beast hunched over the lip of the roof, his hair and claws were singed off by an electric zap pulsating from Yvette's fingertips. The girl rose in the air, elevating herself with her *Fée* powers, her glamour fully engaged and glowing with electricity.

The ifrit brushed the burnt hairs from his arms before swiping at Yvette as if she were a nuisance gull. But the girl's skills had improved under her grandmother's training. She easily maneuvered out of the demon's reach without losing her balance. When he came at her a second time, she reached in her endless pockets for her atomizer, then sprayed him in the face with the weaponized perfume as the witch had done. The creature gagged and snorted, wiping his nose and mouth to be rid of the horrible smell assaulting his senses.

Jamra shouted at the ifrit. "Kill her!"

The beast snorted a stream of mucus from his nose and charged. The girl, her ire glowing, delivered a bolt of electricity, shocking the swollen-eyed ifrit off his feet. The creature swung his arms wildly, as if unable to see, then dissipated to escape the electrifying jolt still crackling through his body.

Jamra turned on his bootheel and marched toward Sidra. "The dagger. Now!"

Free of the ifrit, the girl lunged when he did. He threw an arc of fire, cutting her off and forcing her to retreat with her hands over her face.

"Come and take it," Sidra taunted and leaped from the bell tower onto the roof of the building below.

Thank the All Seeing, Jamra gave chase, leaving the girl behind. The tiles rattled as he landed in a crouch behind her. She was playing for time, though what that would gain her she didn't yet know. Around them the storm spun out. The fury of the wind and sand receded even as her heartbeat sped up. All she knew was that she must lead him away from the girl.

Sidra veered left, then right, zigzagging over the ancient rooftops, breaking tiles and brushing the crowns of the highest palms with the soles of her sandals. Layers of sand covered the streets and windowsills, collecting in flowerpots and filling downspouts with their grit. Jamra's hot breath remained at her back. But where to go? The market square came into view as the air cleared of dust. Sidra dissipated and escaped through the ether, leaving the rooftops for the narrow lane where Yanis lived—a village canyon only an arm's width in places, walled in on either side by the buildings whose roofs she'd just run over. She swam through the air invisible, looking for a nook or crevice in the plaster she could hide in before she hit the village boundary and was sent flying back to the town's center. *Curse Jamra and his sorcerer!*

As she fled, the narrow uphill street suddenly descended. It twisted left and then right, going around another corner until she no longer knew which direction she flew. Had she taken the wrong alley? Impossible. She'd been traveling toward the upper village, but now she was heading straight for the fragrance factory in the center. The scent already floated to her on the wind. But what had brought her here? In her panic to escape Jamra's fire, had she missed the influence of some unseen energy around her, turning her, guiding her?

Sidra paused. Was it possible? Had she somehow been swept up in someone else's magic yet again? It had happened before, being delivered to a place she did not wish to go because of the force of someone else's desire. Is that what the tail she'd seen in the birds' omen meant? That her will was once again being buffeted by the whims of others? Turning her around and around until she was too dizzy to know where her own feet would materialize?

Heavy foot stomps on the rooftop behind her told her she hadn't fooled Jamra by going to ground.

"Show yourself, *jinniyah*!" He landed on the cobblestones in front of the spot where she had stalled in the ether to get her bearings. "I know you are here. Understand that the fair one will die a painfully slow death if you do not come out."

A chunk of golden hair sailed down in front of Sidra. Above, an ifrit held Yvette on a chain. The foolhardy girl hadn't got away after all. An iron ring had been fastened around her neck to control her *Fée* powers. Jamra paced in his soft boots, moving nearer the factory with each step. Could he feel the lure of the sigil within the village? Even in her disembodied state, she felt her heart squeeze for all that had gone wrong. But most of all she missed Hariq. Why did she let him talk her into such a mad scheme? The deception had always been doomed to fail.

She stared at the strands of yellow hair. Let him have what he was after, she thought. Let him have the dagger and be done with the charade. All of it. At least he might keep his word and feel indebted enough to let the girl go. Maybe then he'd leave, and the rest of her friends—yes, that's what they were—could return to their homes unharmed. There would be hardship and suffering for others in the world, but maybe Jamra had a point. Maybe some mortals deserved retribution for what the jinn had suffered in the past.

Sidra materialized. There was no more reason to run. If the All Seeing wished to play them all for a fool, so may it pass. "I am here," she said and walked toward the factory, following the trail of mysterious fate that had brought her to its door.

CHAPTER
THIRTY-ONE

The funicular had been blown off its rails and was now wheels up in a patch of weeds, which meant that witch, sorcerer, and mortal had to walk. The steep climb to the village would have proved hard enough without being pelted by jinni magic, but the wind only made the effort that much more difficult. Elena rested a moment beside a door tucked within an archway. Jean-Paul, still fever-weary, gave no complaint at stopping to shelter out of the storm for a moment. Nor did Yanis, dragging his false leg behind him, his breath coming in great gulps of effort. The dog had followed them up the hill, only reluctantly resting when they did.

Out of curiosity, Elena peeked in through the window to the side of the door. Two young men, their hair and skin dusted white with grit, slept sitting up in front of a stove that had yet to be lit. One of them still held a box of matches in his hand. "It's like they're frozen in time," she said.

The dog stood on his hind legs and pressed his nose against the glass beside her to see the mortals for himself.

"You could reveal yourself," she said. "If there's something you're not telling us, now would be a good time."

"Isn't that the same dog I saw running in the vineyard?" Jean-Paul asked, wiping his forehead with the lacy tail of the *fichu*.

"Yes. He's also the one who saved me from my abductor."

The animal dropped from the window and stared at them with a nervous energy that suggested he didn't think they should linger much longer where they were.

Jean-Paul reached out to pet the dog's head. "What did you mean by asking him to show himself?"

"She means he's jinn," Yanis said while the dog keenly avoided eye contact with him.

Jean-Paul retracted his hand, as if he thought the dog might bite. "Oh, of course," he said. "I should have realized. What was I thinking?"

The dog trotted a few feet down the lane before turning back, encouraging them to follow a different street from the one they'd been taking.

"He wants us to go that way," Elena said, gazing ahead.

"Can we trust him?"

Yanis stood. "In this, I think we can," he said. "Quickly, the wind is dying down. We should take advantage of the break in the storm."

The animal barked and trotted up the narrow street, his ears alert, tail high. The pace was still slow going, like a recurring dream of Elena's where she put one foot in front of the other but never seemed to make any forward progress, eventually crawling on her stomach, clawing for an inch of ground until she awoke.

Finally, after what felt like an hour of slogging, they'd nearly reached the market square. Exhausted, they'd meant to sit and catch their breath when a crash like the breaking of clay tiles sounded overhead. Elena glanced up and saw a flash of red and gold leap over the gap between buildings. "It's Sidra!" The dog growled as the others tilted their heads back in time to spot Jamra jumping from one rooftop to another in pursuit. Hot flames erupted from the jinni's feet when he landed on the opposite side.

"Follow them," Yanis said and darted through a narrow passageway that wound between apartment buildings.

It was impossible to keep up. Even though the storm had died down, sand covered the streets and back lanes, making them trudge twice as hard as normal to cover the same ground. They were going to lose the jinn.

"That way." Jean-Paul pointed ahead where Sidra hurdled over another gap.

Restricted by the corridors of an inner-village maze, the group couldn't maneuver fast enough even to follow the rare glimpses they caught of the jinn leaping overhead. Sidra was in trouble, likely running for her life, and yet there was little they could do even if they could catch up.

Elena stopped in her tracks. She tugged the makeshift scarf away from her mouth. "You have to help us," she yelled. She waited for the dog to lift his ears and turn around. "I don't know what you're waiting for. I don't know whose side you're on or what you have to gain by leading us, but if there's something you can do to save Sidra, you must do it now."

The dog checked the roofline, bent his ear to the right, and sniffed the air. He stuck his nose in the other direction and drew in a deep whiff, testing the scents on the wind. Concern rested in the dog's eyes as he lowered his head. He understood her, she knew he did, but for some reason he continued to hesitate. Instead he kept his nose pointed toward a side alley, growing more agitated the longer he sat. Elena rounded the corner to see what he was reacting to, and there, hobbling forward, was Camille.

Elena ran to meet her, followed by the others. "Are you all right? What happened?"

"They ambushed us. At the shop." Camille's hair hung in her face. Tears had left tracks through the dust on her cheeks. "Those *things*, they dragged Yvette and me to the top of the bell tower." Her body shivered, remembering. "There was a jinni. He tried to kill us, but Sidra . . . she saved my life. I sprayed that *thing* in the face with my scent spell, and she helped me to the ground." The perfume witch leaned against the wall and took a deep breath.

"But where's Yvette?"

Camille shook her head. "She was still on the roof. I don't know what happened to her. There was a flash of lightning. I'm sorry. That's all I saw."

"You're alive after tangling with an ifrit," Yanis said. "That's no small feat."

"Yes, but if they've still got Yvette, that brute will kill her if Sidra doesn't give him what he wants."

The dog circled the group, sniffing the air as if seeking a lost scent. He tried four directions before pausing and letting out a small whine.

"What's wrong with him?" Camille asked Elena.

"He must've lost Sidra. We were following her. Jamra was chasing her on the rooftops, but we couldn't keep up."

"But he could," Yanis said, gesturing to their four-footed friend. "If he wanted to, he could keep up."

The dog grumbled low in his throat.

Elena had seen the animal move with the speed of the jinn. It was true—he could have left them behind at any time to catch up to Sidra. So why hadn't he? Why did he need them to follow so badly?

"Jamra has bound Sidra to the village," she informed him. "They can't have gotten too far."

The dog looked up sharply and bared his teeth.

"Do you want to go after them alone?" she asked.

The dog shook out his fur and sat on his haunches.

"In that case, mind if I try finding them my way?" Following a hunch, Elena rested a hand on the animal's fur and closed her eyes, testing the boundaries of her connection with the shadow world, if not the dog's tolerance as well. Though he kept himself veiled, she sensed intelligence, loyalty . . . and love. Yes, deep love. Transcendent love. The kind poets write about. That's what guided him, what drove his urgency. But for some reason he remained hidden behind his furry masquerade.

Still, using that thread of emotion from the animal she was able to trace a connection to Sidra. Elena sank deeper in her trance, deeper in the shadow world, until she was following an invisible trail that veered one way and then another. Racing. Panicking. Darting down a narrow alley only to turn around and go back the other way. Though she couldn't see her, she knew it was Sidra's energy. Her fiery spirit in the ether. But something was interfering with the jinni's free will of movement. Forcing her to move in a direction she didn't want to go. Turning her around so she was no longer in control of her destination.

Elena absorbed the feeling of panic, her heartbeat speeding up as she followed the jinni through the streets, under arches, searching for a crevice to hide away. She feared she might not be able to hold on at the disorienting speeds the spirit flew. But then a familiar scent wafted in the distance. The fragrance of flowers, pressed and drained, stripped of their purest essence. Camille's factory. She was staring straight at it. And there was Jamra pacing the street, searching for Sidra. Elena's breath sped up. She could sense Sidra trying to hold back, to not show herself, to be strong. But she couldn't turn away from the lock of blonde hair on the flagstones.

All hope fell out of the bottom as the jinni stepped from the ether and into the path of certain death.

CHAPTER
THIRTY-TWO

They had barely animated inside the lobby of the perfume factory before Jamra began complaining of the smell. Sidra could have said the same about the sulfur-like odor lifting off the ifrit who led Yvette on a chain. If only there were a scent to revive the girl. She'd wilted from the touch of iron against her skin, wanting to collapse to the floor but held upright by the beast's tight rein.

Jamra covered his nose and mouth with his sleeve to avoid inhaling directly. "I'll never understand what brought my brother to this place. I would have flown a hundred miles around such a stinking village to avoid that smell."

Sidra twitched her lip at him. Was he so self-involved he couldn't understand the underlying benefit to her in his opinion?

"This way," she said and passed through the wall to the shop where the factory's many perfume bottles lined the shelves to sell to the wealthy tourists. The smell to her was intoxicating. Love's elixir, he'd called it. She'd teased Hariq about his work at the factory, calling it frivolous dabbling in inferior spell magic. But the truth was that she'd been as enamored of the possibilities as much as he. The way nature's essences could elicit both emotion and memory by a single inhaled molecule, depending on the combination of a flower's most intimate identity, was a delicious sorcery to contemplate.

Per fumum. Through the smoke. It had been their private love talk while Hariq perfected his scent with the help of the witch until one day he presented Sidra with the bloom of his efforts. Her very own fragrance. Fleur de Sable in the witch's tongue. Sand Flower. *Zahrat al sahra'*. His flower of the desert.

If this was where she was meant to die, she was pleased it was as near to Hariq as events would allow.

The jumble of fragrances seeping from the bottles inside the shop made Sidra's head float. She had to concentrate on not dissipating in front of Jamra again. She would have to give him what he wanted. He'd grown too powerful for her to deny him much longer. There, too, Hariq had played too frivolously with his plan. With their future. With the security of the dagger. With her life too.

"Where is it?" Jamra stood in the center of the shop and folded his arms.

Sidra approached the shelves lined with green glass bottles wrapped in metal filigree. Crystal birds topped them all, each an exquisite piece of art that caught the light and promised all the beauty in the world. The girl squeaked in protest despite the burn of the iron ring on her neck. As if *she* could read minds. "The sigil is there," Sidra said and pointed to a bottle on the third shelf, the fourth one over from the left.

Jamra snatched the bottle in his hand and tore out the stopper, tossing it to the floor, where the birds' wings shattered on the marble. He tipped the bottle over and shook it, expecting a shrunken dagger to fall out. Instead, a pungent stream of perfume dripped and spilled over his fanciful jacket. She hoped it had ruined the silk forever. Sidra may be facing her final moments of life on this earth, but she didn't have to change how she felt about this camel's ass.

"My mistake," she said and took a final ounce of pleasure at seeing Jamra's eyes water from a cloud of perfume once dedicated to her.

CHAPTER THIRTY-THREE

Elena hurried down the narrow lane, her feet slipping in sand as she rounded the corner. The steps leading to the *parfumerie* were straight ahead. It couldn't be too late. The vision had taken place only moments ago.

"This way," Yanis shouted.

The sorcerer moved deceptively fast over the stones, maneuvering his false leg in a step-drag motion. Camille limped behind, ignoring for the moment her injuries, fatigue, and the obvious shape of a body buried beneath a blanket of sand beside a lamppost. The dog trotted alongside Elena and Jean-Paul, restrained for the moment from his usual supernatural speed. He deliberately kept pace with them, waiting for something. Holding back, yet herding them forward as if they were sheep he was shooing into a pen. All the while his eyes watched the rooftops as he kept his ears bent skyward. His lack of panic was the only thing giving Elena hope that they weren't too late.

The group reached the perfume factory, out of breath and ragged from the ravages of the wind against their skin and the adrenaline rushing through their veins. The plaza in front of the *parfumerie* was the last place Elena had seen a vision of Sidra. The scent of toasted orange rind and frankincense still lingered in the swirling air, as did the odor of meat left too long to scorch in the fire. She and Jamra had to have been in the plaza mere minutes earlier, but where had they gone?

The dog sniffed the air too. Instead of following the trail to the *parfumerie* as Elena expected, he spun around and grumbled at the sky.

"Wait, something's wrong," Yanis said.

The dog's shoulders tensed and he growled. At first Elena worried she'd led them to the wrong place, but then a dark smudge appeared in the sky. The figure grew larger as it descended through the haze of dust. The clear outline of fiery wings and a tail came into focus. In a matter of seconds the air churned with the beating of half a dozen wings as two more ifrit dropped from the sky to circle the courtyard.

"Run!"

The group sprinted for the factory door, only to find it locked. Camille, her hands shaking, fumbled for the key in her coat pocket as the dog barked and snapped his teeth at the creatures.

"Come on, Camille! They're swarming."

The witch slipped the key in the lock and jiggled the door open just as a pair of scaly feet landed on the flagstones beside them. Camille sprayed her perfume at the beast, making him gag and swipe at his nose. It was distraction enough for the group to get inside and slam the door shut.

All but the dog. Their guide and guardian hadn't made it inside.

Elena peered through the glass in time to see the animal get plucked up in an ifrit's arms and carried away to the rooftop across the courtyard. She squeezed her eyes shut as her heart sank for the poor fellow. If not for him, none of them would be alive.

Inside, Jean-Paul waved a hand in front of his face. "Does the perfume always smell this strong in here?"

The overwhelming fragrance polluted the air in the factory lobby, affecting the nose keenly but none so much as that of the perfume witch. She inhaled in alarm at the full degree of scent floating in the air. "My perfume," she said, tracing the source with her nose. "It smells as if . . . oh, no, no, no. What is he doing in there?" She flinched as the sound of smashing glass hit the floor and a fresh cloud of Fleur de Sable billowed out of the shop.

Camille marched toward the entrance to the shop until Jean-Paul took hold of her shoulders, keeping her back a mere second before she would have been seen. And he was right—they couldn't just barge in there. Who knew what Jamra might do if cornered? The perfume witch relented and held her trembling fingers over her mouth as she worried over her precious goods being destroyed on the other side of the glass.

The group tucked themselves out of sight to figure out what they must do, while the wings of even more ifrits battered the side of the building. On the other side of the wall, Jamra raised his voice. They tensed, waiting for a violent outburst or the sound of shattering glass, but heard only his mocking laugh cut through the aftermath. Something had changed. The urgent panic Elena had sensed while following Sidra through the village had morphed into something else: sheer survival.

But something else had shifted, too, almost as if a layer of static electricity hung in the air around them. Camille caught the sensation as well, raising her hand to test the air. Above them, a cloud of light appeared in the lobby, shimmering as it swirled in a clockwise motion.

"Is this your magic, Camille?" Elena whispered.

The perfume witch shook her head.

"Yanis?"

The sorcerer swallowed. "No, and it's unlike anything I've ever encountered."

"Is it friendly?" Jean-Paul asked as he scanned the room for a weapon just in case. He grabbed an umbrella from the stand by the door, where a janitor snored from the sleeping spell, and gripped it, ready to strike.

Elena held her hand out to test the air with her shadow vision. She sensed no danger from the odd cloud of light, no spell magic, though it hovered ominously and deliberately above them. As she pondered what to make of it, a mumbled angry squeak escaped from the shop.

The lock of blonde hair. Yvette. It had to be. She was in there too. He had them both.

They were past the point of restraint. Jinn magic or not, they couldn't abandon Sidra and Yvette to that lunatic. The cloud seemed to concur as it whispered in her mind: *Ready your sorcery.*

Had Yanis heard the message too? He urgently searched his belongings for his chalk and talismans while Elena felt for the comfort of her grimoire in her satchel and whispered a protection spell.

And then the world inside the *parfumerie* exploded.

CHAPTER
THIRTY-FOUR

Jamra's temper no longer intimidated. He could make the wind howl. He could bury her under a mountain of sand. Sidra was done with his tantrums. She was done with their feud. Let the families fight among themselves until Jahannam swallowed them in the afterlife. A curse on them all. And a curse on Hariq for dying and leaving her alone to face this beetle-hearted brother of his alone.

No, she took that back. Hariq had always tried to do the right thing. He had lived a good life and made her a part of his world. They may have had only a few brief centuries together, but it was enough to prove she had loved deeply at least once. Her life had been fully and completely intermingled with another's. And soon they would reunite. With her death the dagger would fall forever from her enemy's grasp and into the unwitting hands of its meek savior.

Jamra smashed another perfume bottle on the floor in search of the dagger. He would not be put off again by false promises. It was time to fight or flee, but first she had to free the girl and balance the scales for entry into the next life. She stepped forward to offer her neck for Yvette's when the air thrummed with the presence of another. Jamra sensed it too.

"Who have you called?" he demanded, his eyes searching the dark corners of the shop.

Sidra shook her head, as ignorant of the origin of the presence as he was, when the outline of a silver cloud shone on the ceiling. The sight filled her eyes with astonishment. "It is not jinn."

Jamra tracked the light as it swirled across the ceiling. "This foul magic is your doing." He lurched threateningly toward Sidra, his face within a blade's width of hers. "Because you keep company with witches and sorcerers."

"And who do you keep company with?" she asked. "Ifrit? Demons? What bond have you secured with blood and flame to carry out your fantasy of revenge against innocent people?"

"Innocent?"

She'd hit a nerve. Jamra's jaw tightened, grinding his verdigris teeth.

"Our people were humiliated. Degraded. We, the superior beings, were forced to do manual labor for a narcissist mortal king whose soft ass no longer fit on his throne from all his years of indulgence at our expense." He pleaded his case before the ifrit restraining Yvette as if he were judge and jury, while bits of spittle clung to his lip from the emphatic tenor of his words. "But," he warned, "his mortal descendants will feel the whip of retribution for attempting to stand too tall on their clay feet."

"And now you wish to wield one of the seven sigils so you can murder unwitting mortals? We're thousands of years removed from this injustice you feel so keenly!" she said, shaking her head, her resolve building. "Your charred heart knows nothing but destruction. Without the dagger you're nothing. Even with the sigil in your hand, you'd still be no greater than a worm in a camel's intestine."

An explosion fueled by petty anger burst on Sidra's right side. Shelves of perfume shattered. The windows burst. The shop door flew off its hinges. Shards of glass shot across the room, barely missing Yvette.

Once the jinni's outburst had been spent, Sidra lowered her scarf from her face. The wall between the shop and the lobby to the factory had crumbled. She blinked at the four dusty and shocked faces that met her gaze on the other side. She had hoped that part of her prognostication had been wrong, but curse the fools, they had come not only when the walls began to buckle but Jamra's mind too.

"Curse this place. Free me of this human stench!" Jamra covered his nose with his sleeve and walked through the cloud of scent created from the explosion. He entered the lobby, where he spied Elena, Yanis the Mostly Honest, and the witch's husband, who seemed to have recovered from his desert-walker spell. They crouched on the floor with their arms protecting their heads after the wall had crumbled. Camille was there, too, huddled under a shower of dust and broken glass. Jamra rounded on them, grinning like a hyena.

"Jamra, wait." Sidra put herself between him and the others. "Let us look for the dagger. In the rubble. You have no quarrel with them. Or with the girl." She stabilized the wall with a flick of her wrist while he looked away, hoping the plaster would hold and the roof would stay propped over their heads. "You only make the task of finding the relic more difficult when you destroy the things around it. This way," she said. "What you seek is here."

Jamra glared past her at the intruders. "Is this who you summoned? These witches and sorcerers you fraternize with?"

"They are nothing. Flies in the ointment. Leave them be. I will help you search for the dagger."

Beside her, the perfume witch rose to her feet. A dazed look of disbelief filled her eyes as she surveyed the damage done to her shop. But her expression transformed to one of pure anger when she spotted Yvette restrained by the ifrit with an iron ring. Sidra watched as the rage traveled from the witch's eyes to her lips. Camille whispered pungent, biting words under her breath. Jamra ordered her to be still, but she would not be silenced as she cast her spell, breathing in and closing her eyes.

When the witch exhaled, a cloud gathered from the spilled perfume and blew toward the ifrit's eyes. The perfume hit him full in the face. His eyes watered as he coughed and spewed phlegm, gagging on the scent of jasmine and musk. The beast smoldered into ash and vanished into the ether, leaving Yvette behind.

"Filthy witch!" Jamra drew his hand up and clenched his fist until his knuckles whitened. Camille, as if stricken by a sudden headache, pressed her fingertips to her temples. A second later her nose bled and she dropped to the floor.

Sidra calculated the risk. Iron was tricky, but the ifrit was no conjurer of sophisticated magic. The inferior metal would have disintegrated eventually. She snapped the ring from the girl's neck with a nudge of her chin before Jamra looked away from the witch.

Yvette gasped for air, checking her neck for damage. Glimmering as her body rebounded from the effect of the iron, she floated in between the witch and Jamra. "What have you done to her, you stupid *cochon*?"

Fire and smoke, the girl couldn't be subdued for one minute?

Jamra appeared amused at first by Yvette's bravado. Then his temper darkened again as she knelt to help her friend recover. "Stand away from her," he said. When she refused, flicking her fingers under her chin at him, his eyes sparked with hatred.

Sidra knew the deadly instinct that coiled inside him. "The girl is brash," she said and waved her hand to downplay Yvette's actions. "Forget her foolishness. She and the witch are nothing but smoke in your eyes."

A thread of tension tingled at her back. Elena and Yanis had both called their power to them. Their energy thrummed in the air, as did the kaleidoscope of odd swirling energy still hovering above. If Jamra didn't feel it too, he was a fool. He formed a fist again as if to make Yvette suffer the same fate as Camille when Yanis shoved him hard with a blocking spell to knock him off balance. "Prophets protect us," she said, knowing the courage it took for him to confront Jamra.

"Careful, sorcerer. One might think you wish to play with fire." The jinni righted himself and hurled a stream of flame at Yanis's wooden leg. The magus managed to deflect the worst of it with a defensive spell, yet the odd angle of the strike allowed a sliver of fire to find its mark. The air filled with the smell of burnt oak. Yanis beat the fire out with his worn *taqiyah*.

Before Jamra could strike a second time, Sidra pushed her sleeves up, emboldened by the sorcerer's courage. She conjured a cobra the length of a man. Unlike before, this one was no smoke-and-air illusion. With one spit in the eye, it could take down an elephant, but she would settle for a single angry jinni. She sent the cobra sidewinding toward Jamra's feet with its hood up, hissing in a low growl. The serpent stood on its tail, ready to strike. She flicked her finger, directing the snake to lunge for an artery, but its prey was quicker. *Damn Jamra.* He shifted out of the way with cursed speed and sizzled the snake to ash before Sidra could send it in for a second bite. Thankfully the others had sensibly removed themselves from Jamra's line of sight as soon as the snake appeared.

"The sigil is near, *jinniyah*, I can sense it. Close enough to find on my own, which means you are nothing but ash to me."

The jinni whispered into the hollow space inside his fist. A whip made of fire appeared in his hand. He snapped the end so that it crackled and smoked in the air, threatening ungodly pain. Sidra shrank back as he flicked the whip, touching the fiery end to the set of powder-blue drapes framing the broken window at her side. Taunting her. Teasing her with his near miss. The drapes caught fire, sending smoke wafting through the main floor of the factory.

Fire was nothing. "Child's play," she said and stood by the flames, calling them to her, drawing them off the curtains. They clung to the hem of her robe, climbed up her sleeves, crowned her head in a blaze of orange. She blew on her fingertips, creating an intense blue blaze, then shook the flames from her body until they turned to smoke and went out.

"You can do better than that." She faced Jamra, turning with him as they circled each other.

"Don't do this, Sidra!" Yvette cried from the other side of the room. "Just poof off!"

The girl didn't know the power of seeing one's destiny in flickering fire and the omens of birds. From her periphery, Sidra spied the silvery light on the ceiling rotate with purpose. Everything seemed to be turning, spinning, coiling tighter. Fate was winding itself up, ready to spring its control on her. Chaos or calm? Life or death?

"Go," she said to her comrades as Jamra lashed his whip. The fiery tip wrapped around her neck. The fire bit. The rope clinched. The room spun as she twisted off her feet.

CHAPTER
THIRTY-FIVE

Sidra had been caught by Jamra's fiery whip and yanked off her feet so that she spun across the room. Elena lunged but was helpless to stop the attack. She waited for her friend to get up, to fight back with her fiery temper, but the jinni remained motionless in a heap on the floor.

Elena reached in her satchel, but a few sprigs of rosemary and a pouch of leftover salt weren't going to be powerful enough to counter Jamra's magic. No illusion she could summon would stop him from destroying everything and everyone inside the building to get what he wanted. Yanis shook his head, as befuddled as she was for a way to stop the jinni with their paltry tokens. Still, the bloodstone she'd tossed in her bag as an afterthought during her abduction called to her, so she slipped it into her palm.

Jamra waited a half beat to see if Sidra would rise. When she didn't, he stood over her, nudging her with his boot as his lip curled over his eyetooth. Breath still moved through her lungs as her chest rose and fell under her robes, yet she did not awaken.

"Hey!" Yvette waved her hand to get Jamra's attention. "I have it. I have that stupid dagger you're looking for. Leave her alone and maybe I'll show you."

"When the *jinniyah* is dead, I will take my prize." He drew the whip through his hands, as if savoring the feel of the flame.

The heat in his eye, the hate in his heart—Elena knew he would strike the life out of Sidra with his next blow. "You can't do this!" she said, hoping to appeal to some sense of decency still residing inside the jinni. "She doesn't deserve this."

He took three steps to his right, deciding the best angle to deliver the final lash. "Deserve? She is a murderer. A thief. And now she will die for choosing to defy me."

Jean-Paul put his arm in front of Elena and forced her back against the wall with the others. They huddled, helpless to interfere. The jinni played the tyrant, brandishing the whip over his head, winding it up, readying to unleash death. The whip drew back for the third time. The arm came forward. A trail of fire arced over the jinni's head. Elena held her breath, cringing in anticipation of the terrible moment, but the sound she braced for didn't come.

Before the whip made the journey to Sidra's body, a window smashed in the lobby. The dog, whom she'd given up for dead, crashed through the glass, bounding inside the shop. Leaping off his power-ful haunches, he sprang with lightning-quick speed just as the jinni snapped the fiery whip. The dog caught the rope of flame in his teeth and tugged until it came free of Jamra's grip. He gave it a violent shake, as if it were a rabbit in his jaws, and the whip disintegrated into smoke.

"Jiminy, where'd he come from?" Yvette said. She and Elena used the distraction to inch closer to Sidra.

Blood dripped from two puncture wounds in the dog's side. Elena would have hugged his furry mane and used her herbs to heal him, but the dog was still on the hunt. He growled and turned on Jamra. The dog's powerful shoulders rolled forward as he set one paw down in front of the other, stalking the jinni.

Jamra backed away, inching closer to where Sidra still lay uncon-scious. "Who are you? This is not your fight. Leave us!"

The dog pressed forward, his growl rumbling into a hair-raising, vicious snarl as Jamra nearly stumbled over the pile of broken perfume bottles. Elena had witnessed fear in the jinni once before when the strange vision of Titania had briefly flashed in her shadow vision. That same look of alarm overtook his face now as the dog advanced, his teeth bared and ready to pounce. Soon there would be nowhere for Jamra to go but the ether, though Elena's instinct told her he would be followed and hunted even there.

"What did he do to her?" Yvette glowed softly as she stroked Sidra's forehead. "She's not waking up."

Obeying her intuition, Elena placed the bloodstone on Sidra's third eye. Known for its restorative power, the stone could invigorate the circulatory system, cure a broken heart, or rid the body of toxins when matched with the correct spell. At least in humans. Because jinn were made of fire rather than true flesh, she reasoned the psychic gateway was the best position to apply the stone for maximum healing of her spirit.

The dog stopped his advance, tipping his ears toward Elena's efforts. Jamra seemed to interpret the pause as a gesture of carelessness by his attacker. He stuck his hand out and grabbed Yvette by her hair, hauling her to her feet. She twisted in his grip and screamed until he put his arm around her neck, securing her in a choke hold. He pressed his lips close to her ear. "If this one means anything to any of you," he warned, "the jinn mongrel will back away." Jamra waited for the dog to decide. He tightened his grip on Yvette's neck until her eyes squeezed shut in desperation. At last, the dog reversed his step. "Now," Jamra whispered in Yvette's ear, "give me that dagger."

Yvette opened her eyes and searched everyone's faces for what to do. "Now!" Jamra jerked Yvette off her feet.

Elena drew her athame from her satchel. It was sacred to her. A tool for ritual work. But it also had a very sharp blade. She did not know for certain if jinn bled, but if he made one more threatening move, she would find out.

Suddenly, the silver light that had been hovering overhead began to flash and spin. Jamra halted his assault long enough to let his attention shift to the ceiling. "Who called this magic?" he bellowed.

No one answered as the light pulsed and sparked, though the dog padded toward it unafraid. The light continued to spin, and as the center dropped to form a twisting thread of glimmering filament, everyone else took a step back. The whirlwind lightly touched down on the marble floor, kicking up a cloud of silver dust. From it, a woman in an iridescent gown adorned with beetle shells and butterfly scales emerged. On her head sat a crown made from dragonfly wings held together with silver wire and tiny seed pearls.

"Titania!" Yvette cried.

"Nonsense," she said. "Call me Grand-Mère, child."

Yvette clawed at Jamra's arm. "Let me go!"

Jamra tightened his elbow around Yvette's throat. "Why does the witch queen stand before me? What business have you here?"

The queen of the *Fée* replied with a smile, then gestured to the dog.

The dog ruffled his fur and twitched his nose. Like a shimmering haze rising above the parched earth on a scalding day, the air blurred where he stood. The effect was momentary. A mirage that disappears after blinking to see more clearly. When the animal came back in focus, he stood as a man. He wore a sleeveless black robe with gold threading that exposed his broad shoulders and a pair of black-and-gold slippers that curled up slightly at the toe. A curved dagger, its hilt encrusted with rubies, decorated his belt. Restored to what Elena assumed was his natural being, his brown eyes telegraphed a warm sincerity, though perhaps weighted with a world of regret.

Except for the fuller face and healthier complexion, the man standing before them bore an uncanny resemblance to Jamra—the same dark, wavy hair, thin beard, flash of white teeth, and intimidating height.

"It cannot be." Jamra blinked, disbelieving. "You're dead."

"Clearly I am not." The jinni in black did not take his eyes off Jamra as he spoke over his shoulder. "Sorcerer, do you have your paper and chalk?"

"Stop. What are you doing?" Jamra wrapped his arms tighter around Yvette.

Yanis and Elena exchanged a look of disbelief before he replied, "Hariq, but how are you here?"

Hariq?

"Witch, do you have your spellfire?" Hariq asked.

"I said stop!" Jamra grew jittery, taking a step backward and pulling Yvette with him. "Why do you address them in such a manner?"

Elena snapped her fingers and a flame appeared in her palm. "I have my fire."

Titania matched Jamra's retreat, closing the distance with him as though she floated on the air. "Release my granddaughter," she ordered.

Jamra blinked and looked from Hariq to Titania. "No."

Behind them, Yanis drew his symbols on a square of paper. He nimbly made a mark on each corner, then drew a circle around them but left an open space in the middle.

Hariq had to know his brother's true name. It was the only way. Elena mouthed to Jean-Paul to find her a bottle. Something small. While he skirted the broken glass in the shop to search for a container, the sorcerer slipped a blade of sweetgrass loose from his braided bundle and tied a knot in it.

Titania continued to stare down Jamra, outwardly unafraid of him or his magic. "Do you really wish to say no to me, little jinni?" She let mockery slip into her voice as her face contorted into a ghoulish mask of gray skin with black eyes and fangs dripping with red saliva. "I have walked in your dreams with this face when your heart yearned to be a purveyor of fear and destroyer of peace."

"Get away from me, you hag!"

"But really just a little boy afraid of the creatures in the night," she said, advancing. "Cowering under your covers. Crying out when the nightmares descended."

"I'll snap her fairy neck, I swear it!"

Titania let the mask fall away again and clapped her hands together sharply. "Concentrate, Yvette. A fool like this cannot hold a daughter of the *Fée* lands."

Yvette, her eyes still wide with shock at what she'd seen her grandmother become, stopped struggling against the jinni. *"Merde!"* She closed her eyes and shimmered into a gold mist and slipped out of Jamra's grasp, transmuting on the far side of the room.

The jinni pushed up his sleeves. He blew fire across his fingertips, and a pair of ifrit flew to the broken window as if summoned like a pair of hounds. Their eyes blazed as they stalked the fairy queen.

Hariq flinched, ready to fight, though Titania stood remarkably at ease even as the first of the fire demons prepared to lunge. With barely a finger twitch, the fairy queen flung the iron ring that had been around Yvette's neck at the window. The band transformed in the air, becoming an iron bar that flew through the window and impaled the ifrit who'd tried to jump. The beast shrieked as the metal eviscerated his fiery core, his insides oozing onto the windowsill like lava, where it cooled and turned to lumps of stone. Outside, the second ifrit screamed in fury but did not cross the threshold, where the fairy queen's magic still lingered.

Jamra crouched and backed away. Titania advanced, daring him to lash out at her.

Hariq called to the sorcerer. "He is called Shayik. Quickly!"

Yanis scratched the name in the center of the circle on the paper. He placed the knotted blade of grass on top, folded the paper, and nodded to Elena. She relit the flame in her hand and held it forward as he sang the words of a spell in his native tongue.

"A curse on you all!" Jamra screamed and dissipated from the physical world into the ether.

214

Yanis hovered the paper over the fire, letting it catch. "You must follow him."

As the smoke rose, coiling like a snare, Elena doused her fire and sank into a trancelike state to let her mind walk in the shadow world. She found him there, sensing his invisible energy thrashing about in anger. Somewhere in the physical world a mirror fell from a wall and broke. Ceiling plaster cracked and popped. A door came off its hinges. Elena refocused her mind and chased Jamra's reckless energy. He was fleeing quickly. Before he could vanish to the farthest reach of her vision, she spoke his name, his true name, the one that would bind him. The smoke from Yanis's spell floated beside her through the ether, following the projection of her voice until the name perched in the jinni's ear. The spell-smoke found him, bound him, and held on.

Now Elena grasped the rope. She reeled herself back to consciousness, pulling the jinni with her. He attempted to resist, but the binding had rendered him weaker than a newborn lamb. Returned to the physical world, she opened her eyes. The smoke from Yanis's spell twisted in the air before her. Jean-Paul held out an opaline glass perfume locket he'd taken from the lobby display. Cupping her hands over the miniature vessel, Elena directed the smoke to flow into the mouth of the locket. When the last wisp disappeared inside, Elena put the cap on and screwed it shut. The glass warmed from the heat of the jinni's temper trapped inside, so she let it dangle from her fingers by its chain.

The jinni who wished to command chaos in the world now ruled an empty chamber scented with an old woman's rosewater.

CHAPTER
THIRTY-SIX

Warmth filled Sidra's veins, not with the welcome heat of a crackling fire, but with the damp, muggy oppression of a humid day. Like a wet rag that needed wringing, her body was sluggish to respond to her thoughts.

At last her eyes opened, yet something still weighed heavily on her sight. A stone. On her forehead. She palmed the stone—oddly veined like a salamander's skin—and sat up. Across the room, the witch, the one who made wine, held a tiny bottle on a chain as a trail of smoke poured into it. Where was Jamra? Where was the sorcerer? And the dagger?

Wasps took wing inside her head. She wasn't seeing straight. Jamra stood only a few feet away, but his clothes had changed and he smelled of oud. Somehow the fairy queen had appeared too. She shimmered beside him, her eyes following the smoke into the bottle. Sidra checked her head for blood or a tender spot. She felt no lasting physical damage or pain—that is, until the girl shrieked in her ear.

"You're all right! Look, everyone—she's awake." Yvette scrambled across the marble to squat beside her. "He's gone. They got him. Jamra's been trapped."

Sidra knew she'd heard the girl correctly, yet she couldn't reconcile her words with what she saw. Jamra stood clearly before her. His hair was longer and his beard fuller, but it was him. Who else could it be? His head turned to follow the girl's words. He lunged toward Sidra. Must she die on the floor at the hands of this camel's ass? But instead of attacking, he knelt and swept the hair back from her face.

"Habibti."

His face came into focus. His skin-and-bone face like a mortal's. The one that had met her every morning since they'd married. She used to run her hand through his long hair as the dawn light revealed the glints of red and gold strands in the ebony curls. But that man could not be here. Hariq was dead.

The man took her hand and bowed his head. "There is much I must explain," he said. "And may I earn your forgiveness in the telling."

"You're alive?" She did not know until that moment that elation, confusion, and anger could be intimate bedfellows under one coverlet. "How are you here? Is this sorcery? Did Yanis do this? Has he made a deal with Mother Ghulah and the dead?"

"Sidra, listen to me," Hariq implored, but she ignored him, her emotions too unsettled to even know how to look at him without becoming dizzy.

She backed away and rose to her feet. The wasps in her head swarmed. She pushed up her sleeves, needing to unleash a storm of magic. She didn't know what kind or at whom; all she wanted was to cast pain back upon the confusing world she'd awoken to. Unable to hold it in, she shot the stone in her palm across the room as if by gunfire, shattering the terra-cotta planter with the potted palm in it. The tree toppled to the floor.

She marched across the floor to the pile of broken bottles, nudging the mess away with her toe. "Where is Jamra? He must be stopped."

"We got him," Yvette said. The girl pointed to the locket in Elena's hands, the one that she wasn't sure had been illusion or not.

Elena held the necklace up by the chain as proof. "Hariq gave us his true name. Yanis bound him inside."

"We both did," said the sorcerer.

Sidra held out her hand, supporting the perfume locket so it rested against her fingers. Prickling heat snapped against her skin through the glass. "And the dagger?" she asked, meeting the sorcerer's eyes.

"As far as we know, it's still safe."

"Here it is." Yvette reached in her endless pocket and drew out a perfume bottle with a pair of crystal birds for a stopper.

Elena balked. "You mean you really had it all along? I thought it was a bluff."

"I swiped this little beauty off the floor when he wasn't looking. Knew the bottle was Sidra's the minute I saw it." She pointed out the dull finish on the filigree from where it had worn away from so much handling. "Not a chip anywhere."

Yvette. Usually such a clever girl.

Hariq stroked the hair on his beard. "The dagger is in the bottle? But to think it could have been smashed on the floor and released. A very near miss."

Hariq. He truly was alive. But then where had he been hidden all this time? Why had he left her? Lied to her?

"How are you here?" she asked as searing heat rose in her eyes. "Why do you call me *habibti* when you are the one who abandoned me alone to this fate?"

He reached out to her but Sidra pulled away, not wanting to feel the heat of him against her. Not yet. Not while her mind still buzzed with the confusion of a thousand angry wasps.

"I will tell you," he said. "I will tell you everything. Please, just sit and listen."

The fairy queen interceded. "We haven't yet finished this business with the dagger."

"It's safe for the moment," he told her, glancing at the intact bottle. "But first my bride must know the truth to put her mind at ease."

Hariq spread his fingers and waved his hand in front of the shop. Amid the broken perfume bottles and the potted palm lying on its side, he produced soft poufs for all to sit on. "Please, come sit."

Sidra took her perfume bottle from Yvette and sat with the crystal birds in her hands. It was true—the filigree decoration had tarnished from the months and years she'd treasured the gift. Holding it, admiring it, thinking herself the luckiest woman alive to have a man who made a scent just for her. The girl sat beside her and placed a hand on her back. She didn't protest the touch or complain about the fair one's soft glow that inexplicably rid her of the last of her soggy sluggishness. Nor did she mind when Elena sat on her other side and pressed a piece of amethyst into her palm.

Hariq sat on his pouf opposite with his hands loosely clasped together between his knees. He didn't avoid her eyes as he began. His voice, absent of the shrillness that so often accompanies excuses, remained calm yet commanding.

"The plan was likely doomed from the beginning," he said with a quick glance at Yanis. For the benefit of the others he added, "My wife and I have a complicated history with our families. There's a feud between her people and mine. No one remembers how it started, yet neither side will relent. Those walls were built long before we came into the world and fell in love." Hariq caught her in his sight again. "Our marriage was opposed. There was no place for us among our people. And the bickering from both sides, like ravens fighting over a dead mouse." He made a gesture with his hands as if to throw it all away. "To be free of it we left, but perhaps you know all this?"

Yvette nodded, knowing the story, as did Elena.

"You are good friends for her to have told you," he said with a light smile. "And you know, too, of the dagger and the responsibility we inherited to keep the sigil safe after it was discovered. And the new danger it introduced into our lives from my brother, Jamra." He looked at his hands and wiped them on his thighs, as if he could rid himself of some unwanted feeling. "It's why we decided to fool the world and pretend to be dead. To relinquish our association with the relic and free my brother's mind, and anyone else, of the need to hunt for us any longer. But . . ." He stopped and braved a withering stare from Sidra. "To truly convince one as cunning as Jamra of the charade of death, we required the credibility only sincere loss and pain could bring. Which meant one of us must survive in ignorance of the truth. For that, we sacrificed honesty, with you, for deception."

Sidra's eyebrow twitched. Her nose flared. Who was this "we" he spoke of?

Hariq went on to describe how he'd diluted Sidra's potion so that she would wake a day before him. He had to appear to the world to be dead. She had to take the blame in a lovers' quarrel. That was the only outcome that would have convinced Jamra to accept the lie, because he was predisposed to already think her capable of such a thing, coming from the family she did.

"In that way, we hoped to use the long-standing feud between our people to our advantage." His brow tightened. "But when you thought me dead, you escaped with the dagger."

"To keep it safe."

"You flew to Jamra."

"To confront him. For foolishly thinking he'd somehow killed you, when all along it was a lie."

"The deception was necessary."

"I went to prison for your murder. They were going to take my head. I came this close to being executed for your game of lies!"

"Never," Hariq said. "I wouldn't have let that happen. We had a plan to save you before the blade dropped. An illusion that would have left everyone, including Jamra, believing that you were dead by execution and the dagger lost forever."

She stood and shook her pleading hands in anger. "Who is this 'we' you keep speaking of?"

Hariq, to his credit, absorbed her rage as one who knows he is deserving of the ire. "I will let him explain."

The warmth in the air shifted. The faint scent of turmeric and cumin wafted through the space as Rajul Hakim materialized beside Hariq. For the old one to animate outside his cave was exceptional, but Hariq showed no surprise at the jinni's appearance. He got to his feet and welcomed their adopted clan leader with a quick bow before ceding his seat to him. The ancient jinni settled on his pouf, stroked his long beard out of habit, then produced his *shisha*. The old one never went anywhere without his pipe.

Hurt, disappointment, astonishment—a whirlwind of uncomfortable emotions swirled inside Sidra at the sight of another she had trusted with her heart materializing before her. "*You* also conspired against me?"

"Deception," said the old one, "is sometimes a long, winding thing like a monkey's tail." He took a puff from his pipe, letting the smoke encircle his head as he spoke. "Without it to grasp the limb, one would fall from the tree. This I wish you to remember."

Elena and her husband exchanged doubting looks, but it was how Rajul Hakim spoke sometimes when he knew he had an audience. The witch bade Sidra to sit again and listen, despite the quirks of the old man's theatrics. Her ears burned at the thought of listening to more of their lies. Still, she sat and allowed herself to fume.

"We could not tell you our intentions. How would it have looked to one as shrewd as Jamra to have even one shred of falseness in your reaction?" The old one puffed on his pipe and squinted at her. "Our actions were cruel, but they were done to save your life and Hariq's, so that you would not always be wondering when chaos would fall into the hands of one ready to cut open a seam in the world's underbelly."

"We were prepared to intervene in the execution," Hariq said. "But then you escaped your cell before we could carry out the last part of our plan."

"That would be my fault," Titania said, rising to her feet to explain herself at Hariq's side.

Sidra got an uncomfortable knot in her stomach from seeing Yvette's grandmother stand so close to her husband. How could they even be familiar?

"My granddaughter was to be reunited with her family on her sixteenth birthday. But her fate took a different turn."

Yvette hugged her arms around her waist, glowing softly as she nodded.

Titania described how she'd kept track of Yvette after she'd run away, peering in on her periodically at the carnival she traveled with, in the hope a reunion could still be arranged. Then one day Yvette wasn't there. She wasn't anywhere. The fairy queen couldn't find her even with the aid of Oberon's vision. She'd simply disappeared.

"It was only after a chance encounter with a bird, while I reclined beside a country stream, that I found you again. He perched on the branch above and sang the most interesting tale. He said he'd just spoken to a jinni inside a prison cell who'd fed him a daddy longlegs and a silverfish from her fingers. With her was a witch and a foul-mouthed, yellow-haired waif. Well, I suspected right away it was our Yvette."

"I do *not* have a foul mouth," the girl said in her defense, to which everyone disagreed, nodding their heads in the affirmative.

The fairy queen smiled, and radiant light shimmered around her. "The powerful rune magic employed by the jail had shielded her from my sight, but there was no mistaking her golden hair and, shall we say, colorful vocabulary."

"Mon Dieu." Yvette covered the sides of her head with her arms as if she didn't wish to hear any more.

"So, a witch, a fairy, and a jinni together in a cell." Titania pressed her hands palm to palm and touched her fingers to her lips, as if reliving the moment she'd contemplated what she could do with that information. "There had to be a way to work that combination to the best advantage." Her eyes landed on Jean-Paul. "And then I found you, a self-assured mortal fellow," she said. "You have no magic, and yet here you are, perfectly at ease with those around you."

"One of the side effects of falling in love with a witch," he said.

"I knew right away I could depend on you." She leaned forward with one brow raised. "Shall I confess it was I who supplied the matches you found in your kitchen on the morning of your visit to the jail?"

"The matches I gave to Elena?"

The fairy queen tilted her chin in confirmation.

"And I gave them to Yvette," Elena said.

"*Merde*, and I passed the lit cigarette to Sidra."

Titania nodded from one to the other as if following a chain, one linked to the other. "And our jinni lit herself on fire and escaped and yet remained indebted to those still inside."

The old one blew out a string of smoke rings. "We were not expecting that," he admitted.

Hariq crossed his arms. "Now we had a new dilemma. After returning to free her cellmates, Sidra disappeared again. I searched everywhere in the ether but couldn't find you." The warmth in his eyes as he spoke directly to her was magnetic, drawing her in when she did not want to be. Not yet. Not when forgiveness was still a fruit she wouldn't bite. "So, I followed the witch instead in the hope she might lead me to you. That was how I learned she possesses the rare ability to see into the shadow world."

"And you have a remarkable ability to remain undetected," Elena said. "My instinct never once noticed your presence, presumably until you wanted me to."

"Remaining hidden is our greatest talent, Madame Martel." Hariq smiled humbly, his hand on his chest as he bowed his head.

Sidra was pleased to hear Hariq call her friend by her married name, but all this shadow talk began to unsettle her. She'd thought she understood how to read the fire as well as any, but there was so much she hadn't seen. It made her dizzy to think of the spinning world and the multitude of destinies swirling together, fueling the future forward for everyone—individually and collectively. And with so much providence bedded under a blanket of deception.

The old one began to speak again, so Hariq sat cross-legged on the floor near Sidra, close enough that she could smell the intoxicating fragrance of his skin. She made no objection.

"When you escaped and presumably took the dagger with you, we thought we had lost our one chance to outfox Jamra," Rajul Hakim said through a puff of smoke. "We feared, too, for your life. But the long curl of fate had brought opportunity back to us again so that all could be restored."

"How?" Sidra's initial anger had receded, replaced by curiosity about how her life had become a plaything for those with the talent to deceive.

Titania spoke again. "After you freed my granddaughter, my heart would not settle until she was home with us. In the *Fée* lands. Her mother had already arranged a protocol for her to return on her sixteenth birthday. It was still there waiting for her in that wretched mortal's apartment after all those years. All I needed was a little supernatural nudge to help her find it." The fairy queen did her best to feign humility, though on her false modesty hung out of place like tarnished tinsel. "For that I stole a wish. One that brought you both to the city."

"Wait, *my* wish?" Yvette stared at her grandmother in disbelief. "That was you?"

"It was still your heart's desire, but it was I who tapped into the jinni's magic while you were both in flux."

Always the fair ones with their airy ideas and fuzzy lines between right and wrong. It had always seemed incongruous to Sidra that the girl could have manipulated her magic with mere desire. "But how does a *Fée* queen interfere with jinn magic on a whim?" she asked.

"Jinn dream, as do all creatures," Titania said, a dangerous glint in her eye. "Their hopes, fears, desires—they float about in the ether, riding on the same currents of yearning as everyone else's while they sleep. Those currents are where I sail my craft. I slide under men's noses with the scent of desire, spy on lovers dreaming of kisses, and slip over ladies' lips to give them a taste of lust. And sometimes I put the fear of death in little boys' nightmares when they think too much of the fire and pain they hope to inflict on others." Her face flashed to that grotesque figure for half a second. Everyone gasped except for the old one. "Yes, I've long maintained familiarity with the jinn mind, slipping in and out of their dream-thoughts at will. Stealing a wish from a jinni was as easy as plucking a string on a harp."

"The *Fée* queen exercised a privilege few are in a position to take advantage of," Rajul Hakim said with a nod. "But she was willing to pay for her theft, once the wish played out and her granddaughter was properly restored to her people." The old one set his pipe aside and attempted to stand. Hariq rushed to his feet to help steady him. "I have sat too long in that cave," he said, then shooed his assistant away once he found his balance. He took a few painfully short steps until he stood before Sidra. "The bottle, please."

Sidra cradled the green bottle with the crystal doves in her hands. It was the most precious thing she owned, but she handed it to her adopted clan leader without hesitation.

"Such a trifling thing, is it not?" The old one held the bottle up to the light as if he might be able to peer inside. "We had lost track of Sidra yet again after the wish was stolen, except for a brief moment when she entertained the witch at a café in the city, but then Titania was good enough to let us know our jinni had been smuggled into her realm within this very vessel." He gave the bottle a tiny shake near his ear, as if testing for the sound of something inside. "As payment for her theft"—he wagged a chastising finger at Titania—"she kept Sidra safely hidden in the *Fée* lands. And notified us when Jamra's dreams lusted again for the missing relic."

Yvette gaped at her grandmother. "Why'd you send us back if you knew that lunatic jinni was after the dagger again?"

Sidra narrowed her eyes at Rajul Hakim. "Because one doesn't escape a lion by outrunning him. One must set a trap."

The old one nodded. "We already had Yanis, who could do the binding. But now we also knew of a witch, a companion of yours, who could see into the shadow world. Who could snap the trap, once it had been baited properly." The old one took the perfume locket from Elena and held it up by the chain. The two pigeon wings above his eyes knitted together as he studied the delicate glass and metal container keeping the jinni imprisoned inside. "You and the dagger were our lure," he said to Sidra. "And now both are safe." He held his hands out before him as if testing the weight of the perfume bottle against that of the locket. "And chaos and order remain in proper tension."

The old one handed the locket to Hariq for safekeeping, then turned his attention to Sidra's bottle. "I do not mind admitting how nervous I was when Jamra began smashing bottles against the floor. To think what might have happened if he'd broken this one open."

Sidra shrugged. "I would have lost a treasure, but the world would still have been safe."

The old one took the stopper out and shook the bottle so that whatever was inside would fall free into his hand, but his palm remained empty.

"What is the spell to remove the dagger?" he asked.

Sidra grinned so that the intricate gold design in her teeth sparkled. "Sometimes a trap works best with a decoy." The jinni crossed the floor to stand before Yanis. The bracelets on her wrists rattled as she pushed back her sleeves. "Lift your leg."

"What are you doing?" Confused, Yanis extended his good leg.

"Your other one," she said, kneeling beside him.

The sorcerer gripped his wooden leg at the place where it strapped onto his knee and pulled up. Sidra rested the leg on her knee and tapped on the wood with her knuckle.

"You didn't." Elena gawked.

With permission, Sidra unscrewed the peg from the bottom of the false leg. From the hollow center inside, she slid out a curved silver dagger with a black hilt. On the pommel end was a round sigil that showed a sunrise on one side of a median line and a sunset on the other.

"Circumstances forced me to hide the dagger where I knew it would be safest," she said. "With one who had the heart and skill to protect such an object from those who would abuse it."

Yanis, so accustomed to threats and derision from Sidra, pressed his palms together and bowed his head. "I am honored to have earned your trust."

"It's not in my power to give you a new leg," she said in return, "but we can make a false one that won't cause you any more pain."

She met Hariq's eyes, and he nodded at her with the admiration of one who knows the long journey she'd taken to see Yanis for who he was.

"And I cannot take away the heartache my deception cost you," Hariq said, reaching for Sidra's hand. "But I hope, in time, you will also see that it wasn't done to hurt you, my beloved. That there was always a plan to find you, to reunite, so that we may spend the rest of our lives together without ever having to look over our shoulders again."

How many times had she said to herself if only Hariq were alive again, she would forgive him anything? She didn't know the words would stick so hard in her throat when, at last, it happened. Chaos and order rested on two sides of a sharp edge, but so did pain and pleasure. Harmony and discord. There was not one without the other. Always the dance of tension. One could choose which side to lean into if or when the blade tipped off-center.

"I am pleased to see you alive, *habibi*," she said, knowing her heart had always leaned toward forgiveness.

Hariq gazed at her, as if she were the only star worth seeing in a spiraling galaxy, and there, in his eyes, she chose to chart her future once more.

CHAPTER
THIRTY-SEVEN

The physical damage had been easy enough to repair. A bit of broken glass. A door off its hinges. A few dented streetlamps that required reshaping. The sand was the worst. The haboob had blown grains of sand into every street and open window in the village. Flowerpots sat coated with dirt, awnings sagged from the weight of the grit, and the mortals who'd been put to sleep by the lavender potion needed to have their clothes and hair swept clean. But between the jinn and the queen of the *Fée*, the cleanup took little more time and effort than was needed to sweep the cobblestones from one end of the loggia to the other. The villagers woke groggy and confused, and perhaps a few found sand in their ears if they dug deep enough, but otherwise the day resumed as any other. Titania, while still in her moonlighting guise, had made certain the people's dreams bore the blame for the peculiar ennui they felt upon rising.

The train north was scheduled to depart on time. Hariq had taken special care to set the cars upright and clean the sand out of the boiler so that it steamed properly while awaiting departure. The funicular, too, had required righting, but it was a trinket compared to the train's locomotive. Elena and Jean-Paul walked out of the depot, tickets in hand for the return trip. They stood on the platform only a little worse for wear, she in her muddy sabots and he still slightly trembly from the effects of his fever and overexertion. But their mood was bright as they were met by friends at the station to say their goodbyes.

Hariq and Sidra made a stunning couple. He still wore his long black jacket and wide smile and she'd conjured a fine new robe and jangling gold bracelets. The scents of jasmine, burnt citrus, and woodsmoke mingled in the air between them.

Behind the couple the old jinni, his body hunched over as he leaned on a walking stick, shuffled forward. Yanis stood at his side with an ornately carved wooden box on a leather strap secured over his shoulder. Elena knew it was a decoy. The real dagger was hidden back inside his polished wooden leg with the generous new padding, where it would be kept safe for the journey ahead. For he and the old one, with the protection of Hariq and Sidra, were also embarking on a journey. All had agreed with Yanis that the dagger must be returned to the care of the Order of the Seven Stars so that it might remain protected and in balance for centuries to come.

"*As-salaam-alaykum,*" Sidra said to Elena and Jean-Paul as they met on the platform.

Elena reached out to shake the jinni's hand. "You know, I don't think we've ever had a proper hello or goodbye, you and I."

"No, but perhaps we've had everything in between," Sidra said and squeezed Elena's hand.

Hariq shook hands with Jean-Paul, remarking on how he'd admired the vineyard when he'd been there. "I hope one day to sample the fine vintage it produces."

Jean-Paul did a double take before remembering he was speaking with the dog he'd seen lurking in the vines. "Of course," he said. "You're welcome to visit the cellar anytime after *les vendanges*. It would be our pleasure."

Elena noted how her husband took such things like entertaining jinn at the vineyard in stride now. How far they'd come since his first encounter with the gargoyle perched among the grape clusters. He no longer ran from the supernatural, and she no longer resisted the pull of his mortal faith in that which could be proven. *Tawazun*, as Sidra would say.

"We would be most honored." Hariq held up a finger. "But we will not wait until then to return this, which I believe belongs to you, madame." The jinni stepped behind a station post and walked out again holding a rolled-up tapestry that Elena was certain had not been there a minute earlier. "There's a grass stain on the back and a snagged thread from where it caught in the tree branches, but otherwise it's still in good shape for flying." He reinforced his subtle jest with a smile.

"My tapestry. I didn't think I'd ever see it again."

"I have grown too old for flying rugs," Rajul Hakim said with a sigh. "So, they are making me ride in that yellow beast to the coast, and then I am being put on a boat. A boat!"

On the street, Camille waved from her big yellow automobile paid for with the scent of desert flowers.

"It is necessary for the sorcerer's sake. And once we land safe on the other side you will sit in a café under the sunshine, smoke your pipe, and forget all about it," Sidra said to him. "It's a good thing, getting out of the house once in a while."

A bell rang, signaling the funicular was arriving from the top of the hill. They turned to greet it, but before the car even docked, Yvette's hair and soft glow caught their attention. She, too, had found new attire. She had donned a powder-blue suit and a matching tricorn hat with a peacock feather that fluttered over her golden head as she disembarked. Her skin was radiant as she burst onto the platform bearing good news.

"I'm going to study to be a nose!" Yvette said. "Can you believe it?" The young woman held up her letter of acceptance as proof. "Camille arranged it. I'm going to learn to make perfume at Le Maison des

Amoureux. Grand-Mère put her up to it, I've no doubt, but isn't it wonderful?"

"You're staying in this village?" Sidra asked.

"Not getting rid of me so easily, eh?"

Elena waited for Sidra to snap at the news she would be sharing a village with the young woman, but the jinni's face betrayed the hint of a smile, even as she curled her lip. As if admitting a little lunacy in one's life was the necessary cure to boredom. Sidra reached into the folds of her new silk and produced two bronze medallions. She placed one in Yvette's palm and one in Elena's. "One for each. The sorcerer made them for me," she said, pointing to the star and the bird symbols engraved in the center of a pentagram. "Hold the talisman in your palm and speak my name. I will answer."

"What if there's something I need now?" Yvette asked.

Sidra raised her brows, her patience already tested.

"Slip the woman the suffragette pamphlet. The one in the village asking for help. Do that for me and we'll be square."

Sidra glanced up at the hillside village as if listening for something only she could hear before Hariq called over her shoulder that he and the old one were ready to leave. She breathed in the scent of the village that had protected her for so long and said, "It's a thing I can do."

Yvette and Elena both kissed the jinni's cheek and said adieu. She walked away, then turned and waved, her gold bracelets jingling their own tune for one last farewell.

"And, of course, I had to come and say goodbye to you," Yvette said, gripping Elena's hands. "Isn't it reassuring to know we're all just a train ride away?" Yvette winked. "Or, you know, a quick shimmer from here to there for some of us. Grand-Mère swore she'd show me how the portal magic works, now that I've decided to stay."

The young woman gleamed under the halo of her newfound purpose. Shimmering bright and radiating joy. Elena pondered, upon their farewell from the perfumed village, that Yvette was like a citrusy high note in the floral tonic of their rare and remarkable friendship. First to shine, first to see the luster of value in others. And Sidra, with her oft overpowering personality, was without question the solid base that would always be there for them, now and in the future. As for herself, Elena supposed she fell somewhere in the middle, the heart note infusing her influence where she could to bind and keep them all together.

"A mere day away," Elena said and hugged the young woman.

There was a rush of activity as the conductor made his boarding announcement. Jean-Paul took her hand, and together they found a compartment with a window overlooking the platform. The boiler let out a puff of steam, briefly enveloping them all in a cloud of mist. When it cleared, the young woman was still there waving. Yes, Elena thought as she slipped her talisman in her satchel, it was reassuring, indeed, to know there would always be a friend waiting just on the other side of a wish.

ACKNOWLEDGMENTS

I don't know how common it is in publishing to get to work with the same people on all three books, but that was my good fortune in writing The Vine Witch series. More times than I care to admit, the editorial team members were often the ones to point out inconsistencies in details from one story to the next that I, as the author, had overlooked in the writing. That is why I thank them publicly and profoundly, because, as I've said before, in the effort to guide the books to publication, they make me look like a better writer than I am. So, thank you to Clarence, Jon, Karin, Robin, and Laura and the rest of the 47North team for your editorial magic. Thanks also goes to Micaela Alcaino, who designed the three enchanting book covers for the series. I am also indebted to my editor, Adrienne Procaccini, for believing in my witchy trilogy, and to my agent, Marlene Stringer, for plucking *The Vine Witch* out of her slush pile. Whatever fairy hand that had a part in orchestrating that particular magic, I thank them too! And, as always, thanks to Rob and David and the rest of my family for their continued support and encouragement.

ABOUT THE AUTHOR

Photo © 2018 Bob Carmichael

Luanne G. Smith is the *Washington Post* bestselling author of *The Vine Witch* and *The Glamourist*. She lives in Colorado at the base of the beautiful Rocky Mountains, where she enjoys hiking, gardening, and a glass of wine at the end of the day. For more information, visit www.luannegsmith.com.